Th

Written and Edited by Blake Hull

Special thanks to Nick Newton who designed the amazing cover art!

And thanks to everyone else that has lent a hand with this first adventure!

Chapter One: The Broken Soldier

-Seeley Lake, Montana-

-September 1875-

Nathaniel Shepherd stared out onto the meadow near his cottage. A breeze with a hint of frigidity made its way through his pepper like hair and through his faded, black duster coat. He drew in a deep breath and enjoyed the beauty of his home. A distant lake sparkled with the fading red light of the setting sun. A large body of water rested in between a range of majestic snowcapped peaks that glowed in the dying light of the day. The sun was eclipsed down its middle by the murky waters of the lake. The sparsely populated town lingered in the distance; trails of smoke billowing from the chimneys of separate cottages and the other larger buildings, drifting and fading out from a heavy cover of pine trees. One could barely even call it an actual town it was so small.

Nate watched his horses as a chill swept over him. It was getting colder already. Mid-September brought in the beginnings of that familiar winter frost and with it, the snow and bite of frost. Nate would soon have to bring his horses into the confines of their stalls. He kept them out longer in the spring and summer, so they were prepared to enjoy what remained of the nice weather. His thoughts turned to the sensation he had when he saw them stroll and gallop about the meadow and how he missed it by the time winter came. It was the season that ranchers traveled from all over the west to buy horses from Nate. He always hated giving them up. He raised most of them from birth to adulthood, generation after generation. It was a feat for him not to grow attached.

Nate turned his attention to his cottage. Sofia stood outside near the window preparing supper for the evening. Her wavy black hair danced along to the circular rhythm of her stirring her pot. The contents of which sat simmering over a small fire. She cradled their bundled infant daughter Sara with her empty arm. She glanced up at Nate as though she knew he was staring at her. A smile let loose a soft and nostalgic laugh from a distance. Warmth rose inside of him almost as if to spite the frigid winds that swept past him.

...

-Near Fort Ellis, Montana-

-1867-

Nate tipped the brim of his light brown brick styled hat to defend himself from the intensity of the mid morning sun. He glanced down at Ghost. Ghost's black and white spotted coat shimmered in the rays of light as they cruised back home together. A small herd of horses caught his attention as they galloped across the green and brown hills and knolls. He beamed as he appreciated the beauty of the spectacle. A short, portly looking man charged down the path toward Ghost and Nate. The man held his white cattleman hat clumsily to his head with his elbow up in the air. The man bounced uncontrollably along to the rapid gallop of his horse. He gripped the reins with his free hand. As he got closer, Nate saw an expression of genuine panic under the man's thick black mustache. Nate looked back with his eyebrows raised as the man passed. He pulled the reins on Ghost and got him off of the path to avoid the man riding toward him, leading his ride toward the group of horses that stampeded past. Nate rolled his eyes and turned Ghost around. He chased after the man and caught up to him. Nate rode along beside him. The man did a double take. Nate grinned at him.

"Are those your horses," Nate asked loudly enough for the man to hear over their galloping.

The man nodded, "Si, the gate broke at the ranch a few miles down the road."

He had a thick Mexican accent as he spoke.

"You need help catching them?"

The man nodded vigorously. He took his horse ties and rope from the side of his saddle and handed them all to Nate. Nate took the ties and charged ahead of the man toward the herd.

One by one, Nate lassoed the horses with the man trailing far behind. He handed the ends of rope to the man as he brought them back. As Nate brought the last horse, the man smirked and rode over to him. The pair rode side by side again as they headed toward the ranch in a trot.

"Muchos gracias, amigo."

Nate stared at the man with his eyebrows raised again. The man shook his head and stuck out his hand. Nate shook it with a smile on his face.

"Lo siento, my friend. I still new to English."

"Actually, it's pretty decent. From down south, I take it," Nate replied.

"Si- uh, yes! I came up north to Montana por mi familia… my family."

"Have a lot of mouths to feed?"

"Mi hija… my daughter Sofia and me."

Nate nodded and watched the barbed wire fences peek over the horizon ahead of them. A beaten looking covered wagon sat on the inside of the fence near the front entrance of the ranch.

"What's tu nombre, friend? Your name."

"Nathaniel Shepherd. Call me Nate. And you, sir, what's your name?"

"Pedro Cervantes, mucho gusto… nice to meet you, Nate."

The two guided the horses to the pasture and Pedro fixed the gate. They made sure the animals weren't able to escape again. Pedro escorted Nate back out to the front of the Ranch where the wagon sat.

"Alright Pedro, this is where I take my leave. I have my own horses to look after."

"Wait, mi amigo… my friend. Can I do something for you? You saved mi job… mi vida… My life and my familia today."

"It's okay, Pedro, don't worry about it."

"No? Agua o comida for the road?"

"Sorry, Pedro, what was that?"

"Uh… food or water.

"I'm all set, my friend. Maybe you and Sofia can pay me a visit one-"

Nate stopped mid-sentence as a woman with long dark hair and toasted brown eyes climbed from the wagon. She stopped and stared back at Nate. The two stared at each other for an eternity.

"Ah, Sofía, este es Nate, él nos salvó de ser expulsado del rancho en la actualidad. Él nos salvó la vida."

Nate took off his hat and placed it on his chest. He dismounted Ghost and walked over to the woman with his eyes still locked on her. She smiled at him. Dumbstruck, he noticed a goofy grin spread across his face. He held out his hand, and she extended hers. Her skin was smooth and warm in his as he bent down and placed his lips on the backside of it. She covered her smile and tucked some of her long black hair behind her ear.

"Sofia… I… It's an honor to meet you," Nate said breathlessly.

"Papá, dice este gringo que no lo entiendo," Sofi replied.

"Pero, Sofía, les enseño Inglés hace mucho tiempo. estás bromeando con él?" Pedro asked her.

"Quiero ver si él sabe reír…"

Pedro rolled his eyes, "Sorry Nate, no English."

Nate frowned slightly, "Pedro, this might seem a bit forward and strange to ask of you, but can you tell her she is the most beautiful woman that I have ever seen and that I would love to get to know her?"

Sofia looked away sheepishly and tried her hardest to disguise her smile. Nate's frown vanished. He replaced with an expression of confusion.

"You understand what I'm saying, don't you, Sofia..."

She laughed, "No, you listen to my father, I don't speak or know a word of English!"

"Well, shoot, I guess I'll just have to teach you myself... Pedro, I think I have an idea... I think I figured how you can repay me for today if your offer is still on the table."

Pedro smiled as he saw the look on his daughter's face while she peered into the bewildered white man's eyes.

"Nate, I won't give her up without a fight," He said calmly, "You seem like an honorable man, but I don't know you... come back here whenever you can to see her. She will be here on the ranch..."

"Thank you, my buddy," Nate replied.

"Oh, and if you hurt her, you are muerte."

Nate looked at Pedro to explain.

"A dead man..."

Sophia laughed as Nate nervously ran a hand through his hair and went back to goofily smiling at her.

...

As he got lost in these thoughts, Nate ambled, stride-by-stride, to the cottage. He let his palm graze the tops of the tall, dry grass that surrounded him. His hands found their way to his hips. He was jarred by the cold sensation on the skin of his wrist. The cold of winter made the metal of his revolver bite harder than the frosty winds around him.

His hand clenched into a fist when his thoughts turned to a time before Sofia. A time before Sara was born… A time when gunshots and explosions rattled through his head and rang his ears. He clenched his jaw tighter than his fists and listened to his teeth grind. The echoes of war overtook him and sent his mind hurdling into the past.

…

-The Battle of Chickamauga-

-Near the border of Tennessee & Georgia-

-1863-

Nate stood boldly in formation with sixty thousand troops and his platoon against sixty-five thousand confederates.

"Are you ready?" asked Daniel reluctantly.

"I think we both have to be at this point, Dan," Nate replied. "You seem nervous."

"Can you blame me?"

"No."

Nate held out a shaking hand to show Dan.

"Knowing you, its excitement, not fear that shakes you… If I don't make it out of this alive…"

"Don't talk like that. We are both making it back home."

"You know damn well the odds of us both coming out of this… but I think you stand a better chance. Give this to mom and dad if I die. Tell 'em I love 'em."

Dan gave a letter to Nate with a stern look on his face. Nate nodded and handed Daniel a letter of his own. They looked at each other. They both dismissed the lurking thought. It felt like the last time they'd see each other alive. They tried to dismiss the thought, but the effort was wasted.

"I love you, Dan… I'll see you after we win this fight."

"I love you too…brother."

Nate clicked the hammer back on his revolver as it sat in his holster. He unsheathed his twin sabers and held them at the ready.

Far off gunshots rolled like thunder over the valiant and ferocious screams of soldiers who charged with their rifles pointed forward, billowing smoke and led from either side of the battlefield. Cannons bellowed deeper than the storm of gunfire. They sent union and confederate troops flying and careening into the dirt, some in sprays of red and in chunks of limbs and flesh. Nate, Daniel, and the other Union forces rushed into battle with muskets firing and bayonets clashing with the confederates. Union soldiers fell all around, but Nate and his platoon charged onward, regardless.

Nathaniel unloaded all six shots of his revolver into the grey wall of oncoming confederate soldiers. He tossed it aside and unsheathed his two swords. As he rode on, he cut down endless ranks of confederate troops, one sword in each hand. His eyes glazed over, red and burning. They stared coldly, blankly, with no emotion as he slashed through dozens of soldiers at a time. He listened to them as they gasped and gurgled for air through slit throats and watched them clamber for their lost limbs. It sprayed through the air with every slash and swing of his swords. He smelled and tasted the iron in their blood. He listened to their screams vibrate in his eardrums.

Nate's horse took a rifle shot to one of its front legs. The animal screeched and lurched forward, sending Nate flying off the saddle and taking his feet from the stirrups. He hit the earth headfirst. He rushed to his feet with his swords still in his grasp, spitting earth and grass.

Nate's teeth gritted with glee as the killing continued. A devilish grin slithered its way onto his face. Bullets whirred by him. He rammed the blade of his right sword through the bottom of a confederate's jaw. The blade found its way up through the top his skull. Blood sprayed from the wound soaking Nate in a new, hot, and fresh coat of red. The cries of the wounded made his smile continue to grow and the fountains of blood that sprayed him brought warmth to his insides. He recognized it. It was utter bliss. His blood thirst was unquenchable. Confederate soldiers dropped wherever Nate passed on the battlefield.

Nate ignored the hot pain that coursed through the top of his right shoulder, in his bicep and the skin of his left hip. The pain of being grazed by the led pellets faded with every dead enemy.

Nathaniel cleared the battlefield in front of him, scanning for more confederate squadrons to fell. He heard sprinting through the fight in the distance. Footfalls were approaching fast from behind him. Nathaniel switched the way he held his left sword, flipping it so that the point faced backward. He closed his eyes and let his ears do the work. With one swift lunge he sensed the sword pass through flesh and break through bone. Nathaniel put his boot to his victim's chest and freed his sword. He listened to the enemy fall to the ground with a limp and lifeless thud.

He turned to look at his prey, pride smeared on his face. Nate's skin became white under the dried blood caked to his skin. He fell scrambling backward and a splash of vomit welled up from the icy cold pit of his stomach. Nate flipped himself over on his hands and knees, retching what little food he had eaten the day before the battle. Nate eyes were stuck open wide with shock. A brand new pain consumed him and brought rage along with it. His eyes leaked, and his vocal cords tore in a silent scream. Panic made his heart leap from his chest. He tried to un-see what he saw, he tried to pretend… he tried. Nothing could erase the image that was burned into his skull.

…

-New York, the Shepherds' Ranch-

-1865-

Nate found himself in front of his family's large estate just outside of New York City. It was a large Victorian mansion with acres upon acres of meadows and pastures. The house overlooked the city but avoided the noise that was its constant hustle and bustle. He remembered that if you stood still enough, you could hear the wind rustle through the trees and the grass nearby. Nate reveled in the rich memories of the ranch when he was a little boy.

Nate walked up to the large oak doors and knocked with trembling hands. He saw an older, grey-haired version of himself answer the door. When the old man saw who was at the door, his expression was pure joy.

"By god… They're back… They're finally home," Said John.

Nate's father charged forward and squeezed him with all his might. With a grunt Nate wrapped his arms around him.

"Christine, Nate is home!"

Nate let go of his father and looked to see his mother trotting down the stairs. She was a couple inches shorter than John with long flowing brown hair and grey blue eyes much like Nate's. Their elegant and privileged lifestyle had gotten the better of both of them over these past few years. Nate's mother and father were completely the same as when Nate was a boy.

"Nate…" Christine sighed in relief as she charged forward and hugged him as tightly as she could.

"Come in," said John. "We have much to catch up on!"

John and Christine walked merrily over to the kitchen where Nate followed closely behind.

"The army told us you and Dan were missing in action," Christine said. "We're so happy to see you home. Where is Danny? Did he have business in town before he comes over?"

Before he got to the kitchen, Nate stopped dead in his tracks. His parents turned back. Their son gripped an old piece of worn, brown, and bloodstained parchment. Tears rolled down Nate's stern face, but he said nothing and extended his shaking arm outward handing them Daniel's letter. John desperately snatched the letter from Nate and read. His jolly smile faded as he read.

"I'm sorry dad. I was supposed to look after him, but-," Nate whispered choking on his own sobs.

"I had a feeling… I hoped it wasn't the case when you showed up here alone… I… Should've known… Should've prepared myself… I told you to protect him… and I told him to guard you... No matter what…"

"Dad, I- I'm so sorry… I should've-"

"YOU'RE GODDAMNED RIGHT YOU SHOULD HAVE… A SERGEANT IN THE FUCKING UNION, YET YOU STILL COULDN'T BRING HIM BACK ALIVE."

John retreated up the nearest staircase to his study. He looked to Nate as tears flowed down his cheeks.

John said solemnly, “Shepherds always protect their flock,” and turned to walk up the stairs.

Christine tried hard to wipe the tears that sent her makeup streaming down her face, but they flowed too quickly. She walked over to Nate and looked into his eyes. Her son’s gaze shifted to the floor, away from Christine’s. She wrapped her arms around him, held him tight. She let go, followed closely behind John, and said nothing. After a moment of silence and overhearing the cries of his parents from one of the far-off rooms, Nate wiped his tears and quietly shut the front door of the house behind him.

. . .

Nate’s legs were heavier than his heart. Each step was a monumental effort. Soon Nate found himself on the streets of New York City, meandering about. His mind was numb and his thoughts combative and violent. Each notion of warmth, each glimpse of positivity was met with a thoughtful rebuttal in his mind.

Nathaniel slumped into a seat at a bar, unsure of how he got there. The sign above the bar read McSorley’s. He waved the bartender for a drink as he put a few coins onto the bar top. The bartender slid a glass of clear liquid over to him. Nate caught it and slammed it back. The drink filled him with sweet, artificial warmth.

The bar was filled with a group of unsavory looking factory workers covered in dirt, soot, and other unmentionables. Nate discerned that they were Irish immigrants from their heavy accents and by the rate at which they drank. He listened to the patrons speak, trying to get out of his own head.

"I'm thinkin' o' leavin' this city," One said.

"Aye, everybody hirin' here has something against immigrants. Bloody fuckin' annoyin'," The other replied.

"The place is over populated. Bloody immigrants."

The pair roared in laughter.

"Y'know what."

"What?"

"What about headin' west?"

"Like more west than we've traveled already?"

"Aye, like California west, whaddya say?"

"They got any beer?"

Nate stopped listening to their banter and put more money on the counter. Another drink appeared out of nowhere. He gripped it and took a long sip. He thought of it. West. A weight was lifted from his mind. He couldn't tell if it was the drink or the aspect of a new beginning.

"Maybe both," Nate whispered.

...

-Seeley Lake, Montana-

-September 1875-

Nate unclenched his trembling fist and let the tall grass he had ripped out fall back onto the ground. He took his wrist from the frigid gunmetal at his hip to bat away the moisture in his eyes.

"Supper is ready, mi amor," Sofia yelled from the cottage.

Nate looked up to the cottage again. The pain in his chest and the lump in his throat lingered. He shuffled through the door. He smiled at Sofia and Sara who were waiting for him at the table. The typical and intoxicating smell of beans and vegetable stew wafted into his nose as he breathed it in. Nate enjoyed it more every time Sofia cooked it for him. Nate and Sofia sat down picked up their silverware. Sofia looked up into Nate's eyes.

"Nate, are you," Sofia began.

Nate stared off into his meal, a thousand yards through it.

She took his hand in hers and rubbed the cold out of his fingers. He snapped out of his stupor and looked over to his wife somberly.

"Mi corazón… it wasn't your fault. I know you. I know you did everything you could to protect him."

"I was blinded… I couldn't control myself… I was lost in a haze when he-"

Sofia stood up from the table. She walked over and held onto him, placing her head into the middle of his chest.

"You protected him the best... the only way you knew how."

Nate placed his arms around Sofia. They sat in silence.

Nate froze. The pounding, thundering of horses rushing up the road rumbled loudly in his ears. Sofia rose and looked around. He followed her, glaring out of a nearby window.

"Nate, what is it, more buyers?" Asked Sofia.

"Too many to be buyers. Take Sara and hide in the forest."

Chapter Two: The Man with Yellow Eyes

-Seeley Lake, Montana-

-September 1875-

Sofia ran for the tree line close to the cottage, clutching Sara to her chest. Nate stood in the cottage and watched them until they were out of sight from the house. He turned his head to the window where the horsemen were approaching, and a cold sweat collected on his brow. He paced over to his and Sofia's bedroom where he kneeled at the side of the bed. With a trembling hand, he pulled an old wooden chest from underneath it. Images and thoughts of the war swam around in his head as he opened it. The hinges squealed. Nate's Twin sabers glinted in the light of the setting sun, shining from the window as he picked them up. The glint of the blades sent him back. Brought him through time to the front lines. His hands shook. He tried hard to hide the look of excitement in his eyes. He tried to keep the sensation from burying the fear he had for his wife and child.

…

A group of fifteen horsemen neared Nate's cottage on top of a nearby knoll. Greed rode alongside them guiding them to Nate's cottage and horse pasture. A deep, raspy southern accent came from the back of the group.

"So, this is the horse breeder's place."

"This should be it," said Greed.

"Should be?"

Greed sensed a sinister chill every time the man spoke. The gang member gaped at the voice's source. The smooth southern creole in his speech did nothing to comfort her. His head was tilted forward. The brim of his grey Gambler style hat hid his eyes. His seemingly permanent scowl was wedged inside of a thick silver beard that covered most of his face. His grey Gambler's suit donned no stains of dirt or sweat from the long ride he and his underlings had been on. The old man withdrew a book from his coat pocket and read from it. From the same pocket, he took a red wooden poker chip and fiddled with it as he read.

"Good work. This is the place."

Greed's head swiveled back to the road.

The man laughed, "You know where to go from here, I presume."

He caught up and handed the gang member a large wad of cash.

"I'll be takin' my leave now," Greed retorted.

"I'll send my men to fetch you whenever I need you next, but I suspect that won't be for a while… best of luck to you…"

Greed shrank and rode toward town as the others reached the fence of the old soldier's property.

"Gentlemen… find him, keep him alive. If you must shoot him, aim for the arms and legs. You kill him, I kill you. See what else you can rustle up. Let's make this quick," said the man in grey.

The fourteen men rode off in front of him with their guns drawn and ready for anything. The man dressed in grey smiled and sat on his horse as the sun's dull rays disappeared behind the mountains, leaving a shadowy twilight across the land. His horse stirred under him with its eyes glued on the edge of the woods. The man scanned the trees. His smile grew larger. He dug his heels into his ride and dragged his right hand onto the butt of his revolver resting in a holster across his chest.

Seven men in long brown duster coats approached the cottage. Three went through the front door. Four went through the back. The rest of them headed to the stables.

...

Nate no longer heard the masses of hooves against the dirt road. Quickly, he dampened all the lamps in the cottage leaving him in the dark. He crouched in the kitchen with his blades drawn and waited for the raiders to enter. He stifled his breathing. His ears twitched. The front door creaked open.

"We saw you dampen yer lamps. Come out with yer hands up or we'll shoot."

Three men stepped through the front door gingerly to keep from making more sounds.

"Can't see a fuckin' thing…" one man whispered.

Nate silently felt around for a fork from the kitchen table, grabbed it and threw it to the opposite side of the room. It hit the floor with a loud metallic clank.
"There!"

One shot his weapon in a panicked spray where they heard the fork drop onto the floor. Through the flashes of gunfire, Nate saw his three targets. He darted up to two gunmen and skewered them simultaneously through the center of their chests from their backs. They fell to the ground. Nate leaped over to the last gunman in the kitchen, held his left blade to the base of the man's spine and his right to his throat. The raider immediately dropped his revolver and shook where he stood. Four men at the back door entered with a clear line of sight on Nate and his hostage. Twilight spilled into the room. Nate spun him around, positioning the man in between himself and the four men.

"Give it up, we've got the cabin surrounded," said Nate's hostage.

A long-forgotten grin returned to Nate's face and stretched itself wide. A red haze came over his vision.

Nate hissed into the man's ear, "You'd better be bullet proof."

The four men at the back door paused with their guns pointed at him. With a swift jerk of his left hand, Nate pierced his hostage's spine and charged toward them with the man flailing upon his sword just above the floor. The four men opened fire. Bullets whirred past him and his meat shield. The whimpering man on his blade fell silent and limp. Bullets grazed his arms and legs. He ignored the burning, stinging pain. A familiar sensation ran through him. Nate halted his sprint. He vaulted his hostage into the three men, knocking them to the floor. In the same motion, he slashed the man across his stomach with his right blade spilling his intestines onto the floor. With three more swift cuts, those three men on the floor choked and sprayed blood from their open throat wounds.

Nate stood panting. The moon hid just above the horizon as if it was afraid to come out. The light of the moon tinted the red sheen that soaked Nate into a shining black. Nate gritted his teeth. He tried to shake the devilish expression and tried to rid himself of the sensation. His eyes were wide with thirst and glee as he looked upon the carnage he had caused. Through the back door, he saw three more men hurriedly leading his horses from their stables. Without further pause, Nate sprinted down the road with his bloodied swords held up at his sides, blood-drunk.

The three men at the stables dragged the struggling and fighting horses from their stalls and through the pasture.

"C'mon, you stubborn bastards!"

"Were those gunshots?"

"Course they were ya idjit. This is a raid."

"Ya think the rest of the guys took care of him?

"Dunno for sure, so let's git the horses and git the hell outta here."

"Oh, shit…"

Before anyone could answer the question, Nate rushed by in a blur. The two men in the back drew their six shooters.

"Where the fuck'd he go!? He's too fast!"

The leading man fell like a rag doll to his knees as his head rolled from his neck. His neck sprayed like a fountain of glimmering black water. The two other men let go of the horses. They scanned the area. Nate's horses ran across the pasture away from the clamor of the raid.

"Oh, God I don' wanna die..."

"What do w-"

The man in the back let out an ear-piercing shriek of pain cut short by blood pooling in his lungs. A sword shot out from the center of his chest from behind him and was slowly withdrawn. The man crumpled and disappeared into the tall grass. Nate stood behind him, his teeth glinting like white polished blades in the soft and pale moonlight. His duster and his old Union army uniform were soaked in streaks and sprays of blood. The last raider opened fire. Six shots rang out. The raider scrambled to reload his revolver. His hands grew limp from fright. He dropped his weapon. His bottom lip quivered as the demonic looking individual continued to approach. The man sobbed, helplessly.

Nate's demonic grin grew to inhuman proportions as he delighted in his latest victim's submission. He walked behind the raider and kicked his legs out from under him, bringing the raider to his knees. Nate grabbed a large clump of the man's hair after dropping the sword from his left and brought his right to the raider's scalp. He moved his blade back and forth in a sawing motion. The raider screamed and screamed, but it only increased Nate's thirst. With each stroke, he cut through the man's scalp even slower. Nate made the final cut. The man fell. Nate held the scalp by the hair.

He dropped the raider's scalp and picked up his left sword, sheathing them both onto his waist. Nate heard a shriek in the distance.

"Sofia…" He whispered to himself.

Nate rushed over to the treelike back in front of the cottage. He scrambled around for a match and a lantern. He got to the road and skidded to a halt in the dirt and saw six dark shapes silhouetted by the moonlight. Nathaniel could barely make out the shape of Sofia carrying Sara against her chest. Nate's family stood with the remaining raiders. He once again, unsheathed his swords and ran toward the dark shapes in the night. As he got closer to the group, he saw a man seated upon a horse whose eyes glowed a dull yellow under the brim of his hat.

"Very impressive. A bona fide monster like you were before you broke at Chickamauga. Perfect," the man with yellow eyes said. His gravelly voice rolled with a silky yet sinister creole accent.

Nate looked around and saw that three gunmen had him locked in their sights, rifles cocked and ready to fire. One gunman had a rifle pointed at Sofia and Sara.

"Let them go," Nate said. His voice shook with rage.

"Oh," the man laughed. "And why should I do that?"

Nate unsheathed and hurled his right sword into the head of the man that had his rifle aimed at his wife and child. He wound back with his left pointed at the yellow eyes. A brilliant flash of light came from the man on the horse as a bullet dug itself into Nate's left shoulder. He dropped his sword. The other three men waited patiently for permission to shoot Nate.

"Hold your fire. I still want him alive… That was awful rude of you, Nate. These men could have shot your wife, and your beautiful baby girl right then and there."

"How the hell do you know my name? Why didn't they… why can't you all just leave with the horses… isn't that what you thieving bastards want?"

"Answer my question first. I believe I asked you why you think I should let these two lovely ladies go."

Nate's hands trembled harder than his voice, wanting to pierce the black heart of the yellow-eyed man.

"I will butcher every single one of you bastards."

"I don't think you're in any position to butcher anyone... yet."

The man with yellow eyes dismounted his horse and drew a dagger from a hidden sheath on his coat as he walked toward Sofia and Sara.

"No, take me instead… PLEASE."

Nate dropped to his knees and threw his swords to his sides.

"It's a bit too late for that."

The yellow-eyed man stole Sara from Sofia's grasp and cradled her against him with his free arm. She reached out in desperation.

"Sar-," She began.

The man took his dagger from his coat and slit Sofia's throat. She grabbed helplessly at her throat and fell to her knees. Her eyes met Nate's one last time. She grew too weak to keep herself sitting up and laid in the dirt and blood underneath her. Nate lunged forward, screaming at the top of his lungs. The man pointed his dagger at Sara and stopped Nate dead in his tracks. The infant girl cried.

"Don't you just love seeing the light fade from their eyes as they pass on…? Look at her go… look at how peaceful she looks. You've seen it. You enjoy it. You've used that rage before. Use it again. You have potential, Nate Shepherd. Much more than I initially thought…"

"GIVE HER BACK!"

"Seek me out, seek out Sins in every hole that they hide. Go to the eye of the devil and you can have your baby girl back… dead or alive depending on when you get there."

The man with the glowing yellow eyes nodded to his remaining men as he mounted his horse with Nate's daughter in his clutches. They beat Nate unconscious with the butts of their rifles. They left the homestead of the broken soldier with all but one of his horses.

Chapter Three: The Grave of the Scarlet Bride

-Seeley Lake, Montana-

-September 1875-

"Mi amor," Sofia breathed.

She held Nate in her arms as they lay in bed together. Nate looked over. Sofia was bathed in golden sunlight from the window of their bedroom. The light curved over her white silk wedding gown. Her smile seemed as bright as the sun behind her. Her brown eyes locked on Nate's, filling him with an overwhelming feeling of warmth.

Sofia let out an infectious giggle as Nate grabbed her and spun her around in his arms. He returned her loving smile.

"What in the world are you so happy about, my love," Nate said teasingly.

"Well, I just married an older man with lots and lots of dinero. Oh, and he's muy guapo."

Nate laughed, "Well, you'd better go find him before he catches you in bed with a scoundrel like me."

"Esta bien. I have a feeling He'll forgive me."

"Are you sure about that?"

"Of course, I am. He es mi Corazon and I am his."

"And if he's so much older, you'd better respect your elders."

Sofia laughed along with him, "Idiota! You know what I mean!"

"I know, but… I love when you say it…"

"Fine, old man, you are my heart, mi corazon. You give me happiness, love. You are my passion, my soul, my warmth in the cold and my light in the dark."

Nate stared longingly into her eyes as she spoke. He got lost in them with a wide and goofy lingering smile. Nate held his expression and brought his face toward hers.

"Mi Corazon…" he said in a whisper.

Sofia embraced her husband in a deep and long-lasting kiss. The couple looked up and realized it was already sunset. Sofia jumped from the bed and extended a hand to Nate. She dragged Nate along and grabbed a sheet from their bed, holding it with her free hand.

"Come," She said.

Sofia led him outside through the back door of their cottage and out to the pasture, past the edge of the woods. They walked hand in hand to the tallest pine tree on the property. Sofia laid the sheet she was carrying down at the base of the tree. She stood looking at Nate with ferocious affection. She faced away from him. Nate approached and loosened Sofia's dress. The soft hue of twilight showed Sofia's slender figure as her wedding gown fell to the ground. She turned around toward Nate, unbuttoning his shirt.

"You are beauti-", before he could finish his sentence, Sofia placed her index finger against his lips.

"Shhhh… No words now, mi amor."

She guided him down to the sheet and onto his back where she climbed on top of him. Nate looked up at her and she continued unbuttoning his shirt and took off the rest of his clothes. Sofia bent over him and kissed Nate passionately.

He stopped as something warm and wet trickled down his cheeks. Sofia brought her face away from his and sat up upon his lap. Nate took his hand wiped a tear from his cheek.

"You'd better not leave me here buck naked," Nate laughed, "Sofia?"

He looked up at his wife. The vibrant brown of Sofia's skin turned to a lifeless grey. She said nothing and kept perfectly still. She was straddled upon him staring at him, grinding him.

"No…" Nate whispered petrified.

Sofia's throat split open and drenched blood down their naked bodies, drenching them in a dark red. He stared into her cold, wide eyes and saw they flickered yellow like two flames. A low laugh echoed from down the road to the cottage that shook the ground. The blood stopped pouring. She leaned down to him and whispered into his ear. "Shepherds always prot-"

Nate's eyes shot open. He screamed out of his sleep and held his face with shaking hands. He lay on his back, staring at the moon and he could hear the dirt and gravel of the road shifting under him as he got onto his feet. Blood trickled from a gash on his forehead, from his nose, from his arms and legs where the raiders' bullets grazed him. With his head throbbing, he looked down on the road where he dropped his sabers. Nate grunted from the stinging in his wounds and walked over. He picked them up and sheathed them onto his belt. He could feel his rage boiling over and dulling the pain in his wounds. Nate balled his hands into fists and clenched his jaw. The red tinge refilled to his sight. He turned around and felt the salt in his tears burn his cuts as they trickled down.

He gaped at Sofia who was sprawled on the road with her throat cut and eyes wide and locked on the night sky. Her skin was a sickening and pallid grey. Nate walked over to her and bent down beside her. He took his fingers and pushed her eyelids down. Nate picked up Sofia's cold and blood-stained body. He carried her to the tallest tree on the property where they shared the first night of their marriage. Nathaniel placed her under it. He shambled to the cottage where he grabbed a wet cloth, and a shovel. He walked back to the tree. With tears streaming steadily, he cleaned the blood from Sofia as best as he could and dug. Nate placed his wife in her grave using the tree as a headstone. With a sword, he carved the bark away and chiseled a message.

Sofia Shepherd
The greatest wife.
The greatest mother.
The greatest lover.
The greatest woman,
Any man could ever know.
1841-1875

Nate threw the last clump of dirt on her grave and wiped his tears. He looked upon the grave of the love of his life.

"I will get Sara back, I promise you. Rest, mi Corazon…"

…

-Seeley Lake, Montana-
-The Horse's Hand Saloon-
-A few Days Later-

Elaine sat at the bar, tipping back in her seat. She casually gulped her glass of whiskey. Three men talked loudly at a table behind her laughing merrily and getting rowdier as the drinks kept coming. The air was a fog of tobacco smoke that mixed with the stench of cowboy sweat and grime. With a tilt of her head, she downed the rest of her alcoholic beverage. She slammed more bank notes onto the surface of the bar. Her consistent gusto in her actions no longer surprised the bartender.

"Oy, barkeep. Another whiskey. Double it this time." She said with a heavy Irish accent behind her the remainder of her previous glass.

Her long, brown hair flowed from under her stovepipe hat. Her leather coat moved along with her as she fidgeted in her seat. She wore it unbuttoned. The openings of her coat revealed her green flannel shirt paired with her black pants that were in the same rough state. Her knee-high boots hugged her feet and legs. Her feet were perched on the top rung of the barstool underneath her. The bartender stood stubbornly and gestured to her for another bank note.

Elaine rolled her eyes, “Fine, ya greedy bastard,” she said.

She slammed more money on the table. With a smirk, the bartender took her payment and slid it back filled with the amber liquid sloshing toward her.

“Thank you kindly, miss… I think you’re the first one to order a double of an already doubled whiskey,” He said mockingly.

“Yeah, hardy-fuckin’ har-har. Bugger off ‘til I need another one.”

The bartender shook his head and attended to the three other patrons. She gripped her drink and stared at the whiskey moving around the glass. She clenched it tight. Her knuckles turned white. She raised the amber colored liquid to her mouth and took a large gulp as the trio of men carried on at a table behind her. She grimaced and hissed at the taste, but drank it like water, regardless.

“Jesus, Nate. What the hell happened to you,” the bartender asked exasperated.

The three men at the table grew quiet. She looked up from the bar to the saloon doors. There was a gruff, solemn, and wounded looking man with greying black hair and deep scabbed cuts strewn about his face who walked into the bar. He was cloaked in an old and stained duster coat with two swords sheathed at his side. The pounding of his boots on the wooden floor made Elaine keep her eyes glued to her drink.

"Sorry Rob, I'd rather not say," Nate said somberly.

"That's alright, friend. Can I get you anything?"

"Whiskey… please."

"On the house."

"Thank you."

Elaine glanced up from her glass to peek at the man who had just taken a seat at the bar. He sat gazing into his whiskey drink too. He grasped it with one and his other resting on the hilt of his sheathed sword. Elaine could see the pain in his grey-blue eyes. He wasn't staring at his glass; it looked as though he was staring past it, and even past the bar. He was staring hundreds of miles away through the walls of the saloon, lost in his thoughts.

One of the men rose up from the table behind Elaine and walked toward Nate.

"Hey, partner can I buy you a drink," the man asked quaintly.

"Sure. I appreciate it," Nate replied.

"Judgin' by them swords of yers, I'd say you were a sergeant in the war… Am I right?"

"Yes, I was... Now, I'm… just a horse breeder…"

"Which side did you fight fer?"

"Listen, thank you for the drink, but I don't feel like talking about it…"

The man stood looking irritated at Nate. Nate refused to lock eyes with him. He took the revolver from his holster and stuck it in Nate's back. The other two men rose up from the table with their hands ready to draw their revolvers.

"Then I think you owe me a drink, Sarge- err… sorry, horse breeder."

Nate let go of his booze and reached into his coat pocket. Nate noticed the revolver in his back click when the man pulled the hammer. Elaine gingerly unbuckled the holsters of her twin revolvers still looking into her whiskey. Robert stood frozen behind the bar and reached for the sawed-off shotgun he kept underneath.

"Ah, ah, ah."

A man from the table drew his revolver and pointed it at Robert. The bartender put his hands up and returned to his upright standing position.

"Easy, I want no one getting killed," Nate said softly, "I'm getting my money from my coat pocket… Rob?"

Robert got the whiskey and poured the man a drink. Nate pulled a bank note from his pocket and placed it on the bar top.

"Gimme the rest of it too. Don't be stingy, now," said the man with the gun in Nate's back.

Slowly, Nate retrieved the rest of his money.

"Whew, boy. We gotta thank that feller in grey if we see him again. This fucker has a lot on him."

The sound of leather scraping against gunmetal filled the room as Elaine pulled her revolvers from her sides. Before the trio men had time to react, three consecutive gun blasts blared. The barrels of her two revolvers donned thin wisps of smoke. The group of men fell. Large parts of their head were missing. Robert stood where he was, quivering and coated in the brain matter of the individual who stayed closest to the bar. Nate also caught a spray from the bullet that sailed through the man's skull.

Nate looked to his left, still holding his money. Elaine lowered herself into the chair and holstered her weapons. She sat sipping on her drink and tipping her chair back casually.

"Thank you, miss. What's your name," Nate asked, wiping the blood from his face. He stood from his seat and approached her.

"Elaine. My friends call me eagle eye. So, call me Elaine," she replied.

"Alright, Elaine. Know anything about the Eye of the Devil?"

"Not a damn thing. I came here lookin' for your horse ranch. Robert 'ere told me I was pretty close."

"I think it's in Mexico somewhere," Robert chimed in, "I heard those guys you shot here telling stories about it a couple days ago. Supposed to be some hideout for a gang called the Sins or somethin'. Heard them talkin' about a town called Snake River down in Idaho, too."

"You're sure, Robert?" Nate asked.

Robert nodded, pale and shaking. Nate looked at Robert and then to Elaine. He turned his attention to the measly revolver on his hip.

"You're good with a gun and it looks like I'm going to need more artillery," Nate said looking at Elaine with his eyebrows raised.

"What's your offer?"

Nate held up a large sum of rolled up bank notes from his coat pocket.

"Two hundred and fifty."

Elaine smiled at Nate, "We sleep in separate rooms and travel only by the light of day, understand?"

"What about sleeping out in the wild? It's probably best we stick together out there in case of bandits or wildlife…"

"Aye, that reasonable, but we start camp before the sun sets. I need me beauty sleep."

Nate rolled his eyes, "Deal."

"Call me Eagle Eye."

Chapter Four: Whore of the Snake's Leg

-Snake River, Idaho-

-October 1875-

The sun seemed to rise and set repeatedly over the horizon of the American wilderness as Nate and Elaine rode southwest into Idaho. The thick and green pine forests of Montana developed into brown plateaus. Big sky country turned into deep, winding red rock canyons.

Elaine sat wearily on top of her horse. The sun beat down on her where the narrow brim of her hat neglected to cover. Dark circles had grown under her eyes. She swayed back and forth with the trotting of her horse. Her fair skin was cooked bright red from what felt like weeks of non-stop travel. She reached down to her saddlebag and raised her flask to her chapped lips. Her head tilted back and drank a few large gulps. She took it away from her mouth and frowned behind Nate.

"For the love o' god, we need to stop," she said irritated.

"We'll stop soon," Nate replied, pointing in front of him.

Elaine squinted through the rays of the sun to see a series of dark wooden buildings sitting upon the walls of a winding canyon with a slow and lazy river set at the bottom.

"I ran out of drinking water about an hour ago. How's your supply holding up," he asked.

Elaine glanced down at her nearly full canteen then to her empty whiskey flask.

"Aye, I'm runnin' dry too… How much longer do ya figure 'til we get over to there, exactly?"

"We should get there by sunset if we pick up our pace."

"Feels like it's been bloody ages."

With a determined grunt, Nate dug his heels into his horse and sped forward. Elaine followed suit and the two travelers sped toward the town of Snake River.

…

Florence brushed her long platinum blonde hair as she sat in front of her mirror dressed in nothing but her black-laced lingerie. She smiled with plump lips bathed in red lipstick. She reveled in her own beauty. Her skin looked like the porcelain on a doll. She gaped down at the curves of her body with a satisfied smile. Florence finished brushing her hair and walked over to the window. She stared out with her pale, crystal blue eyes over the Snake River canyon and the main road of the town. The sun was setting over the rim of the landscape. It turned the Snake River to dark shades of black, ink-welled versions of themselves.

"Showtime," she said to herself with a proud smile.

She shut the blinds, leaving the only light in the room coming from the lamp she left on the table. Her eyes flickered pale yellow in the dark. Florence made her way down the stairs and to the stage of the Snake's Leg brothel.

…

Elaine and Nate arrived by the time twilight had washed itself over Snake River canyon. Not a soul wandered the dusty, lonesome dirt roads. The hair on the back of Nate's neck stood up. He rested his right hand upon the hilt of his sword, still holding the reins on his horse with his left as he and Elaine rode further into town. Elaine unbuckled the holsters of her revolvers, following Nate's lead.

"What is it," Elaine asked.

"Something isn't right here," he answered, still staring straight in front of him, "This isn't a ghost town… it looks too well kept."

Nate and Elaine drew their weapons as they heard a door shut from one building that stood before them. A portly looking man with wearing a white-buttoned shirt with a black bowtie and pants emerged from one of the buildings. He trotted along the main road to the only lit building in town. His greasy and slicked back hair bounced with every step he took. He hurried along with a blissful look on his face. A thick mustache adorned the silly expression. The man ignored them completely. Nate sheathed his sword and hurried to catch up with him. Elaine followed.

"Excuse me, Sir…" Nate said politely.

He didn't notice Nate. He continued his walk toward the large and well-lit building.

"Oy, ya deft twat," Elaine yelled to the man.

He took no notice and entered the swinging doors to the brightly lit building. Nate looked back at Elaine who shrugged unapologetically. Nate eyed the building in front of them. He saw a sign that swayed and squealed on rusty hinges, pushed from a breeze that ran along the canyon.

The Snake's Leg Brothel and Saloon

Nate and Elaine dismounted their horses and hitched them in front of the saloon. They walked in, ready for anything. The pair squinted as the light from inside hit their eyes. They eventually adjusted to the luminosity. They saw a stage near the back of the room. All the town drunks, outlaws, shop keepers, and even the sheriff clamored and piled on top of each other to be closest to the voluptuous performer.

Elaine scoffed at the sight, "Typical."

Nate chuckled a bit at Elaine's quip and sat down at the bar with her.

"Two whiskeys and some water," Nate said to the bartender.

The bartender stood gaping at the stage, ignoring Nate's request. Nate reached across the bar and snapped his fingers in front of the bartender's face. The bartender didn't even blink. He continued cleaning the glass in his hand, just staring. Nate looked over at Elaine who had already reached over the bar top and grabbed herself a bottle of whiskey. She took pulls straight from it. She wiped her mouth, nodded at Nate and continued to drink. Nate stared sternly at her and pointed his finger to the bar top. She offered Nate another scoff, pulled a couple bills from the wad of bank notes he had given her, and placed some of her money onto the counter.

"Not like he gives a shite anyway. The people in this town are controlled by fuckin' tits," she said behind the bottle, grabbing her chest.

Everyone else kept their eyes glued to the stage.

Nate laughed, "Apparently not yours…"

Nate grabbed a glass from the rack above him and slid it to her. She poured a serving into it and slid it back to him. Nate took a long swig and finished his drink. He passed it to Elaine who poured him another and slid it right to him again.

The clamor of the townspeople grew silent. A pale leg clad in black lace and a matching heeled shoe peeked itself out from behind the curtains of the stage. A tall blonde woman stepped out. A piano in the bar began to play. The pianist's gaze was glued to her as he tickled the ivories in a slow and seductive tune. She danced to the tune teasingly, playing with what little clothing she had on. The audience once again erupted into hoots and hollers as she took off her top revealing her large breasts to everyone there. She playfully jostled them and wiggled them about. Dollar notes flew up and filled the stage.

Florence continued dancing and looked around her audience. Every man in the town was reaching for her. She laughed proudly and wagged her index finger at them.

"That's off limits for the moment, boys… unless you've got more money after the show," Florence yelled over the crowd.

Elaine saw the woman on stage. She gripped her bottle tightly and took another few gulps.

She glanced over at Nate who sat a couple of seats closer to the loud and rowdy crowd. He surveyed the selection of alcohol behind the bar, minding his own business. She walked over to Nate and clasped her hand on his shoulder.

"I'm going to get the horses some water. Unless you got them some already," She said loudly so Nate could hear her.

"Shit, I forgot. I thought I saw a trough on our way into town. You can probably get them some water there."

"Aye, want me to feed 'em too?"

"Yeah, I bet they're starving out there. I put their food in the bag on the left side of my saddle. There isn't much in there, but it's better than nothing. Thanks, Eagle Eye," He smiled at her.

Elaine returned his smile, taking the whiskey from the bar top at Nate's side. She walked out the saloon, her bottle tilted high in the air, the amber liquid pouring down her throat.

…

Florence looked beyond the crowd and saw a darkly dressed and scarred man with two swords. He was drinking a bottle of whiskey at the bar. He paid no attention to her. Outrageous… Curious. She glanced at the piano player and he ended the song. The crowd shared a collective groan as Florence walked off the stage and upstairs. The townspeople departed the saloon. They went back to their inn rooms and homes. Few of the men remained to have a drink. The barber with the greasy hair took a seat to Nate's left. Nate was spinning what little alcohol he had remaining in his second glass of whiskey. He thought about the town. He thought about that strange collective trance they seemed to be in earlier.

"Gin, please", the plump barber requested from the bartender.

The bartender stopped rubbing the same glass he had been cleaning for the duration of the blond woman's strip tease, nodded and grabbed the patron a drink.

"Hohoho, wow," The barber said nudging Nate.

Nate glanced over and looked at him with the slightest hint of irritation.

"What a show, huh," he asked.

"I wouldn't know, "Nate replied gruffly. "I wasn't watching."

"My god, man! How could you not? That there is the most beautiful woman in the west; Florence… I can't stop looking at her deep blue eyes… not to mention everything else!"

"Never heard the name before."

"Ah, you must be from out of town. Let me introduce myself; I'm the barber of Snake River. The name's Geo-"

Nate let go of his drink and held up his hand to stop the barber in the middle of his sentence.

"No need for names. I'm just passing through."

"A drifter… fair enough… Well, friend, what brings you to these parts?"

Nate's free hand dropped to his hip. He caressed the grip on his revolver, hiding it from view under his duster.

"It's like I said. I'm just passing through."

The barber nodded and took his drink from the bartender for a few more bank notes.

"Nice chatting with you, Sir,"

"Same to you," Nate mumbled.

The bartender walked over to a table on the opposite side of the room and started a conversation with his fellow townsfolk. The patrons of the Snake's Leg grew silent. Nate could hear the distinct clicking of heeled shoes on hard wood approaching him. A soft and warm hand dragged itself across his shoulders and a pale white arm wrapped around him as Florence sat down next to him. She winked at him from under a black veil she put on after the show. She put on other articles of less revealing clothing to keep her admirers at bay.

"Howdy, stranger," Florence breathed.

Nate looked up at her after she spoke. In the corner of his eye he saw that familiar yellow glow from under her veil, “Come and keep me company upstairs. It gets real lonely up there.”

Nate said nothing, and his expression did not change. He got up from his seat at the bar. He seemed mesmerized by her words. Florence led him up the stairs of the saloon and Nate sauntered after Florence.

They approached her room. Florence shut the door behind her and Nate. Florence walked past Nate and lowered herself down with her back upon her bed. She untied the silk string that held her top together once again revealing her pale and voluptuous naked figure.

“Well, c’mon sweetheart. I won’t charge… I won’t even bite, I swear… well, I’ll try not to…”

Nate unbuttoned his duster, coat letting it drop to the ground. Florence smiled as he walked toward her. Nate got on top of her. He spied silk ties near the nightstand on the side of the bed and tied Florence’s hands and feet against the four bedposts.

“Ooh, I didn’t take you for that kind of lover,” Florence cooed.

Nate straddled her, “I’m not.”

Florence’s expression turned one of sheer panic as she struggled to free herself from her bindings. Nate drew his sword in his right hand and covered Florence’s mouth with his left. With a swift jab of his blade, he pinned her right hand to the headboard of the bed. Florence’s shriek was muffled through his fingers.

“I'm going to take my hand off your mouth if you can-”

Florence's, yellow eyes darted around the room looking for any means of escape. She whimpered and cried behind Nate's grasp.

"She shrieked, "Fucking bastard! He sent you…"

"If you scream, you die. If you attract any attention or call for help, you will die. If you struggle, I'll cut something off… then you'll scream and then you will die. Do you understand?"

A look of horror combined with panic flooded of her face. She nodded slowly and nervously. Nate released his hand. Florence took heavy breaths. She shot a hateful glare at him. Her eyes flickered bright yellow as she stared intently into his. Nate quickly looked away.

"I guess your little trick doesn't work on me if I don't look at you in those fucked up peepers of yours."

"How did you know?"

"It's pretty damn obvious when you aren't under that spell of yours… and thanks to a certain barber. I'm going to ask you some questions. If you don't answer, I'll cut something off and… you know how the rest goes."

Florence reluctantly nodded again.

"Who are you?"

"Guess you're not his dog after all… I'm Florence… a simple whore from Snake River Canyon."

Nate's smiled. He covered her mouth again and twisted the blade in her palm. Her eyes rolled back in pain. Her muffled shriek turned to a breathy moan.

"I'm adding another rule. If your answers aren't truthful or the whole truth, I will know, and I will cut something off. Same question, Florence…"

"A long time ago, I was part of a crime organization. The sins. I am- was the sin called Lust."

"That's more like it… How many gang members are left?"

"That I remember, five and whoever the leader hires as cannon fodder and for grunt work. Myself, Gluttony, Envy, Sloth, and our leader the Gambler. Our leader had a flair for the cliché… There used to be six, but I never really knew Greed. None of us did. I've only seen him once… and it was brief."

"How did you get your eyes and your powers?"

"I don't know about the others, but I sacrificed a person who was… close to me. I received great power and great looks, but this power comes with… intense urges."

"Urges?"

"I received youth and beauty for blood, but I have to pay a price every day. Like the name Lust implies, I have to fuck whenever I can for as long as I can. I can't get enough. Cute nickname, huh?"

"Where can I find your fellow sins and your boss? Where is the eye of the devil?"

"They're scattered across the southwest. That's about all I know. It's been a hell of a long time. I remember where you can find Sloth. He should know where the others are. He was always a loyal dog."

"You sure are quick to sell out your friends."

Florence huffed at the phrase, “Friends? They were never my friends. Last I saw those bastards... It was years ago. I don’t work for the Gambler anymore and if I had to guess, not a whole lot of us do anymore.”

“Much obliged,” Nate said. He withdrew his blade from her hand and drew his other sword. His smile grew. Florence struggled again trying to squirm out of her restraints.

“I answered all of your goddamned questions. Let me go.”

“We never agreed to that.”

Florence’s face twisted once again in horror as Nate’s mouth donned a wide, gleeful grin.

Chapter Five: Flowers for Jane
-Central Idaho-
-1862-

The satisfying crunch of mud and gravel traveled through Jane's ears as she made her way home from the market. The air was filled with the voices of vendors trying to make a sale over the clamor of bartering customers. Horses pulling coaches zoomed by in the streets.

A bag of potatoes pulled at the strap on Jane's shoulder. They bounced from side to side. She rolled her eyes as she walked. The thought of potato stew or mashed potatoes for supper made her cringe. She clenched her hands into tight fists as she pictured her fingers pruning over while she peeled them. A gentle breeze brushed past her, pulling her short black bangs in front of her face. The wind made her flannel dance. She could feel the wind through her jeans. Jane looked at her hand, bringing it up to her face and brushed her hair from it. Dirt caked the undersides of her fingernails. She couldn't remember the last time she bathed. She dreamt of the warm soothing bath waters.

A circle of young men drowned the distant clamoring of the market out. Jane made herself walk faster, looking at the chaotic circle of testosterone and romantic pleas from the corner of her eye.

She sighed, thinking out loud, "Same spot… every damn day."

Jane caught glimpses of a familiar young blonde woman stood in the middle of the circle of men fighting for her affection. She smiled and laughed as flowers and candies were being paraded around her.

"Oh, miss Claiborne, how your golden hair flows so beautifully. Miss, Claiborne you look lovely today. You're mighty voluptuous. Can I take you to dinner, for sweets?! Oh, miss Claiborne! I wanna ask your hand in marriage and to have lots of babies with you. Blah, Blah, Blah, Blah, Blaaaaaaaaaah," Jane said out loud to herself.

Jane's annoyance faded the further she got. She looked back at the crowd around the blonde woman and down to her own tattered clothing and to her filthy fingernails. She put her head down and continued her journey home, staring at her feet. Jane let the soothing crunch of the mud and gravel tune out the declarations of love and admiration for the tall blonde woman. The more she thought, the more jealous she became. Jane tried her best to deny it.

The afternoon sun hung low, painting the sky with soft hues of pink, purple and orange. The fast pace of the town died down with the sunset. Jane stopped in front of a large brick building and walked through the doors.

The apartments always smelled at the end of the day. The accumulation of human filth and lack of care ensured it. Jane grimaced and made her way toward her room as she typically did. The narrow halls of the building reflected the look of her tattered and dirty clothing. Khaki colored paint peeled in most placed and flaked off, revealing the red bricks and the mortar between them. The mortar behind the decaying paint was more visually pleasing to her, more vibrant than the wallpaper hiding it. The wooden floor creaked under her as she continued toward her room. Aged wood bent underneath her, stressing under her weight. Jane wondered if it was a testament to her eating habits, or merely the failing integrity of the building. She hoped it was the latter.

Jane looked at the end of the second-floor hallway. As always, there stood Thomas. He held his right arm behind his back, revealing old sweat stains on the armpits of his long-sleeved shirt. His face and his clothing were stained with dirt, sweat, and god knows what else. He hadn't bathed in a long time judging by his looks. His clothes sported more dirt and holes than hers.

"Hello, Thomas," Jane smiled. "How were the stables today?"

Thomas smiled back. "Smelly and hot as usual. How were the markets today, any buyers?"

Jane looked to the bag of spuds, "Enough for a few meals and to keep the room this month, I hope."

Thomas nodded in agreement and stared at Jane with that same smile on his face and fondness in his eyes. He snapped out of his stupor and brought his arm forward from behind his back, revealing that same bouquet of wild flowers.

"For you, Jane."

Jane's grin widened. She joyfully pranced over to him and swiped the bouquet from his hand.

"Oh, thank you!"

Thomas' smile grew as wide and as warm as hers.

"You're such a good friend to me, Thomas."

His grin faded as she hugged him. His eyes embraced the floor and his heart sank. Same as always. They finished their hug and Thomas snuck a fake happiness back onto his face.

"Spuds for dinner again?" He asked.

"They're the cheapest food in town…"

"Jane, can I ask you somethin'?"

She looked at him for a moment, puzzled, waiting for him to speak.

"W-would you like to uh… to get some sweets with me after your dinner. It'd be my treat. Whatever you want, I'll pay for it."

"Oh Thomas, thank you… but, how can you afford all these flowers and these gifts for me?"

"Been spendin' more time at the stables to earn extra pay and saving up. Whadda do you say? D'ya want something other than spuds this evenin'?"

"I-I don't know. I haven't had a wash in ages. What should I wear?"

"I haven't either, it don't matter, and you can wear whatever you want. I'm guessin' that's a yes?"

Jane glanced at her potato sack and back to Thomas. She nodded excitedly. She took her key out from her pocket and unlocked the door to her room. Jane closed it behind her. Thomas wiped the faux smile from his face and turned toward the entrance of his apartment. He sighed, threw the door open with a loud creak, and shut it quietly after he somberly walked through.

…

Jane sifted through her rolls of old fabric for something to wear. The smell of boiled potatoes dominated the small space of her room. Unfinished pieces of her work lined the walls and edges of the room. Coats, dresses, suits, pants, shirts and hats covered what little furniture she had. Jane stopped digging and retrieved a somewhat clean navy-blue gown. She threw it on and left her apartment in a hurry, locking it behind her.

She walked down the hall and knocked on Thomas' door. After a moment, he answered. He had his brown hair slicked back and wore a clean, white-buttoned shirt adorned with a black bowtie and a pair of black pants.

"Thomas, I didn't know you had such nice clothes!"

"There's a lot you don't know about me. You look wonderful too, by the way. I never seen you in those colors."

"I've never had the chance to go into town apart from work. Where are we going tonight? Are there any places open at this hour?"

"I think Bart's candy shop, but we have to get there soon before he closes up!"

Jane nodded, and the young pair made their way out of the complex and into the summer Idaho night. The pinks, purples and oranges of the sunset faded. They turned into hues of dark blue and black with white flecks of stars dotting the sky. The town was motionless, and quiet except for the saloon near the main street. Most of the residents had either gone home, were spending their money on drinks, or were working there at the saloon. The streets seemed to be vacant apart from Jane and Thomas. The pair reached the shop door, but no light came from inside the building.

"Damn, looks like Bart closed up for the day," Thomas said.

"That's okay Thomas; we can try some other time."

"Hold on, I think I know one other shop. It just opened up across town. Do you want to try it?"

"Oh, I don't know. I have to be at the market early tomorrow and I have to finish hemming a pair of pants for a customer by tomorrow morning."

"It'll be quick, and I'll have you home before you know it… please?"

Jane crossed arms and looked down at the ground, pondering.

"You said it yourself, Jane, you never get to do this kind of thing."

Jane smiled at him, "Okay, as long as we don't come back too late."

Thomas extended his elbow to Jane. She reluctantly hooked arms with him. He led her down the main street and turned down a lane she didn't recognize. Thomas took turn after turn until Jane couldn't recognize any of the surrounding buildings. They appeared to be more rundown than the apartments she and Thomas lived in. The houses and buildings looked uninhabited. The streets were shadowy despite how clear the night was. The buildings had no light coming from inside their windows.

"Thomas, where are we… what part of town is this?"

He didn't answer. They stopped in front of and old, dark townhouse. The door of the decrepit looking house hung halfway open. He let go of her arm and walked inside, leaving Jane outside in the dark.

"What are you doing?"

Thomas did not reply.

"Thomas!"

Pieces of orange candlelight slipped through the cracks of the decaying walls. The light urged Jane to escape the dark. She stormed into the house to confront her friend. She walked into an antique of a foyer. The furniture was missing and probably already had been for ages. The structure smelled old and rotting. Thomas stood leaning against the wall opposite of the front door and opposite of Jane, watching her enter.

"Jane, I-" He began.

"I just want to go home now, you're scaring me."

"Would you please listen to me just for once?!"

Jane stormed toward the exit, but Thomas caught her arm and pulled her fiercely into the room. He stood between her and the door. He shut it, keeping his gaze locked upon her. Jane backed up and returned his gaze.

"Every day, I work as hard as I possibly can at those miserable fucking stables so that I can come home and see you smile when I bring you something. Whether its flowers, or sweets, all you ever say is that I'm a good friend."

"Y-you are, Thomas, you're my best friend."

"CAN'T YOU TELL?!" He shouted, "All I've wanted is to be more than your friend. I love you, Jane. I've tried showing you my affection every chance that I could… and still, you give me nothing in return."

Jane stood in place frozen as Thomas continued to yell at her.

"I'm sorry."

"Sorry for what, Jane?!"

"I just don't feel that way about you and… I-I wish I could have seen that earlier. I don't love you."

Thomas stood panting. The orange light from the single flame made his tears glisten as his face quivered.

"I saw you every day. I followed you. I see you looking at her as you pass her by, the beautiful Florence Claiborne. I just wanted to make you feel beautiful like her, feel loved like her. You are beautiful."

"Thomas, you're family to me, please stop. Let me go. I need to go home. Please take me home!"

Thomas took a dagger from his pocket and pulled it from its sheath.

"No, Thomas, Please!" Jane screeched.

Thomas strode toward her and raised his dagger. His tears stopped. A look of cold emotionlessness spread over his face. Jane sobbed as he tore the surrounding fabric with his blade. The blue gown fell to the ground and with it, her underwear. Jane stood naked and shaking, covering her chest with one arm and holding her groin with her other hand.

“Thomas, you don’t have to do this p-pl-.”

He brought the knife close to her throat. She fell backward and scrambled against the wall. With one hand, Thomas undid the buttons on his pants and undressed. He pulled her hand away from her groin as her forced himself in between her legs. She wanted to fight, bite, claw, scratch, kick and punch, but she sensed the sharpness of blade on her throat.

He spat on it, rubbed it in, and slid in and out of her, back and forth. She covered her eyes and sobbed as Thomas thrusted harder and faster. Her sobs could not drown out his animalistic grunts and moans. Jane's cries faded into a numb and quiet motionlessness. Her head tilted to the side lifelessly and bobbed rhythmically with Thomas’ thrusts. Jane's breasts flailed on her chest. Her legs drooped to her sides and trembled with each push into her.

Before she knew it, it was over. Thomas pulled out with a final grunt as beads of sweat trickled from his forehead and dripped onto her. The large globs of his semen oozed out of her. It was the only warmth throughout her body. Thomas took the knife from her throat and wiped Jane’s blood and her vaginal fluids from his genitals.

Without a word or a glance, Thomas put his clothing back on, blew the candle out, and left old rotting house.

Jane's eyes adjusted to the dark, as she lay in the same position, paralyzed and nude. She glanced over at the candle that Thomas had left. Its ember still smoldered upon the wick. A trail of smoke danced from it toward the ceiling. The night was quiet except for Jane's short breaths. She felt nothing. Her panic, her fright, her anger, her desperation, her sorrow all turned to nothing. Like the flame, she was so easily put out. Only a remnant of the brilliant and beautiful flame that she was before, now only a dying ember. Once strong, shining and brilliant… Now weak, dying, and dull.

Her legs shook as she managed to pull herself up. She felt the tickle of hot liquid dripping from her groin, and down her legs. Jane braced herself on the wall behind her and grabbed the tattered remnants of her blue gown and pieces of her underwear. She held the torn articles of clothing to herself as best as she could and shambled out of the front door.

…

Thomas wiped the sweat from his forehead as he swiftly walked down the town's main road. He sheathed his knife and slipped it back into his pocket, out of sight. Thomas looked behind and saw nothing but the shadowy blanket of night. He squinted through the light of a lantern.

His eyes darted and stung as they adjusted. He could barely make out the sign above the saloon's entrance.

The Dove's Glove Saloon

Thomas pushed the doors open and looked for a seat. He sat down across from a sharply dressed man. The brim of his hat shaded his face. His eyes seemed cut through that shade. Thomas perspired visibly in the wooden chair; his head darted around the room, following the erratic movement his eyes. The stranger in the suit slid a glass of gin to Thomas.

"Drink this, son, it'll make you feel better," the man said. His southern slaw was palpable, creole like.

Thomas' hands shook as he reached out and accepted the drink. His voice made Thomas shudder every time he heard it.

"Your first time, I gather," The man said.

Thomas nodded and took a gulp from his glass. "I don't feel right, mister. I loved her... and I-"

The stranger looked up. He smiled from under a silver beard and mustache, "We both got what we wanted, son. She denied you every step of the way. All you needed was a little incentive… and a weapon, I reckon."

The man reached into his coat pocket. He pulled out a wad of bank notes and slid it over to Thomas. Thomas reached out and accepted his payment.

"Does it feel right now?"

Thomas took a large drink of the gin and did his best to pull away from the man's penetrating gaze.

"It'd be best if you leave the state… dare I say even these United States. Your payment should get you to Mexico and then some. You can live like a king down there with what I just gave you."

Thomas looked at him with apprehension. The man tilted his head back and finished what remained of his whiskey.

"How do I get there?" Thomas asked, shaken.

"Some of my men are waiting for you outside the saloon. They'll get you started on your way."

"Before I go mister, what's your name and what do you want with Jane? Why did you want me to-"?

The man in the suit raised his hand to stop the Thomas mid speech.

"You shouldn't ask questions you don't want the answers to. Some knowledge is better left unknown."

Thomas stood up and headed out of the saloon doors in a rush with the wad of cash in his pocket. He smiled as he exited the building.

Two large men in dusters sat at the bar. They had their backs to the suited man. They turned to look at their boss as Thomas left. The stranger nodded at them. The two pursued Thomas out of the bar. The man in the suit followed them out after finishing the rest of the boy's gin.

They held Thomas back as he struggled to escape. Thomas met the stranger's gaze once again. Thomas gaped. The man's eyes glowed yellow. He patted Thomas' legs and took his money along with his dagger. The glint in his teeth seemed brighter than the flaming flicker in his eyes.

"Tell me somethin', Thomas, if I didn't give you this money, this means to an escape, and this rather persuasive, sharp piece of metal, would you have been able to rape the girl who never loved you back? Of course… you wanted to, needed to. I saw it in your eyes the day we met, but would you have done it… could you have done it?"

Thomas looked down at the ground as tears dripped from his eyes. The man's grin grew even wider.

"Well, son, I think it'd be a hoot to go see what would happen if you couldn't escape. Wouldn't you?"

…

Jane shambled down dark streets and alleyways for what felt like hours. She shivered at the bite of the cold night and held what little of her clothing was left on her body. Jane wandered the streets of the Idaho town. She stopped as a man came running toward her with a coach following closely behind. He wore a grey Gambler's suit and a Gambler's hat. He panted and bent over as he halted in front of her, covering her with a shawl. Jane wrapped it around herself and kept her eyes down with a dead look in her eyes.

"Are you alright, Miss?" The man in the suit asked between breaths.

Jane stood and remained silent. The man's deep and gravelly voice only brought her more discomfort.

"Let's get you somewhere safe and warm."

Jane limply followed. The elderly gentleman led her by the shoulders to his coach nearby. Two men sat at the top. One held reigns in his hands. The other leapt from the top to open the door for the man in the suit. Warm light inside the coach made her eyes hurt as they adjusted. The stranger closed the door behind them. He climbed back up top. Jane overheard one of them cue the horses to run as they began to move over the dirt roads of the town.

"Can you speak, miss?"

Still, she stared blankly at the floor of the carriage compartment.

"What did that boy do to you?"

Jane's eyes shot up and met the man's gaze with fire and ferocity.

"Why didn't you stop him?!"

"I was too late, I'm afraid. I was passing by in my coach, lost my way to the saloon. I saw the candle light from outside that abandoned house and stopped out of curiosity. As soon as I got out, the candle was blown out. I saw a young man exit the building in a rush. He saw my men, and I and ran for the hills, I could only assume what he did in there was horrible, so we gave chase."

"Did you catch him?!"

"I believe so… Come with me, dear…"

The coach stopped, and the door opened. The man in the suit and Jane stepped out. They were in front of her apartment complex.

"We chased him all the way to this here buildin', caught him as he was scrambling to open his door."

"What'd you do with him," Jane asked.

The man in the suit gestured toward the entrance of the building. Jane stormed into her apartment complex and charged up the stairs onto the second floor. She grabbed the handle of Thomas' door. It moaned open with a push. Hatred burned in her eyes. Thomas sat hogtied and gagged on the floor in the middle of a circle with strange markings around it. He begged and cried. His words were muffled through a cloth gag. A dagger sat on a nightstand next to him. She ignored the strange markings and watched. Tears streamed down his face, soaking his gag. Thomas' muffled pleas grew more desperate and wilder. His eyes widened. He saw her pick up the dagger. The old wooden floor creaked behind her as the man in the suit stood at Jane's back. The man looked at the dagger in her hand, at Thomas, and back to her. The stranger nodded to her encouragingly and stepped out of the room. She untied the gag from the quivering boy's mouth.

"J-Jane Please let me go, he's going to kill me. I'll do anythin', jus-" Thomas cried.

She bent down until her lips were almost touching Thomas' ear. She whispered as she brought the blade to his throat.

"Make me feel beautiful."

She held the back of his head as she slid her blade into the center of his throat. Blood gushed and trickled as Thomas choked on his blood and his cries. The man in the suit murmured and mumbled strange gibberish. Warmth returned to Jane. A sensation washed over her, overwhelmed her. Her body changed. She saw her hips widen, her skin faded to a new, pale, porcelain tone covered by a thick red spray. Her breasts swelled, and her hair lengthened, fading to a platinum blonde. Jane's bones and her muscles bent and contorted into a longer and thinner frame. Her face stretched into a pleasing shape. With it, an insatiable feeling came over her. She gasped and grabbed her irresistible curves. She couldn't stop touching her body. Every touch sent a sensation of ecstasy coursing through her, an overwhelming urge to put something, someone inside of her.

Jane rose and spied the key to her apartment resting onto the floor next to Thomas' bed. She extended her long pale doll like arms and grabbed it. She walked past the man in the suit, feeling her new features bounce with each step. She pushed the door open and saw her flowers resting on a table near a black silk gown for one of her higher paying customers. Jane took another project of hers and wiped as much blood as she could from herself. She then slipped the gown on and paired it with long black gloves of the same material. The gown hugged her new body. Jane gaped into the mirror, leaning against her wall and smiled at the woman she saw.

"What did you do to me?" She asked.

Jane's new voice sounded as silky as her dress looked. The gentleman in the suit leaned against the frame of her apartment door.

"I made your wish come true."

"How long does this last? Why do I feel so…"?

"The feelin' is a side effect. Both the effect and the wish last as long as you're at my side."

The man extended a hand to the blonde woman. With a smile, she took it.

"Where will we go?" she asked.

"Far away from here… There's some other folks similar to you that I'd like to introduce you to."

Jane and the stranger walked back to his coach where his men were ready to get them onto the road. She looked into the man's eyes. They flickered as pale-yellow flames. They strangely comforted her.

"What's your name?" She asked.

"You may call me the Gambler… and you? I believe a new woman should have a new name."

She glanced down at her tight, well-endowed body, and her platinum blonde hair.

"Florence."

Chapter Six: The Giant's Mine
-The Summit of Battle Mountain, Nevada-
-November 1875-

The dusty dirt roads of Idaho turned into narrow, rocky trails. Nate and Elaine made their way up into the snowcapped peaks of Northern Nevada. The brilliant blue skies were filled with billowing storm clouds that belched thick snowflakes. It coated the peaks of the surrounding mountain range and the trail they traveled on. The snow whistled past the two travelers. It was carried by an unforgiving wind. Nate wiped the melting snow from his face as they pressed on. Elaine rode along in front of him. Her head tilted back as she took a swig from her flask. She looked at him with glee. He frowned at her, displeased with how content she was in the storm.

"What're you so happy about," Nate asked, holding onto his frown.

Elaine swung her head around to look where she was going.

"Don't ya love this weather? It reminds me o' home," she replied happily.

"Scotland?"

"Ireland… ya bloody fool!"

"Whatever, you're just warm because of all that damn whiskey!"

Elaine smirked with pride. She sensed Nate's annoyed glare beaming a hole into the back of her head.

"So where are we off to now," She asked to break the silence.

"Battle Mountain. I need information on where exactly we can find and the members of the sins gang. Maybe gather more information about them. Eventually, we need to make it to the eye of the devil… somewhere across the border."

"Pfft, that's a stupid name. What a bunch of ninnies. I guess we're gettin' pretty close then?"

"According to the sin named Lust, we aren't far from it now."

"Lust told ya where to go just like that?"

"I tied her to her own bed and… convinced her to give me the all the information I needed."

"Did ya…"

"I stabbed her."

"With your penis?"

"With my swords. MY SWORDS... in her hands to subdue her."

"Ohhhhh… Aye, I can see that. Ya got the look of a fighter more so than a lover… What did ya do with her after ya got the information ya needed if ya don't mind me askin'?"

"I mind."

Nate remained silent after his last remark. Elaine looked behind her as their horses continued along the mountain pass. His face was as cold as the squall raging above. Nate's grim expression chilled Elaine more than the storm did. She turned back around and pulled her whiskey flask out.

"They slit her throat… the woman I loved most in this world… my wife. They ripped my infant daughter from her arms as she bled in the dirt… I'll be as merciless as they were… I will bring them the suffering and death they have brought me… I will get Sara back and the Sins will suffer before they die… Shepherds always-"

Nate stopped himself mid-sentence and pulled the reigns on his horse, stopping the animal in its tracks.

"There it is. Right where she said it would be," Nate muttered to himself, "The Battle Mountain Mine."

Nate and Elaine peered through the snowfall. The path widened ahead. They could barely make out a series of buildings made of wood and stone. The structures were illuminated by the orange light of torches strewn about the outside each door. As they approached, they saw people; men in tattered old clothing. They worked wearily, hauling ore and stone from a large hole in the side of a slope. Nate and Elaine rode past, watching them toil. The miners kept their heads down with defeat on their faces. They shuffled weakly through the storm. Their cheeks were sunken into their faces and their skin was stretched tightly against their bones.

Nate clutched the hilt of his right saber. He and Elaine made their way to the largest building on Battle Mountain. They dismounted their horses and Nate pointed to a small shack.

“Lust told me the sin here would have the locations of all the other sins. He'd have the exact whereabouts of the eye of the devil. I need you to look around for his maps. See if he has any other information you can get your hands on. Sloth is mine,” Nate said to Elaine.

“I thought ya needed me for my artillery not to be your little errand girl… and how do ya know she wasn’t lyin’ to ya?”

“If there’s one thing I know, it’s that enough pain will bring the truth out of anyone. I’ll need you eventually. Probably sooner than I expect. I can’t keep bringing knives to a gunfight, but it hasn’t been a problem so far. You’ll get your chance.”

Elaine rolled her eyes and approached the shack far to the left, up a steep hill. Nate headed for the wide wooden double doors of the largest stone house. With a forceful push, they creaked open and Nate stepped in. There was a large fire billowing smoke through a chimney. In front of the fireplace there was a desk with various ores and ingots lying on top. A hulking mass of a man with short and curly black hair and a dark complexion sat slumped at his desk snoring loudly. He stirred as Nate approached unsheathing his swords.

“Close the door, you’re lettin’ the warm out, you lowly piece of shit,” Sloth yawned.

Nate looked at the entrance and back to the giant who sat slouched still taller than a standing Nate.

“What’d I just say, slave,” he said more alertly as he picked up his large and drooping head.

Sloth blinked and rubbed his eyes at the sight of Nate. He appeared to be as confused and groggy as the stranger stood near the entrance.

"You a visitor?" his voice boomed with a southern slaw.

Sloth stared down at Nate's blades and frowned in slight disappointment, "I see you fought for the freedom of my people… forced into the Union, weren't you, Sergeant?"

"I joined for my brother," Nate replied.

"I should have guessed you fight only for your own… and where is he now… your brother?" Sloth asked with a smile.

Nate's hands drifted to the hilts of his swords. His stare grew more intense as his rage built.

"… And it doesn't look like you're here to buy metals from me either…"

Nate glared at Sloth, wary that he had some powerful and supernatural advantage over him.

"Your friend Lust told me where to find you. She said you know where the rest of the scum is."

Sloth snorted, shaking the foundation of the stone building, "Ah, so you're hunting sins… Even former members of our gang like that filthy whore… did you become a bounty hunter after your brother died?"

Nate held his position and his tongue along with it, ready for sloth to strike at any moment. He unsheathed his twin sabers.

"Judgin' by how quit you are, I'm guessin' I'm wrong again…" Sloth grinned and rose, looming six feet above Nate from behind his desk. As he rose, the sound of metal clanking came from under his black fur coat.

"Since you ain't no bounty hunter, I guess we sins did you a real unkindness. You want revenge… That's what I wanted a long time ago… and that's what I got… thanks to the Gambler."

Sloth reached over to the mantle of the fireplace and grabbed two iron lined leather gauntlets. He placed them on his hands and listened to the metal ping with the wiggling of his large fingers. Casually, he grabbed the edge of the large desk and hurled it over to the other side of the room with a pull of his arm.

"I won't simply give away information like that pitiful traitor whore did. I remain loyal to the Gambler. That man saved my life and the lives of many of my friends. He gave my brothers, my sisters, my friends their freedom. He granted me my vengeance."

Sloth approached Nate with his fists up in a fighting stance.

"Oh, shit…" Nate said.

Nate sheathed one of his swords and aimed his revolver at the giant's head. The Gargantuan man responded by guarding his face with his hands. Nate's six shots ricocheted off metal plating. Sloth lowered his guard revealing a victorious and vicious smile.

"OH, SHIT."

Nate readied his second sword once again. He took advantage of Sloth's sluggishness. He dashed under Sloth and wildly swung his blades at the backs of the giant's knees. They collided with the more metal plating.

"You like it?" Sloth asked him. "I fight with rather unconventional weapons as you do, so I had to compensate for gunfire and apparently, it works for swordplay too."

With a great heave, Sloth plunged his steel lined fist down. Nate dove and rolled to avoid the impact. Sloth struck the stone floor of the house with a thundering impact. It created a large crater and sent cracks running along the adjacent floor. Nate scrambled to his feet again. Sloth stomped over with another arm cocked back, ready to strike. Nate dashed and dodged around the giant, offering fierce slashes and cuts from his swords to find a weak point. Nate grew increasingly fatigued with every move he made. He knew he would give out soon if he couldn't pierce the behemoth's armor.

...

Elaine kicked the door of the shack open with her revolver pointed it into the small storage room. There was a thick layer of dust caked upon a bookcase to her left. All sorts of rolled papers and documents were thrown about its shelves. A faint light came through the snowstorm and through the window that overlooked Sloth's large stone home. She unrolled a piece of parchment from the top shelf of the bookcase. Elaine opened what appeared to be a map.

She read aloud, "Hideouts and last known whereabouts of the Sins."

Elaine searched around through more of the papers and found another map showing a base in a thin stretch of land near the coast of Mexico. She shrugged and holstered her pistol, rolling the papers up to take them back to Nate. Elaine stopped in her tracks as a small glint of light hit her eye. Slowly, she turned to look across from the bookshelf to see the muffled shine of dusty gunmetal. A scoped breechloader rifle leaned against the wall next to the window. She picked it up and inspected it thoroughly. She cleaned off a layer of dust with the sleeve of her coat.

"Well, aren't ya just the most beautiful piece o' arse I've ever seen," She said cooing to the weapon.

She opened the chamber and saw a round placed perfectly in its center. Elaine brought the chamber back into place and aimed the gun out of the window. She peered through the scope, pointing it down to the large stone house where she last saw Nate. Through the scope, and through a series of windows, she saw Nate fighting with a giant armored man and losing. All he did was cut up Sloth's clothing and scratch his armor.

"You'll get your chance, hasn't been a problem so far," She said in a goofy voice, imitating Nate.

Elaine carefully placed her sights on Sloth. She caressed the trigger of the rifle, her finger hovering just above it.

"Keep him there, Nate… right where I want him…"

A cheerful smirk ran across her face.

"At least I get to kill someone bad for once…"

...

Sloth lunged and swung at Nate vigorously. Nate grew sluggish as evaded the giant's swings. With a fake left punch, Sloth predicted Nate's slow dodge to the right and grabbed him. To Nate's horror, Sloth squeezed him with all his might. Sloth watched as Nate turned white from the asphyxiation. Sloth raised his massive fist again to finish him off.

"Say goodnight," Sloth said with a brutish grimace.

Nate squirmed as much as he could in Sloth's grasp, trying to escape. There was a loud crack of a rifle in the distance followed instantaneously by the shattering of glass. The splat of the sin's brain matter against the wall filled Nate with relief. The left side of his head was caved in. It sent a red spray and the pang of a bullet ricocheting off the right wall of the house. Sloth's grip loosened and Nate staggered gasping for air. The giant fell to his knees, cracking the floor as his large yellow eyes flickered and rolled into what remained of his head. From his knees, he fell onto his back with one final loud clang of metal.

While Nate hunched over, gasping and panting for air, he heard laughter rolling through the shattered window.

Elaine strolled through the open doors of Sloth's stone house fumbling all the rolled-up papers she had collected from the Shack upon the hill. She had her new rifle strapped to her back as she approached Nate with a giddy and childish smile stuck on her face.

"Ya sure got 'em good, eh?" she asked.

Nate looked at her blankly as he wiped the blood and bits of brain of Sloth from his face.

"Well o' course ya didn't… ya know, I think a thank you is in order."

"Thanks. I'm guessing that shot came from your new toy."

"Aye, isn't she a beaut?!"

Nate thought for a second on a sarcastic remark, but hesitated.

"Yeah it is. You saved my life with that shot. I don't know what I'd have done without you."

Elaine was shocked at Nate's genuine gratitude and stood speechless for a moment.

"Well, frankly ya probably would've died…"

"I also need to thank you for that."

"For what… speak up!"

Nate shook his head at her. They smiled at each other briefly as they walked over to the front door. The pallid and weak looking miners grouped outside of the entrance and greeted them. They stared blankly at the pair. Elaine reached for her pistols. Nate waved his hand at her, signifying for her to relax. A thin old man with a long beard and dressed in thick rags approached them. He peered past Nate and Elaine into the house. He gasped and threw his fists in the air as he faced the crowd of his fellows.

"The giant is dead", the man exclaimed.

His southern accent caught Nate off guard. It reminded him of the Gambler's way of speaking.

The large crowd of corpse-like miners mustered up what they could for a cheer. The thin bearded miner turned back to Nate and Elaine with a weak grin stuck to his face.

"Thank you, both. We thought you were just traders comin' to get ore from the giant until we heard that gunshot," said the bearded miner.

"Were you working for him?" Nate asked.

"Enslaved is a better word for it. The lumbering oaf pillaged our homes and had his men burn our… farms. He took us here to work as his slaves givin' us only enough food to survive and keep the work goin' at the mine."

Nate looked around the peaks and saw that the snowstorm ceased and left a thick white blanket across the trails rocks. The clouds remained and put Battle Mountain in a looming dark.

"Do you have any means of getting off of this mountain without hiking all the way down?" Nate asked.

"No. By foot we would more than likely starve before we got anywhere close to civilization… especially in the sorry state the giant left us in."

Elaine unraveled one of the maps she was carrying and peered at its contents for a moment.

"Aye, it's about a few days to the nearest town if you're travelin' by foot. About one and a half days by horseback if ya hurry," she said.

"We can send you a shipment of supplies here as soon as we get to the next town," Nate said.

"That would be mighty kind of you, sir."

"The shipment should be here in about six days' time. Do you have enough to last you until then?"

"I think not by normal standards, but we've managed on the slim supply he was givin' us. He kept the food stored under his house and we can ration it until your supply arrives."

"Will you be able to defend yourselves properly if any friends of the giant show up?"

"Again, in our state, no, but hardly anyone comes up here apart from food shipments every three weeks or so."

"Good. We'll head out to get that shipment here as soon as we can."

"We owe you our lives, travelers. What're your names?"

"That's not important; we'll be on our way as soon as this storm blows over."

"Fair enough. Looks like it'll start stormin' again at any moment. Let's go inside and warm up."

The miners gestured for Nate and Elaine to follow as they made their way to the houses. The crowd dispersed, and the sun set behind the dark grey clouds. The storm made the night dark as pitch.

Chapter Seven: The Bigger They Are
-Jefferson County, Mississippi-
-Walters' Plantation-
-1851-

The air outside seemed thinner to Jacob than usual, like he was trapped in a tight space. The sun and the southern humidity slid a blanket over him and the other workers as they harvested ripened tobacco plants. Sweat poured down his forehead and dripped down the rest of his body, soaking his rags. Jacob stopped and gaped up at the sky, squinting as he gazed upon a wondrous, vast and endless blue. He tried to wipe the stinging sensation from his eyes but ended up getting more sweat into them. He looked across the Walters plantation. Many ensembles of tattered clothing bobbed up and down among a sea of green. The Walters' mansion stood looming in the distance behind a tall and spiked iron gate. As he stared, lost in his thoughts, he found his fists clenched and his jaw clenched tight, grinding his teeth back and forth.

The crack of a whip brought him out of his thoughts. He pivoted to his left. William Walters sat on his horse with his whip readied at his side, staring intently at Jacob.

"Jacob," William yelled, "Quit lollygaggin' boy."

Jacob tilted his head from side to side cracking his neck loudly. He pulled his large arms across his chest, working the fatigue and soreness out.

"Yes, sir, mister Walters."

Will kept his eyes on Jacob as he heeled his horse forward, continuing his rounds on the plantation. Jacob saw the red of William's face under the brim of his hat. It did little to quell the intensity of the sun at noon hour. Jacob continued picking the tobacco, listening to the grunts of his fellow slaves as they worked.

...

As the sun worked its way down to the horizon, the slaves of the Walters plantation heard the ring of the work bell. Jacob stretched his arms above his head and let out an exhausted sigh. Work was finally over for the day. He took his place in line by the well to get water. A man reached up and clapped Jacob on the shoulder as he lined up behind him. Jacob smiled down at his friend.

"Don't you ever get tired out there, Jacob?" asked Andre.

"I reckon, I do," Jacob replied.

"Shit, not as much as us regular sized folk. What the hell is that woman of yours feedin' you, anyhow?"

Jacob laughed, "Whatever she can."

Jacob and the other workers craned their necks. A loud female shriek came from just inside the front doors of the mansion. Jacob's brow furrowed.

"Goddamn Wayne Walters..." Andre said through a growl.

Jacob clenched his fists, "Third time this week."

The mansion doors flung open. A young slave woman in a maid's attire came tumbling down the steps with Wayne Walters walking proudly behind. The young woman cried and pleaded as she picked herself up off the ground.

"Please, Mister Walters, I swear I'll try better-"

"Next time?" Wayne asked.

Wayne picked her up and backhanded her. The smack echoed across plantation grounds. The slaves around the house kept their heads down, ignoring Wayne's assault on the girl.

"You keep this up and there won't be a next time."

Wayne took up his horsewhip and raised it above the girl, about to hit her again with all his might.

"WALTERS!"

Jacob's voice boomed across the plantation, stopping Wayne before he could strike the girl.

"Damnit, Jacob, not again. Think of Chloe and your boy. Don't put this on them. Don't put this on yourself," Andre said.

He put his hand back on Jacob's shoulder, but he simply brushed it away. Jacob walked over to the gates. Wayne smiled and drew his revolver from the holster at his hip, pointing it at Jacob.

"What is it, boy? You gotta problem with the way your masters do things 'round here?"

Jacob stopped with his fists still clenched, staring at the plantation owner and the defenseless girl before him.

"I'll take her punishment, mister Walters."

"Oh, will you, now… a third goddamn time in how many days?" Wayne holstered his pistol. "I never thought I'd see such a noble man in my lifetime and working on my plantation, no less. My word, Jacob, you make everyone else here look like filthy animals, you know that? Takin' all sorts of punishment for 'em."

Wayne waved to William. The young man exited the house. He scooped the crying maid up and held her with his whip in his other hand.

"You already know what chivalry gets you here," Wayne said with a smile.

He pointed at the ground in front of him. Jacob kneeled and unbuttoned his shirt, sliding it off and revealing his back. The sun glinted off the sweat that coated his skin. It ran along the ridges and dips of the long scars. Jacob gripped his shirt tightly, readying himself.

"You know the drill, boy. Since you're double the size, you get double what she would," William laughed.

Wayne held his hand out. William gave him the whip. Wayne snapped it by Jacob's head with a loud crack. Jacob remained still, still gripping his shirt.

"Twenty lashes," Wayne yelled.

Jacob's eyes were glued open and his jaw was clenched tight. His shirt ripped in his grasp as the whip tore at his back. New wounds formed, and old scars reopened. Blood sprayed with the arc of the whip and trickled with the sweat down Jacob's reopened wounds.

Jacob looked over at the maid. She stopped crying and gaped with her hand covering her mouth. As his pain grew, the sound of the whip dulled. His spine throbbed and oozed blood. The crack of the whip ceased. Wayne bent down in front of Jacob, close to his face.

"Damn, boy. I'm startin' to think you enjoy this kinda shit," Wayne said with a short laugh.

Jacob didn't answer. He sat and looked at the ground in front him, breathing short breaths.

"I can't have one of my slaves enjoyin' himself for wrong doin's on this plantation, now can I?"

Jacob looked his master in the eye, remaining on his knees.

"Answer me, boy."

"No, Sir." The anger in Jacob's voice rose.

"That's right… and we can't have our maids not learning' from their mistakes… William, ten for the girl."

"With pleasure," William replied.

Jacob shot up onto his feet, looking down on Wayne and William.

"Best not get too excited, Jacob," Wayne said.

His revolver clicked as he pulled the hammer and pointed its barrel at him. Jacob stopped. He watched as William threw the young woman to the ground. Laughing, he threw the blood-soaked whip back and forth. Jacob winced and looked away and winced with each strike. The girl's shrieks hurt Jacob more than the crack of the whip. He looked at Wayne and William; hate burning just below the surface. With one last shriek, she fell to the dirt bleeding and unconscious.

"You're one of the best workers out here, Jacob. Last thing I wanna do is have to put you down, but you keep playin' the hero…" Wayne looked at the hanging tree and then to Jacob with a shrug.

Wayne and William strolled into the mansion. They closed the doors behind them. Jacob walked over to the unconscious girl and picked her up. He kept his arm away from the gashes on her back as he carried her toward the slaves' quarters. Andre ran up to Jacob walking along beside him. Jacob looked down at Andre. He shook his head in defeat.

"What are we, Andre?"

Andre looked up at his friend with a confused look upon his face.

"What are we if we can't even stand up for little girls?"

Andre kept his gaze locked on Jacob as they walked, sensing the shame and the sorrow in his voice, "I… I guess…" His voice faded.

"If we were all like you, Jacob, we'd be ruling the world and the crackers would work for us… either that or we'd die tryin'," Andre said softly.

Jacob looked down and returned Andre's gaze. He saw the somberness and the sincerity in Andre's eyes.

"We need you, Jacob. We need you just as much as the rest of us out there."

The two friends broke eye contact to look ahead. They inhaled deeply through their noses, as they smelled their home cooked meals drifting toward them. The scent filled their mouths with drool.

Andre clapped Jacob on his shoulder once again as he left to his shack a couple doors down from Jacob's.

"Keep them safe, brother," Andre said.

Jacob looked down at the girl in his arms. She shook as she came to. Her jaw quivered as she wept from the pain. Sounds of weeping brought an elderly woman from her shack. The old woman waddled over as fast as she could. She looked panicked. The girl looked up at Jacob.

"Thank you, Jacob,"

"Can you walk?"

The girl nodded. Jacob let her down softly. She winced as her feet touched the ground. She wobbled toward the old woman who braced her. The old woman helped her walk to her shack. She looked at Jacob and nodded. He raised his hand in acknowledgement and headed to his own home.

Tattered cloth blocked candlelight from the outside as a makeshift curtain. The cloth wavered back and forth in a gentle breeze as Jacob brushed it aside. Chloe stood stirring the pot facing away from the entrance and facing away from Jacob. Ed lay in the corner under the sheets napping before dinner.

"Supper's almost ready." Chloe said without looking.

Lightheaded, Jacob leaned against the frame of the shack's entrance. The shack shifted under his weight with a loud scrape. Chloe turned around and approached Jacob, taking him by the hands and leading him to the nearest chair. As he sat down, the chair creaked. She grabbed a bucket of water and took a rag that hung on a line near the fire. Chloe went behind Jacob and cleaned his wounds.

"Is Ed still feelin' ill," Jacob asked quietly.

"Boy's been sleepin' all day, he's gettin' better though," Chloe replied.

"Who'd you rescue this time?"

Jacob recognized the irritation building in her voice, and looked at the ground, "Nobody."

"I bet nobody has you to thank for comin' home all scarred, bloodied and beaten just for 'em. Who was it?"

Jacob sat still for a moment. Chloe spun him around. She looked him in the eyes. He remained silent as tears rolled down his face.

"I couldn't save her, Chloe… not this time… I couldn't save anyone… fuckin' William and Wayne Walters made that girl howl n' bleed even after they agreed to let me take the whippin'… you know I can't help it. I'm bigger and stronger than anybody here. I can't stand by and watch them do that."

Chloe reached over and held him. Jacob held her too.

"One of these days, Jacob, you ain't goin' to come back. I need you… Ed needs his father to protect him like he protects everyone else."

Chloe felt him nod his head as they embraced. They let each other go. Jacob wiped his tears. Ed stirred in his sleep and pulled his sheets over himself. Jacob smiled at his son and at Chloe. She continued cooking.

"I will keep you both safe," Jacob whispered to himself.

...

The carpet lining the mansion floor muffled the footsteps of the servers as they brought food back and forth from the table. Wayne Walters dabbed sweat from his forehead as it trickled down his sunburnt cheeks. Will looked at his father nervously. They sat with their guest quietly at the table, munching on an assortment of Mississippi delicacies. Their guest wore a fine grey suit. The two Walters were shaken by something in the man's voice despite the familiarity they sensed in its southern twang.

"Mr. Walters, have I thanked you for this wonderful meal yet? That'd be mighty rude of me, if I have not already. I haven't had such fine seafood since I was just a young man," Said their guest.

Wayne coughed nervously, "Why, you are most welcome to anything in our estate, Misterrrr..."

"I wouldn't want to bother you with the burden of pronouncing my name, Mr. Walters, I'm afraid it's quite long and difficult to say. Call me... Sir, if you wish."

Wayne Walters nodded, looking down at the table. William's nervous gaze was locked upon the grey suited man.

"Mister Walters, might I also say that your plantation is marvelous. You keep a fantastic establishment here!"

"Why thank sir, we Walters love to keep our house and farm clean as well as keep our slaves disciplined and happy."

"I'm glad to hear it. Now, let's talk business here… I would like to purchase one of your finest slaves here from the Walters plantation."

Wayne sat in thought for a minute, "Well, we have some women and young men that we might want to get rid of."

"I want one in particular. I believe his name is Jacob, an exceptionally large slave. Works the fields, typically. Likes to stir up trouble."

Wayne gawked, "How did you-?"

"Is Jacob for sale?"

"I- He's… one of my best workers in spite of his insubordinations. I'm afraid I can't sell him to you."

The Gambler threw down his utensils and reached into his coat pocket. With a thud, he tossed a wad of two thousand dollars onto the table.

"I'm sure this'll change your mind," The Gambler said.

"T-This is…"

"Well over two times of your average asking price, I know… sources. Do we or do we not have a deal, Mr. Walters?"

Wayne looked over to William who shrugged dumbly. Wayne then looked back over to the Gambler who smirked while picking scraps of shellfish from his teeth.

"I- well yes, I'll take that deal," Mr. Walters replied, flabbergasted.

The Gambler held his index finger up at Wayne and pulled out an extra five hundred dollars. Wayne and William's jaws dropped simultaneously.

"There is a bonus if you can accomplish a rather shady task for me after I take Mister Jacob into my ownership and away from the Walters plantation…"

"For that collective amount, Sir… Merely ask…"

The Gambler smiled devilishly at Wayne and William, folding his arms in sheer glee.

…

Jacob winced at the incessant pain in his back. He got up and looked over at his wife and son to make sure he hadn't woken them up. Chloe snored with her mouth open and drooling. Ed lay on his side, returning to sleep right after he ate. Jacob's head spun as he walked out of the shack. He did his best to snap himself out of his lightheadedness. The cool night air caressed him. The moon shone in the sky. Tiny twinkling stars varying in subtle hues of reds and blues accompanied it. The plantation was quiet. Jacob listened to the distant chirps of insects and the occasional splash of bayou fish. The soft patter of footsteps approaching in the grass disrupted

Jacob's sense of tranquility. In the dark, it appeared as though a single lantern was floating toward Jacob, but he knew better. His anger welled back up inside of him.

Wayne and William Walters came stumbling from their home. William was armed with a double-barreled shotgun and chains hanging from his belt. Wayne followed with his revolver and lantern. They saw Jacob standing in front of his home and jumped, surprised to see him. They pointed their weapons at the giant slave.

"Mister Walters," Jacob whispered, "What is this?"

"Come quietly, boy, no need to make a ruckus, now," Wayne whispered back, "You've been bought."

William Walters approached, tucking his weapon under his arm. He pulled the chains from his belt and revealed a pair of iron shackles, Jacob looked at his shack, shaking his head.

"Easy, now. You get any funny ideas, and you'll never be able to see 'em again, I'll make sure of that."

"Just… let me say goodbye," Jacob said.

William stopped and lowered the restraints in his grasp, nodding at Jacob in approval. Jacob approached the shack. Chloe and Ed lay next to each other still fast asleep on the floor. Jacob bent down as he could, kissing his son and his woman on their foreheads without waking them.

"I love you, Chloe… Ed," He said faintly. Jacob wiped the tears from his eyes before they could drip onto the sleeping pair.

"Don't you go nowhere, I'll be back as soon as I can."

With one last look at his family, Jacob shuffled sadly outside of the shack. He approached William who put the iron chains around his enormous wrists. Wayne and William prodded the giant slave with their guns, making him walk in front toward the Walters' mansion. There sat a coach with an individual in a grey suit in leaning against it. The man looked up at Jacob and handed the Walters their twenty-five-hundred-dollar end of the bargain.

"You must be Jacob," Said the one in the suit, "I've heard a hell of a lot about you."

Jacob stood glaring at him. The man kept his eyes hidden from view underneath the brim of his hat.

Wayne… William, this is where we must part ways. It was an absolute pleasure doin' business with y'all."

The Gambler shook both of their hands, took the key to Jacob's restraints, and gestured for the newly purchased man to squeeze into the cabin of his coach. Jacob did so with some effort. He barely fit. Jacob felt the rumble of the coach as it rolled over the gravel path leading away from the plantation.

The Gambler looked up at Jacob as they sat together in silence. Jacob glared down at the man, his head thudding against the ceiling with every bump.

"Jacob, do you have a last name or a name you'd rather go by?" the Gambler asked him. He fiddled with the key in his pocket and brought it up to Jacob's Wrists, undoing the shackles. They fell to the floor of the coach's cabin. Jacob looked at the man puzzled.

"Jacob is… all I've ever known," he replied, rubbing his wrists.

"I bet you're wondering why you're all cooped up in my coach with me and I bet you're even more curious about why I just unshackled you when you could undoubtedly kill me right here and right now."

Jacob sat and listened to the man, keeping eye contact with him as they bobbed up and down on the road.

"What I want from you, Mister Jacob, is your notorious strength and endurance, but I don't want you as a slave. I want you to choose what I offer you, and you have the freedom to deny my offer or negotiate our terms, of course. It is all up to you. If you say no, I will have some of my men escort you north to safety."

Jacob remained in thoughtful silence for a moment as the Gambler looked at him inquisitively.

"First, I don't even know the name of the man who freed me… Who are you?"

"I'm the Gambler," He replied with a smile.

Jacob looked at him blankly.

"A nickname I was given a… long time ago," He reassured Jacob.

"Okay, Gambler, I will work for you on the condition that my family comes with me wherever we go and that they'll be safe no matter what. I want them to be free. Can you promise me that?"

The old man opened the coach window and poked his head out.

“Turn around, back to The Walters’,” The Gambler yelled.

The coach swung around, and the two passengers braced themselves.

The Gambler smiled, “You’ve got a deal.”

…

Jacob and The Gambler pulled up in front of the Walters’ Mansion once again. One of his drivers pulled the door open on the Gambler’s side. Jacob got up. The Gambler held up a hand to stop him.

“Stay here, Jacob. I think things might get a bit messy if they see you out of your shackles,” The Gambler grunted.

“I thought you said I had a choice…” Jacob replied.

“You do, it’s merely a strong suggestion. Slave owners… especially these Walters don’t take too kindly to the freedom of black men... especially their former slaves… and especially if I just bought you a few moments ago. I’m goin’ back to buy your family and I want this deal to go as smoothly as possible. Don’t want Wayne and William getting’ their drawers in a bunch.”

Jacob reluctantly nodded and let the Gambler conduct his business with the Walters. The Gambler gestured for his two drivers to follow as he made his way to the front doors and knocked. A young slave woman answered the door. The Gambler smiled at her.

"Grab Wayne and William Walters for me," he said.

"I'm sorry, sir, they went to bed just a moment ago," She replied, smiling back at him.

"I'm afraid that the matter is urgent, wake them up."

The maid eyed the man's holster strapped his chest. She nodded shakily, raced upstairs, and woke the Walters. They descended their staircase in their long-johns, holding candles at their sides.

"What is the meanin' of this, Sir, I thought you'd left already," Wayne said rubbing his eyes with his off hand.

The Gambler raised his head from the ground as his men stood behind him. His they glimmered yellow at the two tired Walters.

"The other part of our arrangement. Is it complete?" the Gambler asked.

Wayne stood more upright, "Why, yes, Will and I took care of 'em right after you left with Jacob."

"Good," he grinned, "Now, where did you put 'em?"

"Left 'em up in…"

Wayne's voice trailed off. The clicks of revolvers from behind the Gambler shut Wayne up instantly. The Gambler looked at William and pointed the barrel of his gun in the young man's face. The Gambler held his index finger up to his lips. He forced himself inside with his armed men.

"You, keep your guns trained on 'em. They move, put a bullet in them. You, gag them. I'll get our new friend and tell him the terrible news," The Gambler ordered.

He stormed outside around the corner to where Jacob stood at the side of the coach. Jacob looked at the Gambler who wore a solemn expression and took his hat off. He placed it against his chest, shaking his head slowly while looking at the ground.

Jacob rushed toward the Gambler, "WHERE," he shouted.

The Gambler pointed. Jacob ran as fast as he could to the backyard of the Walters' mansion.

Chloe and Ed swung by their necks in the willow tree. Jacob's bellow echoed across the plantation. He rushed over to the tree to bring their bodies from the branch. Jacob untied the rope and let them down into his arms, bringing the nooses from their necks. Their skin was cold to the touch. Jacob wailed. The cries brought the slaves out from their quarters, frightened at the ferocity and desperation of Jacob's wails.

The Gambler peered from behind the side of the mansion, at the man holding his family inside of a large red circle drawn crudely in the grass. The Gambler whispered his incantations. He approached Jacob carefully.

"Jacob, I- I am sorry. What they did was… if there's anything I can do, just-" the Gambler began.

Jacob stopped his screaming. He looked over to the Gambler tears still streaming, his family still in his arms.

"I want power… I want the power to free my people from this. No more suffering. No more death. I want the power to stop it all… and bring them the suffering and death they have brought on us…"

A strange feeling came over Jacob. His eyes fluttered open and closed. He could barely keep them open. His anger kept him awake. Jacob's large frame swelled. His bones snapped to grow thicker and longer. New muscles tore along with the clothing he wore. They swelled and expanded wildly. Jacob raised himself, the earth straining and crumbling under his new weight. He turned his head to the Gambler who stood admiring the giant that loomed over him.

"The Walters…" Jacob said his voice now inhumanly deep and loud.

The Gambler walked back toward the front doors of the house, leading the giant through them. As Jacob walked, the earth shook under him and with it. The Walters squealed and cried behind their cloth gags. A giant approached. The Gambler stepped inside the doors and out of the way as Jacob smashed through the entrance, standing six feet above the top of its frame. He sent planks and broken wood splintering at Wayne and William who were kneeling on the floor, whimpering. Jacob looked down at them. He picked William up, fitting the boy's entire head and neck in the grasp of one enormous hand. He pinched the gag off with his fingers and looked stoically at the boy who babbled at him in a panic.

"N-n-no, Jacob please it was-" William began.

Jacob cut him off. He squeezed. William Walter squirmed in his grasp, his eyeballs bulging and his face turning purple. The boy stopped crying. Jacob's hand covered his mouth. Jacob looked Wayne in his eyes.

With a final clench, blood and pulped brain matter popped from William's orifices with a sickening splash onto the floor. Wayne vomited into his gag and scurried toward the front door, still crying and choking on the remnants of his dinner. He crawled into the threshold of the door, but the giant caught him by the collar of his pajamas and hoisted him into the air. With one hand, Jacob held the man by his torso and with the other, he gripped Wayne's arm and tore it off. Wayne screamed at the top of his lungs. Blood gushed from the base of his shoulder. Jacob tore off his other arm, his legs, and his head, squashing it in his palm. He flung Wayne's torso across the room.

...

Jacob walked out to the willow tree. He dug graves for Chloe and Ed. The Gambler waved his two men to help the giant. Before long, they buried Jacob's Family and went to the coach. The Gambler's men readied it for departure. Jacob sat tiredly at the mansion steps; his eyes fluttering open and closed, as they were earlier. The Gambler stood by his coach and looked at Jacob.

"Jacob, we're headin' west to Nevada where you can fill your end of the bargain. Is there anythin' you need before we leave?" The Gambler asked.

Jacob looked up and nodded, "I want to say goodbye to a friend of mine and add a condition to our deal," Jacob replied.

The Gambler waited for Jacob to speak his mind.

"I want to take every man from here to Nevada with a whip. I... we will make them feel what I felt when I worked here."

The Gambler nodded. He hoisted himself into the coach and looked out at Jacob who started toward the slave quarters.

Dozens of slaves cowered at the sight of him and the booms of his approaching footsteps. Only one came forward. Jacob kneeled as Andre looked up at him.

"Jesus Christ, Jacob what did they do to you…"

Jacob looked at his new immense features with uncertainty and looked back down at his friend.

"I don't know, Andre, but I'm giving power to you, our brothers, and our sisters," Jacob thundered, "We have the power to free them now. I can help. Go take them up north, it's safe up there."

Andre shook his head; "I think I got a little work to do in these parts before I go north. Seems a lot more of our people need help like you gave 'em tonight."

Several other men approached from behind Andre. They placed their hands on his shoulders.

"What'll you do?" Andre asked.

Jacob looked toward the coach and then at Andre, "My place is in the west… with the man who bought my freedom. Along the way, the slave owners will know our pain. They will know what it's like. After I take them, do what you can to free our brothers and sisters…"

Andre stepped closer to Jacob and clapped him on the shoulder, "Good luck my friend. Stay safe."

"Same to you, Andre."

With a final exchange of looks, the freed men parted ways, and the giant wiped his so that no one could see.

Chapter Eight: Forsaken Ground
-Coyote Springs, Nevada-
-December 1875-

Nate and Elaine made their way down dusty and sandy trails. Withered Joshua trees were strewn scarce throughout the desert as far as they eye could see. Battle Mountain towered in the distance behind them. The incessant pounding of the horses' hooves on the sand was driving them both insane. Regardless, Nate and Elaine rode on.

Eventually, they spotted a wooden sign post through the heat waves and the blinding, blazing sunlight. It was a titled, worn and disheveled sign pointing to the nearest town. It had been too long since they last stopped and restocked their supplies. Help was on its way for the miners of Battle Mountain. Nate and Elaine were on their own in what seemed to be the middle of nowhere.

Coyote Springs 5 miles

"That's the place. The last known hideout o'… Pride accordin' to the map," Elaine said while straining her eyes.

"Let's find him," replied Nate.

The pair of riders dug their heels into their horses. The Nevada wastes were filled with abandoned buildings reminiscent to the state of the sign they had passed. Charred inns, shacks, and saloons filled the horizon.

Nate and Elaine rode down what remained of the main road of Coyote Springs. They passed a well. Nate got off his horse and picked up a small rock. He dropped it down the well and heard a splash.

The smell of decaying oak planks filled the air. Structures creaked and moaned in an arid desert breeze. The living monuments shrieked in an imaginary pain as the wind pushed them and the sand wore them down. With the arid wind, came the smell of soot and ash. Nate looked around and spied aged bloodstains splashed about the burnt oak buildings. Nate ran his hand along the stains of the nearest building. He could almost see the tragedy seeping from the wood. He imagined thriving streets one day… and the next, a smoldering graveyard.

“Do you think Pride left?” Nate asked.

“By the looks o’ this place, aye. It looks like everybody here either died years ago or got the hell out o’ here when they could.”

“Alright. Any of those maps say where the next settlement is?”

“Southwest from here. About thirty or so miles… hopefully, it's not another bloody ghost town.”

“Let’s set up camp here for the night, we’ll head out in the morning.”

“Sounds like a plan.”

Nate and Elaine pried what they could from the decrepit structures for firewood. They built a small bonfire in front of an old inn where they discovered dusty wire frame beds. Elaine poked the fire to keep it alive.

Nate stared into the fire and got lost in his thoughts as he lay in his bed. The man could not get to sleep despite his best efforts. His restless mind haunted him with images of the past flickering in the flames. He wished that they'd burn away.

The sun set, casting a long shadow along the night. Elaine unpacked her things from her horse. She threw down her old bedroll and put her hat over her face, trying to wind down. The woman could not close her eyes no matter how hard she tried. The silence of the ghost town was unnerving to her.

"We've been traveling together for about a month now and I still don't know all that much about you," Nate said, still staring into the flames.

"And why may I ask would ya want to know about me," She asked, her voice muffled by her hat.

"Curiosity, I suppose, but I'd also like to know who you are before I should trust you."

"Are ya fuckin' kiddin' me, Nathaniel? I saved your sorry arse back there on that bloody mountain."

Nate tuned his gaze from the fire to look at Elaine, "You did, and I thank you for that. But who were you before I hired you? How did you get so good with guns? How do you drink all that liquor?"

Elaine paused for a moment before answering his question. She gaped at the charred buildings and then into the fire with her brow furrowed. She pulled out her flask and took a long drink.

"I…"

A low mumbling whispered its way through where they sat. Nate turned his head to the end of the main road. There, he saw a poor excuse of a church hunched in the distance. Candlelight burned in the two large stained-glass windows that were facing them. The small flames weakly illuminated the inside. Nate drew his weapons and approached the beaten down building. He glanced back at Elaine who was sitting slouched, fiddling with her revolvers facing away from him.

"You coming or what," Nate prodded.

"Aye, I'm right behind ya, just reloading these suckers…"

Nate looked toward the chapel once again.

"Did one of those papers tell us anything about Pride," Nate asked, while keeping his eyes on the church.

Elaine caught up to him.

"All these papers say is that Pride is a male. About… sixty years old by now. He made the sacrifice o' the sins and got control o' the lifeless… whatever that means…. Wish these descriptions weren't so damn cryptic. He was a preacher once, and I reckon he still thinks he is by the looks of where he's at. He used to collect donations from the churchgoers for his miracles. Says nothin' else. Think he'll be a threat?"

"Does it matter?"

Elaine shrugged in response. She tucked the documents back into her coat and readied her weapons again.

Nate and Elaine reached the door. The muffled speech was a light whisper and swiftly became a loud uproar of verbal blasphemies. Nate pulled the doors open and they stepped inside. The oak surfaces of the walls were tinged orange by the light of hundreds of candles.

Nate and Elaine faced the center of the church where Pride stood ranting incoherent gospel to his crowd of slouching followers. Two parallel sections of six pews lined the room. In the pews, sat numerous decaying corpses. Their skeletal figures had dried green flesh and skin clinging to their bones. Large bite marks were missing from several places throughout their bodies. Their heads were tilted toward the sermon and with their arms folded in their laps as if patiently awaiting their passage into the kingdom of their lord and savior. For them, salvation never came. Pride stopped his sermon. He finished chewing on what looked like rotten jerky and turned his attention to Nate and Elaine.

"Ah, all ye faithful… we have two new initiates for our lovely little chapel. Let them come and embrace the gifts of god," said Pride with a dry and raspy call.

Elaine stood her ground with her revolvers pointed at Pride. Nate charged to the podium where Pride stood.

Pride lifted both of his hands with his palms up, "So will it be with the resurrection of the dead. The body that is sown is perishable, it is raised imperishable; it is sown in dishonor, it is raised in glory; it is sown in weakness, it is raised in power; it is sown a natural body, it is raised a spiritual body. If there is a natural body, there is also a spiritual body."

The dead cracked and crumbled to un-life. They began to reanimate. Their skin snapped and crunched. They rose and fixed their sightless gazes upon Nate and Elaine. Death stripped them of their voices. Their screams came out as raspy moans and dry hisses. Where their eyes once were, only hollow pits remained. Elaine acted quickly. She unloaded her .357 rounds into the skulls of the skeletal churchgoers closest to Nate. Nate swung his blades barbarically into the ranks of the approaching undead. He severed limbs and skulls as his sabers smashed through dried bones. The corpses that took bullets from Elaine rose again and continued their slow, shambling pursuit. The closer the dead got, the more ravenous they became.

"For our light and momentary troubles are achieving for us an eternal glory that far outweighs them all. So we fix our eyes not on what is seen, but on what is unseen. For what is seen is temporary, but what is unseen is eternal."

Nate lined the ground with pieces of skeletal torsos. The jaws of severed heads snapped at the air, no longer able to attack. The dead marched. They approached Elaine who shot frantically at the deceased crowd. No matter how much led she pumped into them, it seemed to have no effect.

"Elaine," Nate shouted, "Cut off the arms and legs!"

He threw one of his swords in her direction. It clambered toward her and landed on the floor at her feet. She tossed her revolvers aside and scooped it up. Elaine slashed ferociously through the limbs of the dead. She watched as their bones fell into small, twitching piles. Pride's grin soon faded along with his sermon. Nate and Elaine slashed through the entirety of his undead forces.

Writhing cartilage and snapping jaws covered the floor of the chapel. Nate and Elaine stood panting and admiring the mess they had made. Elaine wiped the sweat from her forehead and tossed Nate's weapon back to him. She walked over to her revolvers and flicked the twitching bones from them. She planted the guns firmly in her holsters. Nate did not turn his hateful look from Pride as he caught his sword. He stormed up to the podium. Pride fell with his arms raised, shaking, and guarding his face. The sin wept on the floor.

"David said to God, I am in deep distress. Let us fall into the hands of the LORD, for his mercy is great; but do not let me fall into the hands of men," Pride pleaded, hiding himself from Nate's fury.

Nate crouched over Pride, pinning the sin's neck with both of his blades in a scissor like hold against the floor of the church. Nate breathed heavily and felt anger surging through his arms. He wanted so feverishly to sever Pride's head from the rest of his fragile looking body. Nate's fingers trembled on the hilts of his sabers.

"Nate…" Elaine said, "Nate, look at him… he ain't worth killin'… he's just a fuckin' worm."

Nate paused. Elaine's hand covered his fist. Elaine stood behind him with her head hung low. He looked to his prey. Nate no longer saw a power-hungry gang member, only a demented old man.

Nate roared and plunged his weapon downward. Pride yelped and froze. His sword was stuck into the wood centimeters from the wrinkled preacher's ear. Nate slowed his breathing. He no longer shook. He took his blades from the wood and sheathed them as he rose. With one last glance, Nate shook the urge off.

He stormed out the front doors of the chapel, leaving Elaine and Pride in the room together. Pride lowered his arms and wiped his tears. The sin rose to his feet. Elaine watched Nate as he headed back to their camp.

Pride shrieked and raised his hands again, "For the wrath of God is revealed from heaven against all ungodliness and unrighteousness of men, who hold the truth in unrighteousness!"

The bones and decaying flesh shook violently and reanimated once again. Pride pointed at Elaine.

"None can serve two masters. Either you will hate the one and love the other, or you will be devoted to the one and despise the other. You cannot serve both God and money!"

Without looking, Elaine took up one of her revolvers. She pointed it behind her and placed a bullet into the forehead of Pride with a boom that rolled through the night. The forsaken chapel was enveloped once more by the eerie quiet.

Elaine holstered her gun. She stared long and hard at the floor. Her eyes darted to the entrance. Nate sat with his back to the building, hunched over the fire, staring at his palms. She walked to their camp and tucked herself into her bedroll, turning on her side facing away from the fire.

"Elaine…" He began. His voice shook in his throat.

"Nate…" She responded without facing him.

"Why the hell can't I control myself? Where the fuck does this feeling, this rage come from? … What the fuck am I?"

Elaine let the question die as the words fell from his lips. She stewed in silence for what seemed like ages, not knowing what to say.

Nate climbed inside of his own bedroll. The pair of travelers stewed in their thoughts. They tossed and turned in the unsettling silence of the desert night. Neither one of them slept a wink.

Chapter Nine: The Farce of Father Christopher

-Coyote Springs-

-Nevada 1866-

Beads of sweat rolled down Father Christopher's forehead. He flipped through the pages of the bible that rested on the podium before him. The roof of the chapel provided him and his audience members' solace from the glare of the Nevada sun. However, the small wooden structure did little to protect them from the heat.

It was quiet in the church except for Father Christopher's attempts to search for an appropriate verse to conclude his Sunday morning sermon. The flipping of pages echoed across the room. He ran his fingers through his greying black hair, tugged at his collar, and stared at his audience.

Father Christopher recognized a woman who sat in the first row. She wore the same beautiful dress every Sunday. She was seated with a small smile on her face as she leaned on the pew in front of her, hands folded as she mouthed a prayer. It brought a smile to the priest's face.

His stare shifted to Doctor McGrath who was wearing a white suit as he usually did. He sat in a pew near the middle row. The doctor looked at father Christopher attentively with his legs crossed. He fanned himself with his fine straw hat. Visible wet stains had formed under the armpits of the man's suit.

Father Christopher turned his gaze to the furthest pew from him. He pinched the skin in between his eyes and sighed heavily. A haggard looking individual was sprawled out on the very last pew. His arms were stretched out, his head was tilted nearly all the way back and his mouth was agape. He snored loudly. His chest rose and fell rhythmically, jostling the open bottle of liquor resting in his crotch.

Father Christopher grinned and slid a hand under the left side of his bible. With a loud thump, the priest slammed the bible closed. The drunk shot up with a gasp and choked on his spit. His bottle fell to the wooden floor, spilling the rest of the liquid. The clang of glass against the hard-wooden floor caught the attention of the other four churchgoers. They all turned to look at the man. The drunk shrugged at the priest. They all looked back at Christopher.

"Off the top of my head, let us conclude today's mass with Colossians three twelve to three fourteen… Therefore, as God's chosen people, holy and dearly loved, clothe yourselves with compassion, kindness, humility, gentleness and patience. Bear with each other and forgive one another if any of you has a grievance against someone. Forgive as the Lord forgave you. And over all these virtues put on love, which binds them all together in perfect unity… That is to say, be friendly to each other. Treat thy neighbor as thyself. I thank you all for coming today and all the days before. That concludes today's sermon. May Jesus be with all of you today and these days to come… and try to stay as cool as you can in this heat," Father Christopher said.

The priest grabbed his bible and descended the stairs from his podium. The drunk stumbled out of the room first, leaving his bottle under the pew where he sat. A pair of unremarkable audience members followed. Doctor McGrath stood near the middle aisle in between the two sets of the pew rows. The young woman prayed with her hands folded in the front row. She still had her eyes closed.
"Hello, Father," The doctor said with an Irish accent.

"Doctor McGrath. Thanks for coming again." Christopher replied.

"No need to thank me. A man who tries to save lives needs a wee bit o' faith and hope here and there."

The doctor broke eye contact and glanced around the chapel. Father Christopher looked with him. The state of the structure did anything but improve over the years. The smell of dry, decaying wood filled the place. The rafters were strewn with cobwebs and abandoned bird nests. Rays of light poked through the slats on the roof. Even the pews were missing planks in their seats and in their backs. Father Christopher scratched the back of his head and returned his gaze to Doctor McGrath.

"It's seen better days, doctor."

"I have a proposition for you, father."

The doctor eyeballed the donation bowl behind Christopher. A dusty coin lay at its bottom. McGrath reached into his pocket for his billfold, Christopher raised his palms in front of him to stop the doctor.

"I can't…"

"Well, sure you can! It's a donation to the church, I insist!"

"I appreciate it, but…"

"Is my money not good enough for you?"

"NO, don't get me wrong doctor; your money is more than good enough it's just that… well…"

"Well what?"

"You saw it. Here today in the chapel…" A female voice said from the front of the building.

The priest and the doctor turned to the approaching woman. Her blue dress bounced along with her long black hair as she came toward them. She had her hands folded politely in front of her.

"Not to sound rude father, but… Nobody in town comes to mass, not even on Sundays," the woman chimed in.

The two men stared dumbly at each other momentarily, then back to the pretty lady.

"I'm sorry Miss," The priest began, "but I don't think we have been acquainted yet. I see you here every week, but I'm afraid that I still don't know your name."

"Miss Claire Abbey. Just Claire if you don't mind."

"A pleasure, Claire. I was about to tell Doctor McGrath the same exact thing. There's no point in wasting your hard-earned money on a church that no one goes to regularly… except for you two, of course."

"Have we met, Miss Claire?" McGrath asked the woman.

"Well, yes sir. I'm not sure if you know this, but I think you've treated just about everybody in town… and then some. Everybody knows your name. We met once some time ago. I had a stomach pain, and you prescribed me something I am currently forgetting the name of," Claire smiled at him.

"Most of the people may have given up on this chapel, but I think there's a way we can bring them in here and make that empty donation bowl into an overflowing and full-fledged donation bucket," Claire said.

McGrath and Christopher looked at her with puzzled expressions, waiting for her to finish her thought.

"But, I don't think you're going to like it very much, Father…" She said with hesitation in her voice.

"Uhh… Why not," The Father replied.

"Well…"

Father Christopher folded his arms and gave Claire a stern look while Doctor McGrath appeared to be a bit more interested in what she was about to propose.

"Hold on, Father, let's hear this young lady out. I know you don't wanna see this chapel of yours torn down or re-purposed for a brothel or somethin'," The doctor said, "What exactly did you have in mind, Claire?"

Claire smiled mischievously at the two men. Father Christopher looked at the poor state of his church again. Uncertainty settled in the pit of his stomach. He already didn't like it.

…

Coyote Springs had its streets populated with both travelers and residents. They filled seats at the saloon, huddled around the general store, and bartered in the streets. They traded for furs and other valuable commodities. There were probably hundreds of them walking the streets, in and out of the town's buildings.

Claire stood in the middle of the main road with the sun beating down on her. She flicked a fan out and cooled herself off. Her emerald green blouse fluttered in the desert breeze. Claire scanned her surroundings and made sure she was the center of attention for at least one onlooker. A man in denim pants, leather boots, and chaps tipped his hat at her from a distance. She smiled waved, batting her eyelashes at him.

"Perfect," She whispered to herself.

Claire looked over at Doctor McGrath's office next to the general store and at Father Christopher who awkwardly browsed dried meats and jerkies inside of the general store. The priest kept his attention down at the food spread out before him. Claire glanced at the cowboy. He was still making eyes with her.

Claire's eyes rolled back into her head. She collapsed in the middle of the street. The cowboy and some other townsfolk took notice to her dramatic fall. Surrounding people formed a tight circle and clamored around her in a panic. The cowboy pushed everyone aside to get to her.

"Quick," The denim clad cowboy yelled, "Somebody grab Doctor McGrath, he'll know what to do with her!"

A man closest to the Doctor's door pounded on it until the doctor came out looking confused.

"What is it?"

The bystander at the door pointed to a circle of people in the middle of the road. The doctor nodded and stormed in that direction.

"Out o' the way, c'mon move," the doctor shouted, shimmying and shoving his way past the crowd as they watched frozen.

The doctor brushed aside the circle of onlookers to see Claire cradled by the cowboy. There was panic is his eyes as he looked to the doctor.

"Everyone, back up! Give her some air," Yelled McGrath.

The crowd retreated a few steps all at once. McGrath picked up her wrist and held it for a moment. He took smelling salts from his coat pocket and brought them up to her nose. Claire didn't respond.

"Shite…" Doctor McGrath cursed to himself.

"What's the matter with her, doc," the cowboy asked with a shaky voice, "I-I was just standin' outside the saloon and I saw her fall over all of a sudden."

"She's still gotta heartbeat, but it's faint." McGrath eyed the fan on the ground next to her and nodded at the young man, "Use that to give her some more air, boyo."

The cowboy frantically grabbed the fan and waved more air into Claire's face. The doctor coughed to cover up his laugh. The sight of a macho cowboy waving a lacy fan like that was too much.

McGrath brought his right ear down to her mouth. The doctor shook his head and gripped his hat tightly against his chest. The crowd gasped and held their breath. Father Christopher sighed from the back of the general store. He glanced up and made the symbol of a cross on his chest, shoulders and forehead.

"God, forgive me…" The priest whispered.

Christopher made his way to Claire and McGrath in his clerical attire. As people saw him, they murmured to themselves. McGrath looked up at the priest and then down to the limp young lady.

"Here to give last rights?" Doctor McGrath asked.

Christopher had a look of determination glued to his face. He shook his head and pulled his rosary from his pocket.

Father Christopher kneeled beside Claire. The crowd behind them leaned in to see what was happening. Christopher placed the cross of his rosary on her forehead and took a deep breath, closing his eyes. He leaned, arching his body toward the sky.

"He gives strength to the weary and increases the power of the weak. Even youths grow tired and weary, and young men stumble and fall; but those who hope in the lord will renew their strength. They will soar on wings like eagles; they will run and not grow weary, they will walk and not be faint…" Father Christopher whispered.

Claire did not stir; she remained motionless as the crowd leaned in closer still waiting to witness the outcome.

Then the priest yelled, "Surely, he took up our pain and bore our suffering, yet we considered him punished by God, stricken by him, and afflicted. But he was pierced for our transgressions, he was crushed for our iniquities; the punishment that brought us peace was on him, and by his wounds we are healed!"

Claire's fingers twitched slightly, and then her arms and her mouth began to move. The crowd gaped in astonishment. The girl was brought back to life.

Then Father Christopher boomed, "The LORD protects and preserves them — they are counted among the blessed in the land — he does not give them over to the desire of their foes. The LORD sustains them on their sickbed and restores them from their bed of illness…. RISE. RISE FROM YOUR SICKNESS AND BE WELL!" Claire jolted herself awake into a coughing fit. The people around stared with their mouths agape.

"This man is a servant of God," somebody declared loudly from the crowd.

"Praise Jesus, it's a miracle," a feminine voice yelled.

"Mary, mother of God…"

"By all that is holy…"

The crowd murmured in prayer and in awe as Father Christopher rose and stared heroically out into the

crowd. McGrath stood next to him still clutching onto his hat.
The cowboy looked on at the priest beguiled while fanning himself. Claire shot the cowboy a look and snatched her fan back from him.

"Sir, you saved this woman's life. You are a hero," McGrath said, "What is your name?"

"My name is Father Christopher Rhodes, but it is not I who saved this poor young lady… It was by prayer and by the grace of the lord Jesus Christ himself that this person breathes again!"

Claire, the townsfolk, and Doctor McGrath all watched in amazement as the miracle worker walked straight to his chapel down the road.

Claire and McGrath smiled coyly at each other. People immediately dropped what they were doing to follow father Christopher into the chapel. Father Christopher looked at the crowd flocking behind him as he neared the steps of the chapel. His brow furrowed. Guilt washed over him.

…

- A few weeks later-

"Now from Luke six twenty-seven to thirty… But to you who are listening I say: Love your enemies, do good to those who hate you, bless those who curse you, pray for those who mistreat you. If someone slaps you on one cheek, turn to them the other also. If someone takes your coat, do not withhold your shirt from them. Give to everyone who asks you, and if anyone takes what belongs to you, do not demand it back."

Father Christopher gazed at the pews in his chapel. There wasn't an empty space in the building. Some churchgoers even stood lined along the rear of the building for the entire Sunday mass. Nearly everybody in the building had their hand clasped together and their heads hung in prayer and thoughts of their god. Every man, woman, and child looked up at him intently, with bright smiles on their faces.

Father Christopher watched as the donation bucket was being passed around. Bills rustled, and coins jingled as more churchgoers made donations. Claire and McGrath sat on opposite sides but in the same front row of pews. They smiled up at the priest brighter than the rest of the crowd. He returned their smiles and closed his bible.

"Thank you everyone for hearing the words of our lord on this beautiful Sunday and I can't thank you all enough for your generous donations toward this chapel. Renovations will continue and there may even be more pews coming in for those of you standing up in the back! Keep Jesus in your hearts as we part."

The chapel roared with applause as the priest walked away from the podium. A chorus of pleading requests bombarded him.

"Father Rhodes, please heal my son," A man shouted as he reached out from the chaos of the crowd.

Christopher grabbed his hand and held it, “Bring him in tomorrow and we will see what the lord can do for him.”

“Father, please cure my alcoholism!”

“Father Heal her!”

“Father Rhodes!”

“Thank you, Father Christopher!”

“Father I need your healing hands!”

“Father, Christopher, I-”

“Father, help us-”

The people roared with pleas as Christopher walked down the center of the chapel. He hurried down to the entrance of the chapel and flung the doors open. He spoke to the audience as they quieted down and flooded out of the old wooden building.

“Come to me individually, my brothers and sisters and the lord will do his best to heal your ailments. I’ll do my best to see all of you, but I am merely one servant of God,” Father Christopher yelled over the crowd.

The last ones to leave the church were Claire and Doctor McGrath. They walked by the priest. Claire hugged him, still smiling at the faith’s success. McGrath gave him a sly nod and shook his hand. Christopher Rhodes let out a sigh, stepped inside of the chapel, and closed the doors behind him. He looked into the empty building, enjoying the silence. He glanced over to his donation bucket. It was filled to the top. He gaped up at the rays of morning light peeking through the holes in the ceiling with an expression of worry upon his face. The stunt he, Claire, and McGrath pulled in town did not sit well with him. He shuffled over to the back row of pews and sat down. Father Christopher Rhodes hung his head not in prayer, but in regret. His eyes grew heavy. He rested against the pew in front of him and drifted off.

…

The sound of gunfire rolled like thunder over the town of Coyote Springs and sent Father Christopher hurdling out of his sleep. He raised his head from the pew. The cries of people filled the silence in between shots that grew louder with each moment. Christopher ran to the window of the church to see what was happening outside. Shadows flew by the church in the night, screaming, raving. Others gave chase, cutting through the dark with each shot. Dozens of torches were lit in the street, illuminating the faces of those who lit them. They stood waiting for something, a sea of orange beacons in the street.

…

The Gambler smiled down at his men. He rode into the main street of Coyote Springs. He gripped the reigns of his horse until he heard the leather creak under his grasp. Somebody in a duster coat lingered behind the Gambler. The gunfire died down.

"We took care of the sheriff," The man said between rapid breaths.

"Anyone else that knows how to use a firearm left alive?" The Gambler asked.

"I reckon we're just wrapping that up, boss."

"Good. Take everything you can. Burn the rest, but leave the church… oh, and have fun."

"You heard him, let's get to it, you dirty bastards!"

A mob of gang members shouted in delight. The man ran off and took twenty others with him to sweep the town for valuables.

The Gambler looked to his left. Two sets of fiery yellow irises flickered at him. A chill of satisfaction ran through him. The distinct ping of steel filled the air. Sloth stood and played with his newly forged armor. From the lower set of eyes, came the feminine giggle of Lust as she eyed the Gambler in anticipation.

The Gambler looked to his right and his smile grew even wider. Two yellow flames returned the look. Greed pulled the hammers back on the revolvers in their hip holsters and cocked the Winchester rifle strapped to the saddlebag. Greed glanced up at the rooftops and then to the Gambler. The Gambler nodded at Greed and the rest of the sins. The night came alive with the orange glow of torchlight.

…

Father Christopher ducked at the window as he saw the large cluster of torches scatter. To his horror, the orange light flew through the windows of the buildings and onto their rooftops, thrown from the streets below. The black of night was replaced with a dancing inferno. Houses and shops were soon filled to the brim with flames. Men came rushing out, their hands and arms clutching loot, weapons, even food.

Screams of terror came rushing from behind the looters. People engulfed in fire ran flailing through broken windows and crashing through smoldering doors. Women and children sprinted like crazed animals from their homes into the streets covered burning and charred. Their skin cracked and split. They fell to the dirt wailing and moaning as their vocal cords burned.

Christopher could not look away. Amid the burning carcasses and the screams of the townsfolk, loomed four eerily still silhouettes. The demonic flicker of their eyes danced along to the rhythm of the fire behind them. There were two on horseback and two on foot. The rider in the middle gave the other three a nod.

The priest whimpered, "I saw when the lamb opened one of the seals… and I heard, as it were the noise of thunder… the four beasts saying, Come and see…And the kings of the earth, and the great men, and the rich men… and the chief captains, and the mighty men, and every bondman… and every free man, hid themselves in the dens and in the rocks of the mountains…"

The other yellow-eyed rider kicked its steed. It took off with blinding speed between the flames that devoured the town. It fired all six shots from each of its twin revolvers. The shots were so fast, it sounded as though the rider wielded a Gatling gun. In a blink, it rode off, gone in an instant. In its wake, twelve rifles dropped ownerless from balconies and rooftops. The lifeless bodies of their operators followed. Some had holes in the center of their foreheads. Some had their faces caved in. Most had their heads completely missing.

The giant yellow-eyed figure stomped forward. Somebody fled from the saloon and mounted his horse, spurring frantically. The giant cocked his arm back and swiped at the man on top of his horse. His frame collided with the giant's swing. A sickening crunch filled Christopher's ears. The escapee flew through the window of the general store and into the blaze. The priest searched for his screams, but he was dead as soon as the giant touched him. The horse seized and squirmed on the ground. The giant stomped on the creature's neck once and it was still.

The third figure sat casually looking to the rider in the middle and then to the crowd of Coyote Springs townsmen who followed it in a stupor.

The last rider looked straight into the church window. It dismounted its horse and walked straight toward the chapel.

The priest retreated from the window. He backed into the aisle between the pews of his chapel and toward the podium. He stood staring at the doors. His hands shook as he struggled to pull the rosary from his pocket. The doors of the chapel flew inward as two men in dusters masked with black bandanas rushed in with their revolvers at the ready. A man in a grey Gambler's suit and a grey hat walked in with a wide grin in between his silver beard and mustache.

Father Christopher's voice shook, "...For the great day of his wrath is come; and who shall be able to stand?"

The man in the suit stared at Father Christopher as he approached, the same wicked grin stuck to his face.

"My word, a man of the cloth in these parts? I never would've thought. What a sight to behold," he snickered.

His voice filled Christopher with dread. The priest held his rosary up in between himself and the Gambler.

"Even though I walk through the valley of the shadow of death, I will fear no evil, for you-"

"Are with me; your rod and your staff, they comfort me. You prepare a table before me in the presence of my enemies; you have anointed my head with oil; my cup overflows..." The Gambler chuckled, "Oh, spare me your clichéd prayers, preacher," The Gambler raised his arms with his palms in the air, "You should be proud... I'd have lost my faith right about now if I were in your position. Your god is absent, Father Rhodes... mine is-"

Someone covered in soot and ash ran in and slammed the door behind her, sobbing. She peered out the window unaware of what awaited her.

"CLAIRE, RUN," Christopher yelled.

The woman gasped and scrambled. The two men fired their revolvers at the door. Claire fell and scrambled backward into the chapel. Father Christopher dropped his rosary and fell to his knees.

"-Here…" the Gambler said, "Why don't you take a seat right next to this prideful preacher of the Lord Jesus Christ…?" he mocked.

One of the Gambler's lackeys walked over and dragged Claire by her hair. She shrieked in between her sobs next to the priest.

"Clear some space for me and keep these two from goin' anywhere," The Gambler barked to his men.

A man kept his revolver pointed at Christopher and Claire while the other dragged the pews from the middle of the room to the sides. The Gambler took a knife from the sheath in his belt. He stared at the pair on the floor. Claire and Christopher flinched at the sight of the blade.

The Gambled chuckled and ran the blade across his palm, hissing in pain. He circled the man and the woman. He closed his eyes, muttering in a strange language. A streak of the Gambler's blood created a circle around them. After a moment, the Gambler re-opened his eyes. Claire eyed Christopher and he returned her gaze. Her soft blue irises made him comfortable as he looked into them. She took his hand.

A flash blinded him for a second. Christopher's ears rang. He could hear nothing but the high pitch squeal. He gaped at the Gambler. The barrel of his Schofield revolver was pointed next to Christopher. The weapon belched smoke. The entire world seemed to go by slowly. From her knees, Claire had arched her spine. Her weight shifted backward from the force of the bullet. The left half of her head was a dark red pit. Chunks of her brain, skull, and hair flew. It all dripped down her dress in the aftermath of the shot. The hollow sound of her skull hitting the floor numbed him. The muscles in her fingers loosened and twitched as the bullet passed through. Christopher did not let go. He sat in the circle with her, still holding her hand. Warmth faded from her flesh.

The Gambler holstered his weapon and stared at the priest, his grin wider and more sinister than before.

"Pray to your God," The Gambler ordered, "Tell Christ what you want most… beg him for it."

The Gambler waved at his men. The man with yellow eyes and his two lackeys left Father Christopher in the dark of his church. Flames continued to rage throughout the rest of Coyote Springs. It brought a shadowy orange glow to the chapel.

They left him on his knees in the circle of blood. The mob grunted and yelled at their horses in the distance. They galloped away, the gangsters with the torches, the yellow eyed demons, all of them. Christopher fell forward onto his palms. He stared at the floor. Coyote Springs fell silent… Eerily so.

"Please… give them back…" The preacher wept.

Father Christopher rose. His eyes opened inhumanly wide and darted all over the floor. He gripped the hair at each of his temples. He panted, crawling hurriedly over to the nearest wall. He tore tufts of his greying hair out and screamed at people that weren't there. He held his knees, teetering back and forth. He swiveled his head around the room wildly trying to see what wasn't there.

He slammed his skull against the wall, trying to be rid of the silence that dominated the space in his psyche, but it was a vast wasteland, stillness, and nothingness. No matter how hard he tried, he could not think. His intuition, the voice of thoughts. It left him there… Just like everyone else that night. All Alone.

He stared to the middle of the church. His eyes flickered yellow. Claire's body shifted and contorted. Her arms and her legs snapped underneath her weight with loud pops and cracks. Claire rose, shaking and twitching in the soft glow of the flames outside. Her body was bent and contorted. She shambled toward Father Christopher. He looked at her corpse twitch and shuffle over.

By the light of the inferno outside, he saw her tilted head drip pulverized brains onto her pale grey skin. Chunks and strings of coagulating blood dotted her clothes. Her jaw hung by a thread and her tongue flopped from her mouth. Tendons pulled her digits and her arms tightly, awkwardly across her chest.

Claire stood gurgling and swaying in front of him. Father Christopher raised his hand. The bones in Claire's arm snapped to match his commands. Tears streamed down the priest's face as he smiled, his jaw trembling. Claire's mouth moved with his. He reached up and placed his hand back into hers. Father Christopher Rhodes strode slowly to his podium with Claire at his side. His laughter prevailed over the inferno of the forsaken town.

Chapter Ten: Once A Sin

-Lake Morena, Southern California-

-January 1876-

Nate and Elaine watched the surrounding scenery change. Over the time they traveled, the desert ghost town of Coyote Springs transformed into the lush and green Californian settlement of Lake Morena.

The Joshua trees and sand dunes turned into rocky fields of grass and oak trees that surrounded a large brown body of water. The lake cooled the air around them as they approached the town.

The wind caressed the two travelers. It cooled the sweat that coated them and soaked their clothes. Nate and Elaine stopped at the crest of a hill that overlooked the town. Elaine unraveled the piece of parchment from her saddlebag.

"Welcome to the last known whereabouts o' Gluttony," Elaine said through a large, bored exhale.

"What info do we have on this one?" Nate asked.

"Well, let's see 'ere… Male. He's about thirty years old by now. He owns the Lake Morena Inn. Sacrificed to get the power to heal 'imself in an instant. He trained the Gambler's men in pickpocketin', lootin', stealin'... basically how to be proper degenerates. Says this is where the Gambler initiated and trained his hired guns before draggin' 'em to the eye o' the devil. At some point, the

Gambler stopped sendin' men 'ere for training, but it doesn't say why."

"… If he's anything like that demented old man we'll leave him be."

"Oh, look at ya bein' so merciful all of a sudden. What happened to the wrathful Nate that I've come to know?"

"Merciful?"

"Aye."

"In his state, it would have been cruel to let pride live. You saw to that after I walked out of that damn church."

Elaine laughed as she continued to focus on the paper.

"What, is that funny to you?" Nate asked.

"No, its somethin' else. It's a bit o'… information about Gluttony. I don't think this'll be much o' a fight at all… Gluttony's price for making the sacrifice; his urge is extreme hunger… and as time went on, I think I know why The Gambler stopped sendin' recruits over here… You're goin' to love this."

…

The scent from the kitchen wafted into the flared nostrils of Gluttony. His eyes rolled back in delight. He thoroughly enjoyed the smell of his immense meal. The sensation never got old.

The meal was comprised a platter full of creamy garlic mashed potatoes garnished with chives and a huge helping of butter. It was accompanied another platter containing stacks of steak seared to a rare perfection. He gripped a fork that was dwarfed compared to his bulbous hands. He raised his first bite to his and plump face.

With every one of his movements, his body jiggled profusely. Sweat rolled down his freckled brow. Fiery orange hair cropped his swollen head. Every movement of his jaw brought the sound of loud smacking as he shoveled his morsels down as fast as he could.

Gluttony's breathing was labored even while he was seated. Scraps of his meal were strewn about his gut as it heaved up and down with every breath. Every so often, he would take a pull straight from a bottle of wine to wash down his food.

When the waiters at the Inn had to bring him more, they were repulsed by the stench of a heavy and prominent body odor that stained the surrounding air. Gluttony's seat creaked underneath him as if to cry out in excruciating pain from the great pressure that his posterior created.

"NICK," he cried out for the waiter.

One waiter rushed out from the kitchen hiding his expression of disgust, "Pat… y'want more?"

"I need more butter for the taters. Make it snappy, these ain't getting any hotter sittin' out here."

"At this rate we won't have any for the guests…"

"What was that?"

Nick sighed without answering and made his way back into the kitchen. He held his nose to block the stench that hung perpetually around Patrick as he left.

Patrick turned his head to squint through the double doors. The sun was beating down through the door. It made the two figures that had just walked in appear as silhouettes.

"Hello," Patrick said through a particularly chewy piece of steak, "Welcome to the Lake Morena Inn. If you talk to Nick, he'll get you a cozy room upstairs right away."

Nate and Elaine strolled toward the table. Nate smiled and mustered a small laugh, "You're right. The only fight here is keeping ourselves from vomiting."

Nate and Elaine chuckled.

Patrick dropped his fork, stopped eating, and rose surprisingly fast from his seat, "Whoa, whoa. Fight? I ain't looking for no trouble here, mister."

"Neither are we," Elaine said with her hands on her hips.

Patrick spied the swords on Nate's sides and the firearms strapped to Elaine's back and sides.

"Oh, Jesus Christ, this is a robbery… Help, somebody… NICK… SHERRIFF!"

Nate sighed and waved his hands at Patrick to snap him out of his panic, "We don't need your money either. We only want some information, Gluttony."

Patrick regained his composure and sat down at the table as calmly and as carefully as he could.

"Whoa, whoa, whoa… I ain't seen or contacted that monster in ages. He just up and left us here."

"Us?" Nate asked. He reached for his swords and Elaine reached for her rifle. They scanned the second floor of the inn for gluttony's back up.

"Relax! Like I said I don't want a fight."

"What about the company you keep here? Anyone else we should know about?" Elaine inquired.

"Listen, anybody that gave a shit about The Gambler… that monster and his business is long gone. It's just me n' Nick that stuck around. He's in the kitchen fetching' me some more fixin's for my lunch. He don't bite neither."

"What exactly did you do for him?"

"He took a percentage… a majority of the loot his men and I would take from other towns n' settlements. Provisions mostly; jerkies, dried meats, furs, weapons, ammo, whatever we could scrounge up and carry back here… He snagged most of the trainees too when he knew they were ready to join up with him."

Gluttony glared down at his disgustingly round figure, still chewing vigorously on food and breathing loudly.

"Believe it or not, I used to train his guys to steal and thieve when I could get up from my seat without having to rest for ten minutes afterward. The men would stay at the inn here while I put them through their training."

Nate and Elaine raised an eyebrow at the man before them.

“You,” Nate and Elaine asked simultaneously.

Patrick nodded enthusiastically, “Yep. You’re looking at the greatest thief in the southwest… well, the greatest a long time ago… and a few hundred pounds ago.” Nate and Elaine chuckled to themselves, looking at each other unable to contain their skepticism. Patrick sighed as he swallowed the last bit of food in his mouth and looked down to his plate.

“I never wanted to be a sin… especially after the Gambler made me into this pile of lard you see before you.”

Nate and Elaine stopped their laughter.

“Could you tell us about the curse he put on you and the other sins to give you your… abilities?” Nate asked.

“All I know is that the Gambler has to keep you in a circle of symbols while he speaks his gibberish. He asks you want you want most, like a wish or something. Then, his spell kicks in and you get the side effect immediately along with your new powers.”

“What did ya wish for,” Elaine chimed in.

Gluttony frowned, “I-… I just wanted to be able to get away from him… no matter what he did to me.”

Patrick gaped past his plate. His brow furrowed, and his breathing got harder, lost in the memory of his first encounter with the Gambler. Nate glanced back at Elaine. She looked at him and shrugged.

"The loot you and your trainees took… did you send it to the eye of the devil?" Nate asked, breaking the silence and the tension.

Patrick snapped out of his trance, shaking his head, "Yes, and to Battle Mountain, Nevada for Sloth's slaves," Patrick replied.

"Do you know about the place?"

"Battle Mountain?"

"No, the eye…"

"Y-yeah, it's in Baja California near a strip of land on the west coast. The locals call it El Soldado."

"We know where it is. Do you have any other information on it?"

"My information is a bit outdated, but it's an old Spanish mission that he had converted into a makeshift fortress last I saw it. Heavily guarded with the Gambler's goons that I trained... or maybe he's already replaced them. Odds are that he has more hired guns inside. He's probably stashing more sins there too, like Greed or Envy. He enjoys keeping the powerful ones close by and … more controlled."

"What can you tell me about the gang members there; Greed and Envy?"

"I ain't got a clue, rumors at the best. I just know that they exist and they're really damn strong… scary strong. The Gambler always kept those two real secret."

"Thanks for all the information. Is there anything else we should worry about when we get there?"

"My God, you're planning on going there?!"

"Yes, we are. I have some… let's leave it at unfinished business with The Gambler and his sins. Speaking of which…"

Patrick gulped at Nate's last remark. Nate rested his hand on the hilt of his sword maintaining eye contact with the frightened sin. Elaine caught a glimpse and followed suit, unbuckling the straps of her holsters.

"Gluttony, what do you plan on doing in the future as a member of the sins… former or not…?"

Patrick stammered trying to form the right answer into words, "Uh, uh… I-I d-d-don't really have any. As far as I know, I'll be here at the lake maintaining the inn and dealing with my appetite. I keep sending supplies up to those poor workers on Battle Mountain too. That's the way it's been for years now. I assure you, I won't do you or anyone any wrong."

Nate took his hand from the hilt of his sheathed sword and let it dangle to his side. He nodded approvingly.

"If you ever do any wrong to anyone, I will find out. I will come back for you without any hesitation."

"I doubt you can kill me, mister. I think you already know about my power judging by how you knew my name and where to find me."

"I am well aware, but I don't have to kill you…"

"You don't?"

"As much as I'd enjoy it, no I don't. What I can do is hurt you, make you bleed, make you suffer slash by slash and cut by cut. I can stab you as many times as I want, and you'll feel every movement of my sword through your flesh and guts. You may have sacrificed for regeneration, but you're still able to feel pain. Aren't you?"

Nate glared at gluttony with a cold expression and an even colder smile. Gluttony trembled and jiggled in his seat as it continued to creak and moan underneath him.

…

Nate and Elaine stormed out of Lake Morena inn and left the frightened sin to wallow in his fright, his sweat, and his foul stench. Nate unhitched his horse and mounted it with a swift vault of his leg. Elaine looked at him, puzzled.

"Where are we goin' to stay for the evenin'," She asked.

"You saw this place from the hilltop. It's huge, there ought to be another place to stay around here somewhere. I can't trust a sin… even one like Gluttony."

A terrible sensation washed over Elaine as she listened to Nate. A cold sweat collected on her forehead.

"Ya saw the fat fucker quiverin' at the sight of ya. I've seen saloon whores more vicious than gluttony."

"Like I said, it's not a matter of how dangerous he is, it's a matter of trust. What would you do to something you're afraid of?"

She huffed in frustration. She and Nate both knew the answer.

"Fight or flight," Nate finished, "and god knows, he isn't running anywhere. There's an inn up ahead, just be patient."

"Hopefully with a goddamn saloon close by," Elaine Remarked.

…

Elaine mounted her horse and rode by Nate's side until they found another place far enough away from Gluttony. The pair reached a saloon and inn called the Mermaid's Heel near the shore of the lake. They dismounted their horses and hitched them to a railing close by.

Nate's stomach churned and rumbled as he and Elaine walked to the swinging doors.

"You hungry?" Nate asked.

"Aye, all that standing there and doing nothing while ya did all the talkin' has worked up quite the appetite for me."

Nate laughed and clutched his stomach, "C'mon it's on me tonight."

Elaine frowned and grabbed her flask from her coat pocket.

Nate glanced back at her, "Drinks too."

With a smirk, Elaine followed Nate into the Mermaid's Heel and dumped the remainder of her whiskey down her throat. She put her flask into her coat pocket and she stared through the back of Nate's skull. Her fists and teeth clenched. Her head swam. She walked past Nate as he held the swinging doors open for her without looking at her. It was bright and warm in the Mermaid's Heel, but she wasn't there. Elaine's thoughts were somewhere much colder and much darker.

...

Elaine stirred as the light of the morning sun hit her. She rolled over and tried to fall back asleep. Nate snored several feet away in his own cot. She squinted hatefully at him and sat up. She rubbed her eyes and grabbed at her throbbing temples. She searched the floor for her flask, so she could remedy her hangover.

Elaine shoved Nate's pack aside to rifle through her own things. She stopped. Streaks of fresh blood lined Nate's blades. Silently, she took one blade from its sheath. Strands of short red hair sparsely lined the sword. She slid it into its sheath and crawled into the cot, watching Nate closely until he woke up.

Chapter Eleven: Rags to Riches
-Lake Morena, California-
-1859-

The sun tucked itself behind the hills around Lake Morena. The town was lit with a grey hue. The moon robbed the sun of its position in the sky. The pale light bathed Patrick as he walked down the streets. He looked back at the town's bustling gravel roads.

Coaches roared by with well-dressed people riding along inside. Men and women of the same wealthy nature strolled outside on the street. They strode with their arms interlocked on their way to dine at fancy inns and restaurants. Patrick glanced down at himself. He put his hands out and spied the dirt and grease lining the insides of his fingernails. Splotches of grime covered most of his arms and, undoubtedly, the rest of his slender body. Patrick's withering black slacks and his sweat-stained shirt missed buttons in various places. They left parts of his chest and stomach exposed. His pants were held up by an old piece of twine he took from a bundle of newspapers and the legs sported more holes than a block of Swiss cheese. His shirt looked much the same.

Patrick fumbled around in his pockets for the rest of his loot. He sighed as he pulled out a piece of dirt with lint tangled in it. He stood still, and no longer heard the slap of his bare feet on the wood of the buildings' porches and walkways. Patrick eyeballed the wealthy visitors. Their noses were held highly up in the air, ignoring everything below them.

Patrick grabbed his stomach with both of his arms and hunched over. That familiar empty pain ran through him. The smell of grilled steaks, baked potatoes and various other Californian delicacies made him swallow the spit pooling in his mouth. Patrick leaned against the railing outside The Mermaid's Heel Saloon to rest for a moment. The swinging doors flew open. The bartender stood behind Patrick with his arms at his hips, and an annoyed grimace on his face.

"Pat," The bartender exclaimed!

Patrick turned around slowly to exaggerate his hunger and his exhaustion to the stalky bartender.

"Leo, you got any scraps to spare today?" Patrick asked in the weakest voice he could muster.

"Jesus, not twice in one day. I've got customers to please and you're loitering out on the deck, scaring them off. I've gotta make a living. Just, get outta here for now, alright?" Leonard replied.

"Please, the smell of that cooking is drivin' me fuckin' nuts, the stuff you gave me earlier, it-"

"You gave it all to Rags, didn't you…?"

Pat's gaze fell sharply to the ground. He nodded.

"… Okay, fine. Come to the back. I'll see if we have anything left over from those rich rancher fucks."

Patrick's head came back up. He wore a wide, glowing smile as he clasped his hands together.

"Thanks, Leonard, you don't know how much-"

"Cut the theatrics, kid. I know your game… but I also know you're going to fuckin' die if I don't feed your scrawny ass. That whole pity party shit is getting old, you're growing up. Soon, folks aren't going to give a shit about you… especially not with that stench hanging around you…"

Patrick nodded again and rubbed the back of his head. He sniffed his armpit a subtly as he could. He started toward the rear of the inn and saloon. Leonard shot inside and stormed through the kitchen, yelling aggressive gibberish at the waiters, cooks, and other staff who toiled inside.

Patrick ran to where he was told. He listened to the rapid movements of the cooks clamoring about the kitchen. They yelled orders at each other much like Leonard yelled at them.

Patrick's eyes lit up when he saw the lead cook open the door with a tray of steak bones, vegetables, and potatoes skins. All of which was served on a large silver platter. John smiled and handed the tray to Patrick. The boy licked his lips in anticipation.

"Thanks, John. I'm starving out here."

"Hey don't sweat it, Patrick. We just throw all this stuff away, anyway. I'd rather feed more hungry mouths than see it all go to waste."

John looked at the young man who sat gnawing at the bones and picking at the vegetables.

"Slim pickins out there today, huh," John asked.

Patrick nodded, "Yep. The weekends are when I can actually get a few of those rich bastards. The crowds of people are growing bigger here. There's a sayin' that I was told once with wider nets and more fish or something like that… that's how it works, I guess."

John laughed, "Anybody catch you doin' it yet?"

Patrick smiled and shook his head, scraping the inside of one of his potato skins with his front teeth.

"Not a chance. By the time they figure out I stole whatever's on their person, I'm already long gone."

"Don't know about that… somebody saw you pickin' pockets out there. I heard the sheriff is lookin' for a young guy… looks kinda like you."

"How do you know?"

"The deputy dropped off posters with drawings on 'em at the bar earlier this afternoon. The sketch looked pretty similar to you. They'll be all over town by now."

Patrick stopped chewing at his scraps and froze.

"Just be careful out there. Last place we all wanna see you is behind bars at the sheriff's office," John said grimly.

Pat snorted, "I beg to differ. You, Fred and Rags are the only ones who give a damn about me in this whole damn town."

"When I said 'all', that's everybody I meant… Say hi to Rags for me… and you know the drill, leave the tray when you finish up here… and bring some back for Rags too."

John went through the door to the Mermaid's Heel and shut it. Patrick cursed to himself. Worry sunk into his belly along with his dinner of scraps. He finished scraping the potato skins and picked up the remaining carrots and green beans, holding them cupped in his hands.

Patrick got up and walked toward an adjacent alleyway. He doubled back and picked the T-bones up from the tray to bring for Rags. The emptiness in Patrick's stomach was quelled for the time being, but he knew the hunger would return sooner than he'd like. He brought the vegetables from his hand and threw them into his mouth. The boy chewed happily as he strolled.

Patrick found his way to a road lit sparsely by street lamps. The streets had died down from earlier. All the rich couples found their rooms at the inns and sat in their dining rooms. Patrick stopped at the front of the barbershop. On the outside wall and near the door, a rough sketch of him stared back.

Wanted Alive: Patrick Cunningham
Age 16-18
Offense: Thieving food, clothing, money, valuables…
Reward: $25

Patrick brought his free hand to the top of the poster. With a loud rip, Patrick ripped it down and scanned the area. Not even a coach could be heard rolling down the streets. Only a few strangers meandered here and there with their heads tucked down, minding their own business.

Patrick crumpled the poster and tossed it onto the ground with a smirk, trying to re-instill confidence in himself.

"They look, but they don't see…" Patrick said to himself with a laugh, "What a hack artist… I bet the sheriff drew that portrait of me himself."

Patrick continued down the street confidently toward Rag's alley, looking forward to seeing the excited look on Rags' face as he brings home T-bones for her.

The crunch of gravel against coach wheels running along with the thump of horse hooves rattled the earth. The noise broke the silence of the warm California night. Two grisly looking men in brown dusters rode at the top of the vehicle. They steered the four horses at the front. It was larger than the kinds that Patrick typically saw in Lake Morena. Probably why it was being pulled by double the usual amount of horses.

Ten more followed, riding on the backs of on their own horses. They wore similar getups to the ones who sat at the top. Patrick's fingers twitched over the scraps of bone and pieces of vegetables in his grasp.

The coach came to a stop a couple blocks down from Patrick. An insatiable urge welled up inside of him as he ducked behind the corner of the nearest building. The scent of riches seemed more delicious to him than the thought of more scraps and that coach reeked of large bills. Arguably, the scent of money is soon followed by the scent of a hot meal if stolen. The men driving got down from the top. They opened the passenger door on the cab.

…

The Gambler got out from his ride and stretched, placing his hands on his lower back. He pulled at the ends of his suit and vest, making sure his clothing didn't crease or ride up on him during the trip over. He flicked the brim of his hat and placed it on his head. He stood looking at his drivers.

"Did y'all ready a room for me here while I was sleepin'," The Gambler asked through a yawn.

"Yessir," one of his drivers replied, "Everything is in order."

"My thanks, Nick."

The silver haired man pulled a thick wad of bank notes from his pocket and unfurled ten bills. He handed them to Nick.

"Treat yourselves, get absolutely piss drunk tonight. Do you think you could do that for me and our friends here, Nick?"

Nick smiled and gratefully accepted the cash with a quick nod. He turned and waved the money at the men on their horses. A loud series of approving hoots and cheers filled the air. Nick turned back.

"You're too kind, Sir. Are you sure you don't want any of us to stick around for your protection?"

The Gambler smiled and shook his head. He tugged the end of his suit and vest out revealing the glint of his silver Schofield revolver.

"Nah, I got things covered for the night. I think I might go straight to sleep. These old bones have gotta retire for the evenin'… especially after a nice, big, juicy steak and a bath. I'm goin' to sleep like a big, drunken baby. I'll see y'all in the mornin'," The Gambler said, waving.

The silver haired man entered the inn. His men hitched their horses nearby and made their way to a saloon just down the road, hooting and hollering cheerfully amongst themselves.

The Gambler sat down at an empty table. A waiter raced over and placed silverware and a napkin at the table. The Gambler took the napkin and placed it neatly in his lap.

"What would you like this evening, sir," The waiter asked.

The Gambler sat and stroked his beard, weighing his options silently to himself. He looked up at the waiter.

"I will have a rib-eye steak as rare as you can get it without makin' me sick… with a side of your finest rice if you have it."

The waiter nodded and started toward the kitchen. The Gambler grabbed his arm to stop him.

"Oh, and if the cook has the proper herbs and spices, have him add a little Cajun kick to the beef and that side of rice."

"Right away, sir," the waiter responded.

He headed to the kitchen to put in the Gambler's order and hurried throughout the room to get the orders of other guests. The Gambler took off his hat and placed it on the table. He ran a hand through his unkempt hair. He raised his eyebrows at the length of it and puffed his cheeks out as he let out a long breath.

The Gambler's eyes turned to a dirty looking teenager whose clothes appeared to be worn and tattered. His arms were sunburnt and thin. Without a doubt, the boy lived off begging and scavenging what he could. Pat looked at him and stood in front of him. The Gambler smiled at him. The youngster did not smile back, but held his hands cupped out at the Gambler. The old man took a whiff of the air surrounding the teen. He thought about grabbing his hat to vomit in.

"Can I help you with somethin' boy," the Gambler asked.

"Please, Mister, spare a dollar so I can feed myself and my little brother tonight?" Patrick begged with a shaking voice.

The hairs on Patrick's neck stood up when he heard the old man in the fancy grey suit speak. Something wasn't right about the elderly individual. The Gambler leaned back in his chair, with the same smile glued to his face. His fiendish eyes were locked on the frail figure standing before him.

The Gambler reached into his coat pocket and pulled a large wad of cash out. He slid two bills from the pile and extended his arm to the Pat. He returned the bundle of cash into the same pocket. Patrick stepped forward, and the Gambler bent his arm, pulling his hand and the money closer to himself. The boy stopped.

"Don't go spendin' it all in one place now, understand," The Gambler said.
"Y-yessir…" Patrick replied.

"Get yourself and your brother a nice hot meal, some new clothes and go find yourselves a job."

The Gambler pushed his hand toward the boy again, offering Patrick the cash. Patrick stepped forward again and took the bills from the intimidating stranger. He looked down at two twenty-dollar notes in his hands. Patrick's Jaw dropped. To the Gambler's surprise, the young man rushed him and hugged him. The Gambler raised his arms and inhaled sharply, not knowing how to react and trying not to take in the awful smell.

"Thanks, M-mister, I don't know what to say…"

The Gambler looked around the room awkwardly and patted the street urchin on the back lightly.

"Say you'll help yourself. Get a job, you hear me, boy? Now get off me before you rub your stink all over me."

Patrick retreated from the Gambler, holding on to the money and rushing out of the inn. As Patrick ran out, the Gambler brushed Patrick's dirt and grime off himself. He inspected his clothes with a few sniffs. If a wash wasn't needed before, it was now.

The waiter returned with The Gambler's steak and rice. He set it down on the table and folded his hands.

"Will that be all for you this evening, sir?" the waiter asked.

"A glass of bourbon and a tall glass of water should do me just fine tonight," the Gambler replied,

"Excellent, sir. I'll come back shortly with the bill and your beverages. Have a great rest of your night."

The Gambler nodded, reaching into his coat pocket. He fumbled around for the wad of money. He patted himself up and down. The Gambler paused. He shook his head and a wide smile appeared on his face. He tucked the napkin from his lap into his chest and ate his meal.

He chuckled as he cut his seasoned steak and brought the rare beef to his mouth. The Gambler dropped his cutlery and leaned forward, bringing forth more cash from his pants to pay for his food and drink.

...

Patrick walked with a skip in his step. He went down one of the main streets of Lake Morena with a look of immense pride slathered to his face. He took the wad of bank notes from his pocket and hurried to the general store only a few more blocks ahead. Patrick squinted to look in front of him. Fred was just preparing to close his general store. He was closing the doors and brandishing his key. Patrick hustled to catch him before he locked the door.

"Wait, Fred," Patrick said between breaths. He approached the shopkeeper bent over, sucking air with his hands on his knees. Fred looked around like he was confused and squinted down at the boy panting at the stairs before his store.

"Pat… What're you…"

Patrick held his index finger up at Fred, signifying him to wait as he tried to catch his breath. The teen rose and gaped at him.

"Fred, can I-"

"Nope, sorry, Pat not today. I've finished cleaning up the shop for the day. I threw some stuff out a while ago, but I don't think you should try eating it, it's pretty old."

"No, I wanna buy some stuff to take with me…"

"You, with money? I don't have time for your bullshit-"

Patrick pulled out a twenty-dollar bill. Fred shut his mouth, flabbergasted.

"Where did you…" Fred began to ask.

"Since when do you care?"

Fred sighed and opened his doors up to him, welcoming Patrick into the general store. Patrick went inside, and Fred followed.

After only a few minutes, Patrick walked out with an old potato sack filled to the brim with assorted jerkies, nuts, and breads slung around his shoulder. Patrick struggled to carry it out. He strode happily toward the street outside and looked back at Fred.

"I can't thank you enough…"

Fred locked his door. He swiveled out to the street and faced Patrick. He shrugged and let out another longer sigh.

"Sure, just… just stop stealing shit, Pat. The Sheriff gave me some posters with your face on them… a bad sketch of you if you ask me…"

"I think I'm done, Fred. I know it might be too much, but if you need help at the store, I'll be around."

"Come by tomorrow morning at six, or don't bother coming at all. If the sheriff comes by, I'll put in a good word… tell him you've turned over a new leaf. I doubt he'd lock up some street rat like you, especially a kid… Also, clean yourself up with all that newfound cash. Wear a collared shirt and pants without any holes or dirt on 'em… and, by god, if I catch you stealing-"

"Nah, I'm done forever as long as you keep me working. Thanks for sticking your neck out. You won't be disappointed, I promise."

Patrick nodded with a wide smile. Fred beamed proudly at the boy as he locked the grocery store up.

Patrick started his walk home. If an alleyway could be considered a home… For the first time in a long time, Patrick was as warm as the Southern California air that night. He reached down into his pocket and had the wad of money between his fingers. He hadn't even counted it yet, but he knew it was a hell of a lot. It was certainly more than enough to scrape by.

Town was much quieter as the night carried on. Patrick enjoyed the slap of his bare feet against the wood porches of the shops. He enjoyed the thump of his feet against the dirt and trod over the gravel in the streets. His steps seemed to echo behind him as he walked.

Patrick tilted his head and stopped for a moment. The echoes continued. He looked to his rear. The sheriff followed about a block away, his brown cattleman hat shading his face from the moonlight as he approached and a silver star adorning his chest. The sheriff reached out and pointed right at Patrick.

“Shit!”

Patrick bolted down the nearest alleyway, running as fast as he could manage, lugging the sack of food at his side. He took lefts and rights, taking twists and turns down more alleys. The sheriff’s heavy boots followed closely, gaining still. Patrick did not look back. His neck craned, looking for an escape at every corner.

The bag got heavier and heavier with each stride and his breathing grew shorter. Patrick hurried behind the next corner and slowed his breathing as best as he could, covering his mouth. He remained as still as he could, hidden in the shadows of the buildings. The sheriff’s footsteps grew louder. Then Patrick heard nothing.

“Come on out boy, I know you saw me chasing you… and I saw you steal from that man in the grey suit right at his table,” The sheriff said trying to catch his breath.

Patrick looked to his left.

“I’m armed. Patrick, just come out and we can settle this peacefully, I don’t want no trouble. I’m sure you saw the posters around town. It’s only four months of labor here in Lake Morena. Don’t make this any worse than it is, Pat.”

Rags came out of the dark. She sniffed at the air and trotted excitedly toward Patrick. Her mop like hair bounced along with each of her steps. Her paws patted loudly against the dirt. She panted and put her wet nose against Patrick's bag. She licked her chops, wagged her tail and whined at him, waiting impatiently. Drool leaked from her gums as she looked up at Patrick with her longing brown eyes. He waved her away, but she tilted her head at him. The shifting of gravel under the sheriff's boots started again, approaching Patrick and Rags.

"I know you're there, now, Pat. Come out. We can get this sorted right quick," the sheriff ordered.

Patrick hissed to himself and stepped out from behind the corner. He heard the mechanical click of a revolver's hammer being pulled back. He stopped dead in his tracks. Rags tensed up. Her posture sank, and she bared her fangs. Her growl filled the air.

The moon peeked over the tall brick structures around the alleyways, illuminating them in pale ghostly light. A loud crack echoed through the alleyways. Patrick watched the sheriff standing in the middle of the alley. He clutched his chest with his left hand and fell to his knees, wide eyed. His right arm trembled as he reached for the pistol at his hip. Blood seeped through his fingers on his left. Patrick stood frozen across from the sheriff who spat up blood that dripped onto his chest.

A pair of flaming yellow eyes flickered from behind the sheriff. The old man raised the smoking barrel of his gun. He pointed it at the sheriff's back. Another loud boom rang throughout the alley, making Patrick and Rags flinch. Patrick looked away. The sheriff fell flat on his face into the gravel and dirt with a loud gurgle. Rags' growl filled Patrick's ears as the rolling boom of the revolver faded. The Gambler pulled the hammer back on his revolver again.

Rags glared at the Gambler and approached him. Her head was hung low, ready to attack.

"Speak of the devil and he shall appear… my timing is absolutely impeccable, ain't it, Patrick? That's your name, right? I couldn't help but overhear. Which do you prefer, Patrick or Pat?" The Gambler asked.

The Gambler paced.

Patrick remained motionless with Rags at his side. The color faded from his sunburnt skin, as he stared at the man with yellow eyes, entranced and afraid.

"You look scared, Patrick. I can see it. How does a young fool who is such a coward, work up the courage to steal from an individual like me? Desperation? Hunger by the looks of you."

Patrick knew his legs were growing weak and shaking under him.

"... Never in my life on this earth has any man, woman, or in your case, a particularly frail teenaged boy, been able to steal from me and lived... or at least been able to slip away as you did… and I've had a long life. Hell, if it wasn't for the bumbling sheriff of Lake Morena, you would've been long gone."

The warmth escaped from Patrick's body as the old man spoke to him. Even his veins were icy. He reached for the wad of money in his pocket, pulled it out and threw it in the dirt in front of the Gambler.

The Gambler looked down at his cash and chuckled, "To be frank, I am impressed with you, boy. I came here seekin' somebody else, but…"

The Gambler grabbed a book from the pocket of his suit pants and eyeballed Patrick up and down his small figure.

"… I think you'll do just fine. I could use somebody like you. We'd make a hell of a lot more than what's on the ground there… My men and I, we love a good raid… raping, burning and pillaging as we go, but as exhilarating as it is, this ain't exactly sustainable…"

Patrick followed the Gambler as close as he could with his eyes as he stopped in front of him and his Rags.

"… Sure, it builds a certain reputation, but if we go burnin' down every town we come across, eventually there won't be nobody to steal from… That and killin' an entire town takes a hell of a lot of ammunition and ammo… it ain't cheap. We could use a more far more subtle approach to takin' what we want whenever we want…"

Rags inched closer to the Gambler, still growling in his direction. The Gambler pointed his revolver at Rags. The old man glared into Patrick's frozen eyes and pulled the trigger.

One last bullet left the chamber of his weapon as Rags shrieked and hit the ground with a heavy thump.

Patrick wiped the tears away as they came out. The Gambler took a dagger and a small leather covered notebook from his coat pocket as he holstered his gun. The Gambler slit his hand. He watched the blood roll and drip down his palm and wrist with a wide grin.

The Gambler laughed, “Tell me, boy… if you could have anything I this world… what would you wish for?”

Chapter Twelve: Flick of the Devil's Tongue
-Ojos Negros, Mexico-
-February 1876-

The sun lingered wearily upon the rocky horizon of Ojos Negros. Nate and Elaine rode into the Mexican desert town. The sun cast an orange hue over the hardened clay of the town's pueblos. Saguaros dotted the golden sandstone that surrounded the village. The cacti stood guard on the sides of the desert roads of Baja California.

The people of Ojos Negros smiled and greeted the pair as they made their way down the main street of the town. Children ran alongside Nate and Elaine offering warm and excited sounding Spanish greetings as though they were long lost friends. They returned the children's smiles. Nate and Elaine continued through the town looking for a place to rest, refill their dwindling supplies, and to fill their empty stomachs.

"This is the last settlement before we get to the eye o' the devil," Elaine said riding to the right of Nate, fiddling with her maps.

"Agreed, we should stay here tonight. We're running low on food and more importantly, water. How long of a ride do we have left?" Nate replied.

Elaine slid a large roll of paper out from her saddlebag and unraveled it to inspect its contents.

"Should be a few hours from here."

"Alright. Let's get to it. We'll see if we're able to secure ourselves a place to sleep too."

"I hope ya can speak Spanish… otherwise it's goin' to be pretty difficult to secure a place."

"We'll see. I haven't spoken it in a while… not since…"

"Since when?"

Nate stood frozen and silent for a moment. His heart pumped faster and faster.

"Forget it… I know bits and pieces… enough to get us some food and shelter for the night."

Elaine gripped the reigns on her horse enough to make the leather creak under her fists. She took her flask from her saddlebag and tipped it up. Not a drop trickled into her mouth. She was sickened without the familiar burn and the numbing that followed.

"Hola viajeros. bienvenida a Ojos Negros," A tall man with greased back hair walked over to Nate and Elaine. He wore a colorful shawl over some faded clothing and beaten black boots.

"Muchos gracias. Habla Ingles?" Nate asked with an atrocious Spanish accent and even worse pronunciation.

"Lo siento señor, que solo hablan español."

"Mi español esta muy terrible pero, que esta ciudad tiene una posada para mi y mi amiga?"

"Sí. la posada es por este camino ya la izquierda de la barra. Sígueme."

"Muchos gracias por tu hospilidad, senor."

"De nada."

"Uh…" Elaine said scratching her head, "Bits and pieces, eh?"

"Guess I'm not as rusty as I thought."

"So, could ya explain that conversation for me?"

"Ojos Negros has an inn we can stay at tonight… with a bar… I think."

They followed the colorfully dressed local to the inn. They hitched their horses and got the animals some oats from a nearby shop. Nate and Elaine entered the saloon across from the inn. They thanked the man as he walked down the road.

The place was practically empty. A lonesome looking bartender looked onward at them as though he was staring right through them. He rubbed glasses he took out from behind the bar. Nate and Elaine were the only patrons.

Elaine held up two fingers at the barkeep, "Tequila?"

He nodded and grabbed a couple of clean glasses for his only customers. Nate and Elaine took their seats across from each other. They were at a table near the back of the saloon. The bartender raced over and placed shot glasses on the table accompanied by a bottle filled nearly to the top with a golden liquid. The label on the bottle was a plain black with a splash of faded brown lettering:

La Lengua del Diablo

"The Devil's Tongue. Must be good stuff," Nate said.

He reached into his duster for his cash, but Elaine beat him to the punch. She handed the barkeep a couple crisp bills.

"Gracias," he replied as he continued cleaning his glasses.

Elaine nodded in the bartender's direction and glanced at Nate, "It's on me tonight."

Nate looked at Elaine in disbelief as he folded his arms, "What's the occasion?"

"Tomorrow might be our last day alive. I thought we should be celebratin'… or at least getting' drunk off our arses before we bite the dust."

Nate shook his head, turning his gaze to the floor in front of him as he leaned back in his chair.

"We have nothing to celebrate, Elaine."

She looked at him puzzled, "Ya killed a lot of bad folks on your way here, Nate. I think that's somethin' to be proud of."

She poured them both a shot and slid the glass over to Nate who clutched tightly, almost nervously.

"Right again, I murdered plenty of people."

Elaine downed her drink as Nate stared into his.

"Can a killer also be a decent father?" he asked as he threw his booze down his throat.

Elaine paused and poured then both another two overflowing tequila shooters, "I don't know."

Nate took his second shot with his gaze locked on the bar top. He tried to picture Sara. Elaine stared into his eyes and recognized the anguish he was putting himself through.

"I know that a good parent doesn't sit back and accept that his child was taken from him, Nate."

Nate looked up from the floor to meet Elaine's gaze.

"A good parent would do exactly what you did. They would go find his daughter. They'd make sure none of this shite would ever happen again. They'd put down anyone responsible."

Nate's stoic and lifeless demeanor remained, "A part of me… a large part of me enjoys it, revels in it."

"In… what?"

"Killing shit… People… It's not just that I've killed. I agree with what you said… that I've slaughtered plenty of terrible sons… and daughters of bitches for the right reasons. I'm not so sure I'm doing this from a righteous place anymore… or if I even started this journey in that righteousness. I haven't lost sight of getting my daughter back and keeping her safe, but something I've struggled with since I was young is blurring that sight. Something… or someone I've had trouble keeping at bay for a long time. I feel like I've twisted and changed my determination to protect my family… into a blind, burning hatred."

Elaine continued to pour them both more shots as Nate continued.

"I've watched the color run from your face and the terror in your eyes as they dart around in their sockets. It's the same face I've seen time after time. When the other side of me arrives. It's… a side of me that, I wish, never had to rear its ugly head, but it seems to come more frequently. Overtime, it becomes harder and harder to burry inside me. It's like a wild animal tearing at the lining of its cage every moment it can. With each second that goes by, its prison becomes weaker and weaker. I can't imagine being raised by that. All I wanted for my daughter is to lead the best life she possible… with or without me in it. With Sofia, I knew… we could do it, but now… I don't know… I don't know if I could raise Sara without her… I think that animal in me… that beast might have to be put down."

He gestured at Elaine to take her drink. She gripped her full shot glass on the table and slurped it back as quickly as she could. Nate did the same.

Nate's far away look remained on his face as he stewed in his thoughts.

"Remember when I asked you who you were a while back?" Nate asked.

"Aye…"

"Well, who the hell are you?"

"Do ya sincerely not trust me after everythin' we've been through?"

"I trust you, Elaine. Before battle, the regiment and I would trade stories about ourselves. The war had brothers fighting against each other on opposite sides… actual blood, and friends. Trading our stories helped make new family for them. Bonds thicker than blood. It gave us a good reason to fight as opposed to being forced into the war by the draft. We made brand new friends… New brothers."

Elaine loosened up as she poured another hefty shot for herself and immediately threw it back, "I think we're goin' to have to be really drunk for this story…"

"Fair enough."

Nate handed Elaine his glass as she gladly poured him a new one.

"Where shall I begin?"

Nate shrugged, "Wherever you'd like."

…

Elaine spoke about her past for what seemed like hours. The pair poured each other shot after shot. Eventually, the pair began to slur their words as they told their stories. The liquid in the tequila bottle grew thinner and thinner.

Nate laughed heartily as Elaine finished a small and funny anecdote from her recent past. She watched him drunkenly wobble back and forth in his seat as she sat up straight and composed herself. Nate stopped his laughter and gazed at Elaine who wore a calm and solemn expression. She got up out of her seat and stood next to Nate.

"C'mon, Nate. We've got a big day tomorrow."

She crouched down next to him and threw his arm over her shoulder to help him get to his room. The two rose as she supported some of his weight on her shoulder. The door creaked open, and she tossed him onto his bed where he laid watching the world spin around.

"See Eagle Eye, that wussn't ssso bad, right?" The solemn look stuck to her face like a badge of shame as she took a seat next to him on the side of the bed. Elaine reached over him and unsheathed his swords. He looked up at her in drunken bewilderment as she tossed them into the far corner of the room.

"Nate… I need to tell ya something else..."

Nate sat up and swayed back and forth with a mix of concern and drunken stupor in his demeanor.

…

Elaine's hands trembled on her rifle. "I'm so sorry about this, Nate…"

She drew back and swung the butt of her rifle against the temple of Nate's head. With a crack, he fell to the bed where he laid unconscious. She packed her things and after a struggle, pulled Nate's dead weight onto her horse.

Elaine rode toward the Eye of the Devil. The pale moonlight cast a dark shadow under the brim of Elaine's stovepipe hat. The warm air did nothing to thaw the iciness she had in the pit of her stomach. Her hands trembled at the reins of her horse. She ran the leather strap between her fingers nervously. She remembered the gravelly voice of the Gambler echoing throughout her head. A shade of golden yellow glowed down upon her. Her eyes flickered like dull yellow flames.

Chapter Thirteen: Whiskey Colored Eyes
-The Eye of the Devil, Mexico-
-August 1875-

The old clay walls of the mission helped to dull the sound coming from outside. Crashing waves kept the Mexican coastline in an uproar. The morning sun came through the window in beams. It gave just enough light to the map that sat on the table in the otherwise shadowy room.

The Gambler stuck two men on each corner. Their hands rested on the butts of their revolvers holstered at their hips. The Gambler wore his same old southern gentleman's ensemble. He had one hand tucked into the pocket of his pants. With his other, he held a mug of steaming black liquid. He slurped obnoxiously and watched Elaine enter.

She rubbed the sleep from her eyes and pulled her frazzled, brown hair into a ponytail. She flicked the dirt from her duster coat. Her long and worn black pants were covered to her knees buy her boots. She eyed the Gambler and waited for him to speak. He brought the mug away from his face after a sip and set it down on the table.

"Good to see you again, Greed. I trust there were no troubles gettin' back here," the Gambler mocked.

Elaine shivered. She never got used to the way his words made her heart stop. She swore the room got cold.

"Aye, same as ever. The men you sent knew their way around better than the last ones, brought plenty o' food n’ water too. Seems you’re trainin’ ‘em well,” Elaine replied.

“Well, it would seem that way…”

“Hm… I’m guessin’ that’s why ya dragged my arse all the way back down here, and not just for a cup o’ joe.”

“Would you like a mug?”

“Aye, I’m bloody tired.”

The Gambler looked over to one of his lackeys and nodded. The guard nodded in response and headed across the room. He poured a mug and handed it to Elaine. She sipped carefully and blew on the surface of the coffee to cool it down.

“Gluttony has been trainin’ most of our recruits, but his… habits have made him sluggish and-”

“Fatter than shite…”

“Right... He usually gets some of his better learners to do the demonstratin’ his methods for him recently.”

“What was he teachin’ em exactly?”

“Stealin’ without getting caught. Resourcefulness too.”

“So, somebody got caught…”

“A posse of ten near the border of Texas and Mexico. East of here. One of ‘em managed to get back and tell me about this shit show.”

“Why are they so important to ya? You have plenty of others just like ‘em to fill their shoes… No offense…”

The two men shrugged.

“None taken, as long as we keep getting paid,” one of them chimed in.

“Anyway, it isn’t the man power I’m concerned about; it’s something else that’s important to me. If they’re still alive, I would love to have ‘em back, but what I need most is an object they succeeded in stealing, but failed to bring here,” The Gambler continued.

“So, you want me to play courier and go get it for ya,” Elaine replied.

“And then some. The one that survived said they were ambushed by a squad armed to the teeth.”

“How many exactly?”

“About fifteen to twenty.”

“Did he say where they were… specifically?”

“He was smart enough to tail the squad to a ghost town near the Rio Grande called Portales.”

The Gambler pointed down to the map on the table. Elaine followed his finger with her eyes. She raised an eyebrow at him.

“Why’d they stop there,” She asked.

“He said it looked like they were settin’ up a perimeter, anticipatin' reinforcements, patrolling around n’ such.”

“What makes you think they’re still there?”

The Gambler shrugged, “I can only hope, really. They won’t exactly be hard to track with the amount of horses and men as they have. Start from that ghost town if they already packed up and left. Track ‘em from there.”

“I’ll need a horse with a large saddle bag for ammo mostly… I’m gunna need food and water for the trip too.”

The Gambler glanced behind him and nodded to the guard on his left. He exited to retrieve what Elaine needed.

"Take some men with you," The Gambler said.

"I'll take the one that escaped, but only him," She replied.

The Gambler smiled and reached into his vest pocket. He pulled out a bundled roll of twenty-dollar notes.

"As always," He chuckled, "Half now and half when you get back."

Elaine swiped the cash from the table and counted the money bill by bill. She raised an eyebrow.

"Why double this time?"

"It's little incentive for you to actually give a shit about this task. Like I said... that object is quite important to me."

"Aye…"

She slid the money to the Gambler on the table. He nodded knowingly and handed the bundle of cash to the other guard.

"Same address in New York City as far as I know. Same name. Make sure it gets there. Any word from them yet?"

Elaine and the Gambler looked to the guard at the back of the room. He shook his head and sealed the bundle of bills in an envelope.

"No word from the McCormicks, No letters, no nothing. I'll be sure to send them your regards… if we ever get in touch with them," the man said.

"Be sure to give them this. Tell them that their daughter, their sister is doing well… and that she loves them."

Elaine slid a sealed letter onto the table toward him. He took it and placed it inside of the envelope with the money. Elaine left the room. She went outside, back into the heat and humidity of the coastal Mexican morning. A man stood with a horse and a fully loaded saddle. He gave the reigns to Elaine as she walked over. She put a hand on the horse's face and stroked it. The horse nudged approvingly against her palm.

"Your guns have been cleaned, the horse has been fed and given water. The saddle is all loaded up with food, water, and ammo… like you asked. Is there anything else you need before you leave," the man asked?

"Fetch the one who escaped from that squad in Texas and get him ready. He's going with me as an escort," She replied.

"Right away, Miss Greed."

She turned to her horse and climbed it, holding onto the reigns and waited for her guide.

…

-Portales, Texas-

-A Few Days Later-

The night was quiet apart from a steady wind that blew a cover of clouds over the moon and the stars, inking over the ghost town. Rotting wooden buildings stood looming in the dark, motionless silhouettes standing boldly against the wind. Broken doors swung on their rusted hinges. They offered an occasional squeal that echoed through the Portales. The Rangers, who patrolled the streets, made their way to the barn and retrieved lanterns from it to keep themselves from tripping and falling in the dark. The others paced inside of the abandoned two and three-story buildings and on the rooftops. They scanned the surrounding hills and knolls with their rifles set close by. Some sat in the glow of their lantern light, eating cold beans and tearing off pieces of old jerky to stay awake.

Bill pulled a harmonica from his pants pocket and played the instrument. The noise startled Joshua from his nap. He sat up and punched Bill in the arm. Bill dropped the harmonica and rubbed the spot where Joshua hit him.

"Goddamn, what the hell," Bill said in a whine.

"Yer supposed to be keepin' watch, stupid," Joshua replied angrily.

"Why do I have to watch when yer lazy ass is sleepin'?"

"Just gimme five more minutes and I'll take over."

"Shoot, I don't even know how you can sleep in a place like this… it's givin' me the creeps."

Joshua leaned back and put his hat over his eyes.

"Bill, you're a fuckin' Texas Ranger, do you think you could grow some hair on yer peaches?"

Bill huffed and picked up his harmonica from the sand covered floor. The front door of the building they were in caught the wind. It squealed and slammed shut. Bill shot up and grabbed his rifle. He scanned the room, panting.

"Josh, wake up, did you hear that shit?!"

"Yeah… you know what else I heard?"

"What…?"

"My friend Bill, the fearsome and mighty Texas Ranger actin' like a school little girl."

Bill stood in near the window with his back to it. His eyes darted around the room. Weak orange light danced off the floors and decrepit walls. The abandoned furniture cast long, dancing shadows behind them. With a loud wet sounding thump, a dark red spot appeared on the temple of Bill's head. Blood dripped and sprayed from the new narrow hole in his skull. Bill crumpled to the floor. Josh fell to the floor with him, scrambling for his weapon and for cover. He dampened the lamp next to him. A dull crack rolled over the hills and through the window, following the carnage. Josh took off his hat and got up from his seat.

"Rifleman! Over here! In the south side of town, take cover," Joshua yelled to his fellow rangers.

He listened to the yells and heavy footsteps approach in the dirt road and the scuff of boots upon old floorboards.

"Where at and how many of 'em are there?" He heard a man yell from the streets below.

Joshua peeked over the bottom of the broken windowsill. He scanned the shallow, rocky hills in the distance, but the dark of the clouds obscured the land in a veil of black. He saw a tiny speck of light flash in the distance. His eyes darted to it. A bullet formed a hole in the center of his forehead and travelled straight back out of his skull with a loud splat. The thunder of a rifle's shot followed, marking his death.

The men below hugged their cover as tightly as they possibly could. Captain Brown looked up to the building where Bill and Joshua were posted.

"Josh, Bill, sound off…" Captain Brown yelled.

The wind brushed past him and through the rest of the ghost town, making the buildings moan. Captain Brown cursed to himself.

"Stick to yer cover, douse yer lamps. Seems like there's only one of 'em out there, but he's a crack shot. Let him come to us…"

…

Elaine pulled the handle of her repeater down and slid more rounds into the rifle while she stared off toward the ghost town encampment. The tiny blips of orange lantern light went out all at once. She slid her gun onto the holster attached to her back. She smirked and stared knowingly out into the abyssal night.

"Hm… damned Texas Rangers. Bastards won't give up without a fight…" Elaine said to herself.

The man that led her to Portales walked up to her side with his hands stuffed sheepishly into the pockets of his long black coat. He looked at Elaine then squinted into dark horizon with the tiny black blips of taller buildings sticking up near the horizon. He then gaped at Elaine. She returned his clueless gaze.

“Can I help ya with somethin’, Blake…?”

The guide took one of his hands from his pocket, leaving the other firmly planted. He raised his index finger and pointed weakly in the direction she was firing in.

“Greed-”

“Yeah, Blake, what is it?”

He squinted back to the horizon, “…How?”

“How what?”

“How… I … I can’t see a damn thing from here.”

“Blake…”

“Yes?”

“Are you new?”

“Excuse me?”

“How long have ya been workin’ for us?”

“Uh, not too long, I guess… why?”

“Nothin’ it just… it… explains a lot…”

“I’ve been meaning to ask you…”

“Ask away.”

“Don’t take this the wrong way, but what’s up with your eyes?”

Elaine sighed and grabbed her forehead.

“Don’t worry about it… just listen. I’m goin’ over there and I need ya to wait here for me while I go clean up the rest of ‘em…”

Blake nodded blankly at Elaine while she spoke.

“Once ya hear all the gunfire stop, ride toward the town. You’ll know where to go from there. Do ya understand?”

He gave her a timid nod. She gave him a smile, a nod back, and a pat on the shoulder as she walked by. She mounted her horse and rode straight for the ghost town. When she knew she was close enough, she dismounted the horse and ran her hand up and down its snout. Elaine grabbed all the ammo she could hold from her saddlebags.

“Real sorry about this…” She said to the animal. She hit the horse on its rear. It charged straight toward the town. Elaine crouched low and frowned at her decision.

…

Captain Brown stood with his men at the south side of Portales. They were still huddled under the meager cover of the wooden architecture. He worked up the courage to peek from behind the corner of the wall. He saw a silhouette galloping straight at them. Soon, they could all hear the pounding of hooves on the dirt in the distance.

“He’s riding’ straight for us… Open fire on my signal… we’re gunna light this fucker up.”

The Rangers cocked their rifles and stuck their heads out to see their fast approaching target.

“Now!”

The combatants emerged from their cover. The air was filled with a chorus of gun blasts and strobes of light.

The silhouette charging toward them fell to the ground with a loud thud and skidded to a halt.

"Hold your fire, cease fire!"

They stopped shooting and reloaded their weapons; the eighteen men had their eyes glued to the dark shape lying in the distance.

"Mills, git out there and check it out… somethin' don't seem right. Moore, Wilson, Taylor, Anderson, Davids… cover our rears at the north side of town. The rest of us will cover you, Mills."

The five scanned the town behind them while Mills reluctantly marched out to meet the large black shape they gunned down in front of them. The large shape twitched as Mills approached. He put another round into it.

The squad covering Mills flinched and readied their rifles.

"Mills, what's goin' on out there?" Captain Brown shouted.

Mills ran as fast as he could. He screamed something, but the wind grew too loud and he was still too far to hear.

"… There's- rider- down…," Mills yelled, his voice faint.

The rangers remained where they were. Their iron sights scanned every alley, corner and building to their rear and the area around Mills to their front.

"Mills, say again," The Captain barked out to him.

Mills' voice grew louder as he sprinted back toward the group and the wind died for a moment.

"It's a diversion! There's no rider! It was just the horse, GET DOWN," Mills screamed!

Five rapid blasts went off behind Captain Brown and his men. Five flashes lit the Northern end of the town. Blood and pieces of bone sprayed all over the group. The five that watched the combatants in the rear slumped to the ground and dropped their guns. Between gunfire, they could hear the spray of their friends' blood.

"At out backs! Take cover and open fire," Brown yelled.

Taylor crawled toward the group from his position at the rear. He dragged his bleeding right while he clawed and clawed at the dirt. Another dull flash and a boom rolled through the group Rangers. A sixth shot pierced the center of Taylor's chest. He gurgled into the dirt.

Mills ran up and slammed his back to the wall of a building with Brown. They fired wildly into the northern end of Portales.

"Hold your fire," Brown yelled over the gunfire, "Conserve yer ammo. Don't shoot unless you know where he is."

The wind howled over the ghost town once again. The sounds of gunfire faded away. Dust and sand hissed as it hit the buildings.

"We can't see shit, Cap," one of them declared, sliding more rounds into his weapon.

"He's somewhere in the North part of town judgin' by those shots… We need to put pressure on him. Seven of you close in on him and spread out. He could be anywhere on that side of town. The six of us will make a break for the farmhouse. We'll secure the package and ready the horses. Good luck, Rangers."

The seven men looked at each other nervously and went north. Their eyes and heads darted, searching desperately for the gunman. Brown and his group of five ran to the western outskirts of the ghost town scanning doorways, alleyways and rooftops. Brown's group rounded a corner, severing their line of sight from the others. Rifle fire and bright flashes lit the street where the seven were. They fired their weapons at the surrounding buildings in a panic. Brown's squad aimed them at the flashes they could see from around the corner as they backed toward the farmhouse.

"WHERE THE FUCK-," a man screamed.

The gunfire slowed as one man remained, firing his rifle in random directions. He shambled from around the corner, into the sight of Captain Brown's group. The ranger fell straight onto his back before the sound of the shot reached them. His head was tilted backward from the force of the bullet piercing his skull.

They continued backing up toward the farmhouse, faster and faster in retreat. Their eyes were locked on the intersection where they saw their fellow fall.

The wind died and left the ghost town in silence apart from the scuff of the rangers' boots against the dirt in the roads. They tucked themselves in and out of buildings as they backed up. They followed each other's lead and kept their guns pointed to that same intersection. Mills' repeater trembled as he pointed it. He looked at the ground and put the rifle down. He stopped and leaned wearily against the inside wall of a building.

"Mills, what in God's name are you doing?! We gotta move," Captain Brown hissed.

"We should surrender, Cap…" Mills said.

"You are a Texas Ranger, Mills. Rangers never surrender."

"There were fuckin' twenty of us on patrol out there tonight, Cap and now there's only six of us left…"

"There's still only one of them out there, Mills, what would your brothers in arms say if they could see you bein' a fuckin' coward now. If you don't pick up that weapon back up, they died fer nothin'."

With a grimace, Mills picked his weapon up and caught up with the five others in front of him. Mills froze and looked forward. Two men in the front fell backward. Knives stuck in the middle of their foreheads.

Elaine drew the twin revolvers from the holsters at her hips and pointed them at Brown, Mills, and the two other remaining combatants. Her eyes flickered under the brim of her tall stovepipe hat. She frowned slightly as all four of the rangers reeled in horror swinging the barrels of their weapons toward her. Her revolvers belched two shots each and the four of them fell before they could pull their triggers. Elaine sighed and shoved her revolvers confidently, proudly into her holsters. Her victims crumpled to the floor of the abandoned building along with their rifles.

Blood pooled from the bullet holes in their necks. They clasped their throats, wide eyed and gurgling for air. She turned to face the farmhouse and walked in that direction, trying and failing to wipe the blood from her face and clothes.

"Mills was right… ya shoulda surrendered…" She said.

Elaine walked over to the farmhouse doors. She peeked through, pushing one open by just a hair. The Gambler's men were tied at their wrists and their ankles. Some kneeled and some sat looking around, wondering about the orchestra of gun blasts that resounded from outside their confines.

The last ranger stood near an old workbench. His rifle leaned against the wall to his left. His neck was craned down toward the table as he read a large leather book silently to himself. Elaine took her revolver and gently pushed the door open with her free hand, leading in with the barrel of her gun pointed at his back. The bottom of the door scraped loudly on the ground.

Elaine saw him shake as he reached for his rifle. She pulled the hammer back on her revolver. The ranger stopped with his shaking hand inches from his gun. The Gambler's lackeys cheered and squirmed happily in their restraints.

"Kill the little Bastard, Greed!"

"Get us the hell outta here!"

"Untie us!"

She looked at the men, then at the ranger. He turned around slowly and faced Elaine his hand still hovering near the rifle. Elaine grimaced.

"What the bloody fuck is a goddamn boy doin' on the Texas fucking Rangers," Elaine asked with her sight locked on the boy.

The young Ranger quivered in place. He said nothing.

"They were training his green ass; fuckin' kill him already, Greed," another one man chimed in.

"Would ya dirty bastards shut the hell up for a damn second?! I was talkin' to the ranger lad…"

The boy's golden-brown eyes locked onto hers. They shifted to the weapon and returned to her.

"Don't even think about it, boyo. The last thing I want on me conscience is the blood o' a wee boy… just back away from it. I promise none of these sons o' bitches will lay a finger on ya. We can all walk outta here with our lives…"

The young lone ranger stayed quiet for a moment, piercing Elaine with that penetrating stare. She studied the features on his face past the end of her revolver. His mouth quivered much like the rest of his body.

"M-my name… is Jim Brown of the Texas Rangers… Son of Captain Alan Brown…"

"No. Just listen, we can-" Elaine stammered.

"…Brother and friend to all the courageous rangers that had their lives snuffed out tonight…"

"Don't-"

"I am a Texas Ranger… and Rangers never surrender…"

Elaine hung her head. Jim swiped at his rifle. He brought it up and pointed it at Elaine. She looked up and revealed her two flickering yellow flames. The explosion at the end of the boy's weapon made her ears ring but failed to shake her. Her eyes darted fast toward the approaching bullet. She tilted her neck to the right. The round hit the wall of the farmhouse at her back. The barrel of her revolver already donned thin wisps of smoke.

The last ranger stumbled to the side and fell, revealing the pulverized contents of his head splattered against the wall behind him. He still held his rifle. Elaine let her revolver fall from her grasp and hit the floor. The boy's eyes were stuck wide open. She saw the fear and innocence lingering in his amber irises.

Elaine slouched while walking over to the large leather-bound book on the table. She closed it and cradled it under her arm. The men tied up around her cheered louder. She walked toward the door of the farmhouse Blake stood dumbfounded, peeking from behind one door.

Elaine walked past Blake without looking at him, out into the night where the clouds over Portales dissipated; revealing some ambient moonlight, but the moon remained hidden.

"Go untie them," She mumbled somberly.

Blake nodded and raced happily inside. He untied the first man, and they helped everyone else out of their restraints. They pooled outside after a moment and clapped

Elaine on her back, congratulating her on a job well done. She stared blankly at the ground. One of the lackeys she freed came up with a full bottle of whisky in his clutches.

"Thanks, Greed! Look what these ranger fuckers were hiding from us… here's to the Sins," the man said waving a shot glass of the amber liquid in her face.

She followed it with her eyes, her head still hung low. Elaine took the glass with little hesitation and gulped it down. She inhaled sharply and hissed at the burning liquid in her mouth.

The man with the bottle laughed, "First time, eh, Greed?"

"Elaine," She barked.

"Hm?"

"Don't call me that stupid fucking name anymore, ya dimwitted bastard… Call me Elaine…"

Elaine snatched the bottle from him and began to pull from it. She walked off and stared at the bodies of the rangers lining the streets, silhouetted in the pale light of the moon. Puddles of blackened blood glimmered and pooled next to them. In between her sips she could almost taste the iron of their blood in the air. She thought she smelled their deaths carried on the winds.

Elaine watched the whiskey slosh around the bottle as she tipped it up into her mouth. She peered into the bottle and saw the boy's shining eyes.

Chapter Fourteen: The Sting of Gunmetal
-The Eye of the Devil, Soldado Mexico-
-February 1876-

The sun hung low in the sky. It cast a fruitful shade of red upon Elaine as she rode into Soldado with Nate bouncing unconscious on the back of her horse. The wind blew grains of sand across the beach with a hiss. It also brought the crash of monstrous ocean waves upon the sharp and rocky coast.

Sweat rolled down Elaine's face. She wiped it off with the sleeve of her coat. She came to the hill's crest. Over it, she gazed upon a decaying Spanish mission. Windblown sand chewed at the sides of the clay buildings. The complex sat close to the beach. The ocean beat the rocks there into jagged spears. A narrow portion of the coastline stuck out into the ocean. A rounded rock pillar that stuck itself into the ocean supported the cliff. The odd rock formation and the ocean's surface created the rounded shape of an eye. The sun set perfectly into the center, creating a black socket around a glowing red pupil: The Eye of the Devil.

Elaine watched the patrols of hired guns circling the buildings while she clutched the reigns on her horse. She looked down the road and spied two dark figures. They stood in front of the largest rectangular structure in the center of the fort.

She recognized the figure on the left as the Gambler. The shape on the right stood two feet above the other. His clean-shaven head gleamed in the light of the setting sun. Elaine approached. She did not recognize the bald man. He had no defining features apart from the brown hue of his skin. He had only a stoic and solemn demeanor with a piercing and soulless black stare. He wore a white collared shirt with faded black pants.

The Gambler smiled with delight when he saw Elaine riding up with Nate hogtied on the rear of her ride.

"Ah, Greed, or do you prefer Eagle Eye, now? It has been quite a while, hasn't it," the Gambler chuckled.

"Enough with the jokes. Here's your prize," Greed replied.

"I assure you, the only joke here is that alias you made up for yourself. I trust you brought him back unharmed?"

"Aye, for the most part…"

"For the most part?"

The Gambler's sinister voice reverberated through her ears, sending that familiar sensation of terror up her spine.

"I hit him over the head with my rifle and drank him about half to death. He'll have one hell of a headache when he wakes up."

"But, otherwise…?"

"Otherwise your prize is fine."

The Gambler's Smile grew wider as he walked closer to Elaine. He gestured for the tall, unremarkable man to carry Nate into the large building behind them. He did so.

"…And your part of our bargain?" Greed asked with her open palm extended toward the Gambler.

"But, of course."

The Gambler stuck his hand inside of his coat and grabbed a thick wad of bundled cash. Elaine grabbed it from him, counted it, and stowed it in her coat pocket.

"So why did ya do it?" Elaine asked.

"Do what exactly?" The Gambler asked in response.

"Have me accompany this goddamn killin' machine through most o' the Western United States to wipe us out?"

The Gambler shifted in place and looked off into the distance, thoughtfully stroking his silver beard. Elaine sat still perched upon her horse, waiting for an answer. He simply smiled in her direction. The expression made her skin crawl.

"Does it matter now?" He asked her.

Elaine took the conversation in a different direction.

"Mind if I stay the evenin'? I could use some rest and some food before I head out again," She asked.

"You're welcome always welcome here, Greed. Take as much time as you see fit. I'll have somethin' new for you by sunrise."

Elaine nodded apprehensively and rode to the nearest building with an empty bed in it. She hitched her horse in front.

The Gambler watched as she walked inside and set her things down inside of the room. He gestured to a patrol of his hired guns and they approached.

"Keep an eye on her. Make sure she stays in that room. Let the other patrols know. She leaves that room; you come straight to me…"

The men nodded and proceeded with their rounds. The Gambler walked back to his quarters. The bald man locked Nate up in the large building and followed the Gambler like a dog.

…

Nate's eyes fluttered open and shut as he regained his consciousness. His head pulsated and pounded. When he moved, he heard the rattle and knock of chains against wood. He shimmied his knees against the ground and heard the shifting of sand underneath him. He was chained by his arms. Held up against an old, large, and re-purposed crucifix.

The smell of the sea filled his nose and the soft roar of the ocean filled his ears. He could almost taste the salt on his tongue. Nate opened his eyes to see two figures standing in a dark and decrepit church. Through a broken stained-glass window above, he could spot the stars shimmering in the night sky. The orange flickering of torchlight partially illuminated the large room filled with broken and disheveled pews and benches.

"Good mornin'… or rather good evenin'," the Gambler said behind a smug smile.

Nate's face was formed in a fierce scowl as he spat the dust from his mouth into the sand in front of him.

"Where is Sara?"

The Gambler leaned back and slapped his knee, hooting with victorious, exaggerated laughter.

Nate continued to glare at the Gambler, "WHERE IS MY DAUGHTER?!"

The Gambler put a hand to his chin, feigning deep thought. He pointed at Nate, "Wrath… Fitting."

The Gambler snapped his fingers and the bald man approached, halting at the Gambler's side.

"Wrath, I'd like you to meet Envy, Envy this is our new friend Wrath."

"TELL ME!"

"Envy, fetch the sacrifice."

Envy nodded and walked out of the church doors. Nate's chest heaved up and down. His eyes still burned, fixed upon the Gambler who stared back, enjoying the hate he had fostered.

"You did one hell of a Job tearin' through those Sins… those mistakes I made over the years. Hell, I couldn't even turn you when we first met, you'd have torn through us like tissue paper… me and Envy included… but now that you're here… and I have my new book…"

Envy returned with all the ingredients for the ritual except for one.

“Sir, the child vanished. She isn’t in her room. Most of the patrols have been killed. We have three squads remaining. Greed is missing,” Envy said.

The smile that was stuck to the Gambler’s face drooped into a wrinkled and infuriated mess of a frown.

“Find them both, now!”

Envy once again, stormed out of the room in pursuit of Sara and Elaine. The Gambler drew his revolver from his holster and waited, eyeing the entrances to the old church.

Nate’s lips curled back in a wide grin, “Thank you, Elaine.”

…

-Ojos Negros, Mexico-

-February 1876-

-The Night at the Inn-

-Before the Eye of the Devil-

“Nate… I need to tell ya something else...”

Nate sat up and swayed back and forth with a mix of concern and drunken stupor upon his face.

“What I told ya about my past is all true, but it isn’t the whole truth.”

Elaine reached over and dampened the lamp sitting on the nightstand next to the bed, casting the room in almost pitch darkness. Elaine’s eyes flickered yellow like twin flames in the dark.

"I was with the Gambler when he tracked you to your ranch in Montana. The Gambler told me to lead you to him… to make sure you got to Mexico in one piece after the raid… right from the moment we met at the Seely Lake saloon… we threatened the bartender… told him what to say to you. I stayed with you to guide you down here… and… I begged him not to… your family, Nate… I'm so sorry… I wish I could take it all back, I really do."

Nate flopped out of bed onto his stomach. He clumsily scrambled across the floor to retrieve his swords.

"I knew ya were goin' to react like this, Nate… so I had to get ya piss drunk so ya wouldn't be able to skewer me on the spot… and so I wouldn't have to shoot ya either."

Elaine reached down and scooped Nate off the floor. She sat him back up in the bed. She clambered around for her pack and retrieved her matches from it. Elaine relit the lantern and stood in front of him with that same solemn and apologetic look. He wobbled there once again with a look of pure rage slathered onto his face.

"Welll… what're youu waiting for? Kill mme," Nate slurred.

"I don't want to kill ya, Nate. I could've shot ya many times before this. I just want to tell ya the truth… and to get my point accross."

Nate sat and swayed less as he tried to get a hold of himself, "Shhhit… I caan't even fform a sentennce let alllone murderr you… Let's hear the truth thenn… and yyour point too, I guesss."

"I'll give ya the short version…when I came to the west… From Ireland, I wasn't doin' so well… I had to do some things that… to this day make me shudder when I think about 'em. I did whatever I could for a quick buck and a hot meal. Then one day, the man we know as the Gambler came and saw the sorry state I was in. He could see my sufferin'. Come with me, dear and I can give you anything you desire, he said to me. He held out his hand. The first time I heard his voice, it rattled my bones… still does. Every fiber o' my bein' was screamin' to run the fuck away from this man, but I took his hand. I had no other choice. It was either anything I desired or do just about anything to scrape by. About a year had passed as we travelled around. The Gambler had me doin' burglary jobs and raids with some of his men. He paid well, and I had no complaints. Then the Gambler took me down south to the Eye o' the Devil and told me that this is where all my desires would be fulfilled. I trusted him. He guided me to a worn-down church inside the mission. He escorted me up a long flight of stairs. In a room there was a bound, gagged, and hooded stranger seated in the middle o' a large circle o' blood. I looked back at the Gambler. He closed the door behind us and stepped toward the trapped man who choked and yelled, muffled by a piece of cloth tied around his mouth. The Gambler sat me down in a chair opposite of the hostage. Make a wish, he said, any wish and it will be granted. I didn't question it… any of it. I wished for help for my family in New York, I wished for the ability to earn lots of money and see me loved ones find their way out of poverty. The Gambler took a blade out from his coat. I scrambled in my seat, horrified. The Gambler spoke some gibberish and stabbed the guy in the chair right through his heart. I still remember his muffled screams. Some ungodly power washed over me. The sensation of horror was replaced by a desire for money. The world became so detailed. I could suddenly watch the tiniest speck of dust floating through the air. Out of the window, I could count the number of a man's eyelashes as he walked through his town from miles away. I could pick out droplets of blood flyin' through the air from the stranger's throat for what seemed like hours. After some time, I learned to use my eyesight with rifles and revolvers; any firearm I could get my hands on. I got my wish. My skill made me a successful marksman. It turned me into a successful murderer. The Gambler would send me out to kill anyone he wanted and for the right amount of money, I'd shoot anything that moved if it meant helping my family. If it meant never going back to the life I lived before I met him… If it meant getting more money. I sent half of every payment to 'em." Nate's look of drunken anger softened into understanding. He sat up straight and tried his best to speak properly.

"So, what's your point, Elaine? Why sshould I trust you? Why should I evver forgive you? What made you change sides?"

"You don't have to forgive me. What we did… the sins… it's unforgivable. My point is… I want to kill the Gambler just as much as you do. Under his wing, I did a lot of things… things I try to forget every waking moment. I want to right those wrongdoings."

"Why didn't you blaast himm alreaady?"

"You've seen it, Nate. He always surrounds himself with hired guns. I could never get close to him. I tried sharpshooting him, but it's like he knew I was targeting him. I would set my sights on the building he was in, but he would already be gone. I'd spend hours with my sights trained on him or track the caravan he was traveling with, but he would escape my sights… nowhere to be found. There one minute and gone the next. Some more of his hoodoo bullshite, without a doubt. Even if I could get away with it, he knows where my family is. I couldn't risk trying without my family being threatened."

"How do you think we aare going to kill him nnow if you couldn't fuckinnng do it before?"

"That's exactly it, Nate… We. We can end this together. We can save your daughter back and end this nightmare."

"So, we just rrush into the eye of the devvil with your guns blazing and my sswords slashing?"

"No, we would get filled full o' led before we even breached the front o' the god damned place. The Gambler is expectin' me to deliver you to him on a silver platter and that's exactly what we're gonna give him."

Nate lurched forward to grab his swords, but Elaine placed her hands on his shoulders and held him in place.

"Wait a second, hear me out. We are going to set a trap for him and we'll kill him when he least expects it. I'll bring you in unconscious. The Gambler will no doubt want to toy with ya some more, that sick fuck. So, he'll have ya stowed away and tied up somewhere. I'll come for ya during the middle of the night, killin' all the men I can find without alertin' anybody and then free you. After that, I'll be spotted. I'll be a diversion. That's when you strike. We'll take the son of a bitch out together along with anybody else that's left to stand in our way, and get Sara to ya… where she belongs… I know I've wronged ya, and I know I'll probably never earn your forgiveness, but I still wanna try. Will ya trust me so we can put a stop to all o' this?"

Nate stared out into nothingness and thought. His stupor seemed to vanish as he thought more about it.

"I don't think I'll evver forgive you for what happened that day, but I have no other choice. I gotta trust you. Let's end this and get Sara back," Nate said.

"Okay. There's just one more thing…"

"What?"

"We need to make it look… authentic…"

Nate looked at Elaine questioningly. Elaine's hands trembled on her rifle.

"I'm so sorry about this, Nate…"

She drew back and swung the butt of her rifle against the temple of Nate's head. With a loud crack, he fell to the bed where he laid unconscious.

…

-The Eye of the Devil-

-February 1876-
-The Very Next Night-

Elaine threw her things onto the floor of the lodging at the Gambler's fort. She took a large pull from her whiskey flask and unpacked some beef jerky. She watched as the Gambler followed the bald man into the old mission chapel to restrain Nate. She also watched the blood red sun dip below the horizon.

The wind died, allowing the ocean water to calm itself. The once loud crashing of the ocean waves turned into a calm rolling against the coastline. The absence of the sun turned the sky into a deep and dark shade of blue. The moon was gone, leaving the night in deep darkness.

That worked out nicely, Elaine thought to herself. She looked into the night sky.
Her eyes adjusted to the absence of light and burned yellow. Though the night was as black as pitch, she scanned the mission grounds with ease. Her gaze was set upon the chapel. The Gambler and his bald compatriot walked out from the two front doors of the building. She saw a key ring in the grasp of the bald man. He stopped a patrolling guard with a large ten-gallon hat who was patrolling the area. He handed him the keys and gave him some orders. The hatted guard nodded and sped off toward the back of the mission.

Elaine reached into her bag for her last meager piece of jerky. She threw it in her mouth and made sure that there weren't any guards peering through the window at her.

She pulled the curtains closed and got ready. With a swift flick, Elaine unrolled her sleeping pack. Nate's sheathed twin sabers clambered to the floor. She buttoned her coat up and removed the top hat from her head, letting her toasty brown hair flow down her back. She pulled a black bandana from her bag and tied it over the bottom half of her face, stifling the sound of her breathing. Elaine fastened Nate's belt around her waist with his swords resting at her sides. She grabbed a small piece of cloth and tied her hair up to keep it from being a distraction. She took her revolvers from her holsters and pulled their hammers back. Elaine shimmied the revolvers on her waist, so they wouldn't hinder her ability to draw the weapons when she needed to. She looked over at her flask. She bit her lip and let out a long sigh. She had a final swig and left it behind.

With a couple of deep breaths, Elaine dampened the lamp in her room, immersing herself in darkness. She walked over to the door and unsheathed one of Nate's blades with a satisfying scrape. She poked a glowing eye out from the curtain to see if any guards were close by.

A patrol of three made their way across the old chapel. They turned the corner of the building with lanterns in their hands. She gingerly opened the door with a slight creak and stepped outside. Luckily, the loose sand that covered the ground turned the loud thud of her boots into a hissing whisper with each footfall.

Elaine slithered across the wall as she heard the conversation of guards approaching. She darted to the cover of the next building, tailing the guard with the remarkable hat and keys. She evaded the last patrol by a hair. Her heart pounded, and she slowed her rapid breathing. She peeked around the corner of the wall she hid behind. Another patrol of two approached from her right.

Shite…

She stood still as beads of sweat rolled down her forehead. She drew Nate's other sword without making a sound. Elaine heard the light crunch of sand under boots getting closer and closer.

Elaine lunged from the corner of the building plunging the sharpened metal into the necks of the two guards simultaneously. Blood sprayed. They gurgled in pain, as their legs grew weak. The lantern dropped from the guard's clutches. Elaine dropped a sword and caught the lantern a moment before it hit the ground. As she sighed in relief, her latest victims fell with softened thuds.

Elaine flinched at the sound. She looked around. No other guards followed. She dampened the lantern with a pinch of her fingers and set it down. With a quiet groan, she dragged their bodies one at a time. She tucked them behind the shallow wall, the rear of the structure where she hid before. They left long streaks in the sediment. Elaine shrugged and kicked more sand over the evidence. She wiped the sweat from her forehead with the sleeve of her coat and continued her search for the keys.

The patrols of hired guns came in threes, pairs, and every so often, a single man. Elaine Dodged and evaded the groups of two and three. She crept alongside of the buildings, waiting for the right moment to strike, keeping herself from being discovered by the other men patrolling the area. One by one, and two by two, she disposed of the guards and hid their corpses as best as she could. She was rapidly running out of places to hide the guards' bodies. Guards that passed by called out each other's names, searching for each other patrol. Their calls received no response.

Three patrols o' three. About nine men left.

Elaine made her way to the southernmost edge of the mission that bordered the coast. One of the three squads approached as Elaine ducked behind a shallow segment of wall. She overheard their brief conversation.

"She escaped. Find 'er before the boss finds us or else we're as good as dead. Me an' Gabe'll head this way. Go tell the other patrols what's goin' on and make damn sure we keep that kid from 'er."

Elaine slowly peeked over the wall and saw the group of three splitting up in opposite directions, leaving the guard in the ten-gallon hat walking toward her alone. Oh, thank bloody Christ…

Elaine heard the jingle and clank of metal against metal as the guard strolled past her without seeing her. Swiftly, she rose and plunged her right sword into the man's back, covering his choked cries with her hand. Blood seeped from his mouth and through her fingers. She struggled to carry his dead weight for a soft and silent fall. She dragged him behind the wall and stuffed the keys into her coat pocket.

Elaine ran, keeping low. She stayed hidden in whatever cover she could find. The guards were desperate now. They had their guns drawn, holding lanterns with their free hands. They searched for her in every nook and cranny of the mission. She shifted from building to building until she reached the back door of the chapel. She pulled the door open and stepped inside.

The air was heavy with the stench of old wood and the salt of the ocean. Elaine entered the chapel from the podium. In the dark, she saw Nate on his knees chained to an oversized cross. She rushed over, fumbling with the keys. She unlocked his cuffs. He fell forward. She held him up and kept him from hitting the ground.

"Nate, wake up. We have to find Sara and get the hell outta here," she whispered.

Nate's skull throbbed painfully as he looked up at Elaine. He shook his head at her and looked at the sandy floor of the chapel.

"What the fuck do ya mean, no?!"

"You need to take Sara and leave before the Gambler comes back with more men."

"Fuckin' damnit, Nate. That's not what we had planned!"

"Change of plans. You and I both know the Gambler will find us again if we don't end it now."

"Fuck sakes, Nate… I don't like this-"

"Find Sara and take her to Ojos Negros. I want her to be safe encase he wins. I'll finish this and meet you there in two days. Don't wait any longer."

"We can finish this together, Nate. We need to."

"No, I need to know she's safe... out of this goddamned place. If we both stay there's a chance, you could die, and I'd be stuck here in chains… He wants me alive… if he didn't, I'd be dead already."

"… And what if ya don't come back?"

"Get her to John and Christine Shepherd in New York… The last of my family."

Elaine looked at Nate, "You're bloody well sure about this?"

"Trust me like I trusted you. Leave me one of my swords, and I'll take care of the rest."

Elaine placed one of Nate's Sabers behind him. He pushed sand over it to hide it. She took of Nate's hand into hers and placed it over the hilt.

"Good luck, Nate… I'll see ya soon."

"Goodbye, Elaine…"

She propped Nate up onto the cross and tightened the cuffs on his wrists just enough, so they appeared to be locked. With one last look, she headed out and searched for Sara. Nate's eyes grew heavy as he struggled to keep himself awake. The thought of keeping Sara safe burned in his mind and kept him conscious as he waited to spring the trap. Fear worked its way into his mind. Fear that the animal he was would return.

…

Nate's lips curled back in a wide grin, "Thank you, Elaine."

The loosened rattle of chains startled the Gambler. Nate rose to his feet. He grabbed the hilt of his sword that was buried in the sand behind him. Nate lunged forward at the Gambler before he even had time to turn around. He placed the blade against The Gambler's throat.

"Drop it," Nate whispered.

The Gambler did as Nate said and dropped his weapon with a soft thud against the sand. Nate kicked the revolver away and stepped in front of him, still pointing his weapon at him. He gestured to the Gambler to get onto his knees. Nate locked the Gambler into the chains of the cross.

The Gambler's crooked smile was still slathered across his face as he whispered something that Nate could not hear. Nate brought the sword to his throat again.

"Get rid of that goddamn smile… you're as good as dead," Nate demanded.

The old man closed his eyes and muttered more gibberish. Envy threw the doors of the church open and stormed back inside. He stared at Nate. Envy's flesh twisted and contorted. His features turned to that of Nate's down to the clothing and weaponry. The only feature he kept of his own was his burning yellow irises. They switched between a hellish yellow glow and soulless black. Nate stared at a copy of himself.

Envy drew a sword in his right hand and charged at Nate with all his might. Steel clashed and sent sparks flying. The two blocked and evaded each other's swings and slashes. With every successful slice Nate landed, came a response from Envy wounding him in the same place.

The two staggered away from each other in pain, clutching at the seeping cuts on their calves and arms. Ignoring the pain, they struggled on, their jaws clenched and their teeth grinding. Nate's fighting grew weaker and weaker with every ferocious slash, and block. His chest heaved. He grew increasingly fatigued. Envy kept up his pace and his ferocity cutting Nate all over where he missed his blocks and evasions.

With another swing of Envy's blade, Nate fell to his knees, dripping blood from various cuts all over his body. He grew weary and tired as his vision blurred. His limbs and extremities tingled. Warmth was leaving his body. Envy held his sword to Nate's neck waiting for an order from the Gambler.

The Gambler chuckled victoriously, "If you would be so kind as to undo these shackles, Envy…"

Nate wobbled while kneeling. His head was getting light and he could feel himself bleeding out. Envy's weapon dropped to the ground and dissolved with his likeness of Nate. Envy turned his back to Nate to free the Gambler from the cross.

"Not, now! Kill him," The Gambler ordered!

In a haze, Nate picked up the Gambler's gun from the sand, struggling to point it at Envy. The cold sting of

Gunmetal on his wounds brought Nate out from his stupor. He could see clearly for an instant.

The Gambler's laughter was cut short by the blast from his own Schofield revolver. Envy's head exploded, sending red shards of brain matter and skull flying across the church. It splattered on the walls and pews behind the Gambler, coating his suit.

Nate shambled to his feet, propping himself up on the blade of his sword, using it as a cane. He pointed the smoking barrel of the revolver at the Gambler who kneeled under the chains of the cross. Nate kneeled next to the body of Envy whose headless body still spurted with blood. Nate took his blade and cut strips from Envy's shirt. He tied the strips tightly against his deeper cuts to stop the bleeding.

Nate turned his attention to the Gambler. He crouched in front of the man and looked him dead in the eyes with his sword hanging loosely in his grasp. The Gambler stared back at the injured horse breeder, the broken soldier. He stared at his wrath. The malicious smile returned to the gang leader's face.

"What," The Gambler said laughing, "You expectin' me to beg?"

Nate leaned closer to the Gambler. The Gambler gazed fearlessly at the frigid pits of Nate's Icy cold blue eyes.

"You know why I chose you," The Gambler laughed from his restraints, "Just as well as I do. It's funny you believed that you could ever be a father to that child… did you really think you could be anything but a killing machine… an animal… a monster like you? You'll never be able to wash his blood from your hands. You can never bring him back. You're better off takin' that weapon, stickin' the barrel in your mouth, and puttin' the beast down."

The Gambler let out one final loud and maniacal cackle. Nate stood. He slid the blade of his sword across The Gambler's Stomach. Nate watched The Gambler's eyes roll into his head and heard his intestines flop out onto the sand.

The Gambler hissed in agony and writhed in his restraints, "Forgive me, Renee…"

The old man's bones cracked, and his cries were choked off. His skin and flesh withered atop his bones and tightened around them. The Gambler's hair and fingernails grew rapidly. His writing corpse turned to ash and was taken by the wind. His empty clothes fell. From his coat pocket fell a worn leather book and an ancient looking, red wooden poker chip.

Nate watched until all the Gambler's remains flew off. He limped out of the chapel. He sheathed his sword upon his belt. No devilish grin worked its way across his face, no demonic glee worked itself over him.

Nate staggered out of the church to see the last of the hired guns fleeing off as the sun rose over the sea behind them. They were under hire no more. No reason to stay. The Eye of the Devil was abandoned.

Nate went to the nearest building where he found a bottle of whiskey and a spooked horse hitched outside. He grabbed the bottle, took a few large gulps, and poured the alcohol over his wounds with a wince. He did his best to calm the horse.

Nate looked down at his hand. Polished gunmetal directed the morning light into his eyes. He looked at the weapon in his grasp for what seemed like a lifetime. His thoughts shifted to Sara, to Sofia… to his identity… what he wanted so desperately to be… for his daughter.

Nate pointed the barrel of the Schofield revolver under his chin.

Chapter Fifteen: The Memory of Marcus Laveau
-The Eye of the Devil, Mexico-
-Late September 1875-

Envy turned his tan colored hand back and forth in front of his face. He sat bent over against the wall. It was one of the largest rooms in re-purposed mission. He picked up his head and looked out the window. His ears twitched. Rain beat hard against the glass and pooled against each pane before running down. The rain obscured the rocky coastline behind the window. Envy could tell it was much darker than normal. The black clouds blocked out the sun and left the coast in the dark.

The ocean was stirred up by the storm. Waves grew fiercer and crashed further up the shoreline. Ocean water had turned as black as the sky, obscuring the horizon. No matter how hard or how much closer the waves crashed toward the mission, the rain did its best to block the noise out with its own constant slamming against the clay rooftops and walls around him.

The Gambler and his other men remained still, preoccupied in their own business. Envy's eyes wandered over to the old man who sat writing something at his desk. It was typical for an afternoon, stormy or not. The Gambler stroked the silver beard on his chin. He pulled a book from his coat pocket along with a sack of what looked like roots, dust, and the small flakes of a torn-up bank note.

The Gambler ran his finger along a line of incomprehensible text and muttered ancient sounding words that Envy struggled to understand. He then threw the ingredients into a bag sitting on the floor. From it, he pulled several wads of bank notes. He counted the bills, leaving Envy to sit close by and watch his back while he did so. It left his mind to race.

Envy looked at his hands. He looked around the rest of the large room. Candles flickered around. Four men talked with each other. The two at the front of the room spoke from each corner. They rolled new cigarettes and chewed tobacco as they laughed and nodded to each other. Envy looked to his left. The pair of guards in the back of the room stood close to each other and exchanged a lit cigarette every so often. The guard who leaned against the wall halted his conversation with his friend. He looked over at Envy and walked over to him with a welcoming smile on his face. Envy remained seated in the chair, looking at the approaching guard.

"Envy, right," The man asked.

"Yep, in the flesh… and you are," Envy replied.

"I'm Gabe and this here is Jack. It's a pleasure!"

"Likewise."

The man who talked with Gabe came over with his hand extended toward Envy. The sin grabbed it and shook it. Envy smiled at Gabe and Jack. Jack offered Envy his cigarette to which Envy and graciously accepted. He took a long drag and exhaled with a large, wispy cloud of smoke. He gave the cigarette to Gabe who inhaled more of it. The three stood together in silence, pandering for a conversation piece.

"It's strange to think about, but you are the first guards to come up and talk to me."

Gabe and Jack looked at each other for a moment. They gaped at Envy with their eyebrows raised.

"The last thing we want to do is offend you, Envy, but we've gotta be honest… you're not exactly a comfortin' sight… the way you look… it's probably why no one here has come up to you unless they really had to," Gabe said.

Envy nodded and looked at the floor.

"Yeah, I know. I've looked like this for as long as I can remember."

Envy ran a hand over his unremarkable face, his hairless brow, and bald scalp.

"Tell us about yourself, Envy. Where'd you grow up, do you have a wife or a family at home, do you go by anything other than Envy," Gabe asked.

"I'd love to tell you guys, but I can't…"

Gabe and Jack scratched the backs of their heads.

"Shoot, don't sweat it, Envy, we were mighty curious… we see that the Gambler is a real secretive guy, especially when it comes to you… people," Jack said.

"It isn't exactly that, guys, it's just that… well… I can't remember a damn thing from before the Gambler took me in."

"You get hit on the head or something," Jack prodded.

"I could've been… I have no idea what happened to me before the Gambler brought me here."

"Like… what the hell do they call it? Amnesia?" Gabe inquired.

"That's right, it's like amnesia. For all I know I could've been somebody important before the Gambler found me," Envy laughed.

"Where did he find you?" Gabe asked.

A chair scuffed loudly against the floor. The gang leader stood up. Jack and Gabe froze. The Gambler walked over and held his right hand out to Gabe. He offered the Gambler his cigarette. The Gambler took a long drag and looked at Envy, Jack and Gabe, exhaling a plume of smoke in their direction.

"Sir, how was the trip up to Montana?"

"It was… fruitful. Thanks for askin'… I couldn't help but overhear your conversation. I've told Envy this story before. He was in a panic when he woke up. I had to tell him everything I knew about him right then and there when I found him in the desert near here, actually. It was a couple years back. I stumbled upon him unconscious out there. He was as bald as he is now. I know about as much as he does about where he came from and who he was… I know a bit less than jack shit."

"Less than me, sir?" Jack asked.

The Gambler smiled and shook his head, "Nah, just a figure of speech, Jack... don't sweat it."

Envy looked up at the Gambler sternly as he remembered vividly the night he woke up in the desert.

"That's right," Envy said, "I remember waking up with the Gambler looking down at me and mumbling something while reading from one of his books. I saw I was in the center of a big circle of blood."

The Gambler nodded as he took another drag from the cigarette they all shared as a group. The men at the other end of the room stopped conversing to listen in on the other conversation.

"That's when I gave you the abilities you have now, and that's why I keep you as my body guard now. You're quite a powerful individual, Envy," The Gambler replied.

"Why did you do it," Envy asked the Gambler.

"What, the ritual?"

"Yes… what did you call it, the-"

"The Devil's Tin…"

"That's the one."

Jack and Gabe swiveled their heads back and forth between Envy and the Gambler as they spoke to each other.

"A benefit of that hex is that it restores the recipient to perfect health… in your case, you were dying of exhaustion, thirst and starvation in the middle of that desert. It was the only way I could help you since I was lacking food and water for you… or for myself as a matter of fact."

Envy nodded and held out his hand toward the Gambler who still held onto the group's cigarette. The Gambler hissed as the ember found its way up the cigarette and nestled itself in between his fingers.

"I'll roll y'all a new one," The Gambler smiled.

He strolled to his desk and opened a drawer near the top, bringing out his own tobacco.

"Sir, there's no need we have some over-" Gabe began.

"Nonsense, I wasted most of yours flappin' my gums' with y'all."

"Well, thank you, sir," Jack and Gabe Chimed in together.

The Gambler walked back over with a freshly rolled cigarette. He handed it to Jack who took out a matchbox from his pocket. The Gambler stopped him by holding his index finger up at him. He pulled out his own box and lit it for him. The Gambler tilted his head to look out of the window to the storm that still raged outside.

"I'm not sure how much this storm is goin' to last. I'm afraid I've gone and exhausted my old self at this desk here for the day. Have a good night, gentlemen… Envy."

The five men in the room nodded at the Gambler as he threw his coat on and headed toward the entrance of the building. The guards that were posted at the front walked over. They pulled the door open for him and followed, closing it behind them. The three of them ran to avoid getting soaked to the bone from the torrential rain.

Gabe, Jack and Envy passed their new cigarette back around. Jack and Gabe gaped at the storm. Envy watched the Gambler run to his quarters at the other end of the mission. Two men followed closely behind.

"Wanna get drunk tonight?" Gabe asked.

"Not 'til this damned storm dies down. Last thing I wanna do is get this change of clothes all wet… or pass out in the mud," Jack responded.

"What about you, Envy, you're more than welcome to join the two of us," Gabe said as he puffed on the cigarette.

"Maybe for a bit, but I gotta leave early and take care of some business before I can do my own thing tonight."

Gabe and jack nodded. The three parted ways.

…

Envy stared at the ceiling from his bed. His room was darker than night. The downpour of rain died down with the storm. It left a soft patter of rainfall lingering and falling against the roof. He took in the smell of rain-soaked earth and clay every time he inhaled. He threw his sheets off himself and swung his legs off the side of the bed. The floor was cold under his feet. He grabbed his forehead and brought his hand back along the top of his hairless, sweat covered scalp.

Envy slipped his uniform on and approached his door. He opened the door and let the cool coastal air envelop him. Envy stretched out both of his arms in front of him and leaned on the railing on the porch of his quarters. He looked out onto the rest of the mission. Portions of men were illuminated by the soft glow of their lanterns as they lounged on their decks.

They looked like orbs of separate realities floating in an ocean of black nothingness. Gabe and Jack sat across from each other in their sphere. They competed in a two-man drinking competition. Jack wobbled in his chair and struggled to keep his eyes open. Men separated in other spheres of lantern light stood leaning similar to Envy against the railings of their quarters with cigarettes in their hands, laughing and chatting amongst themselves.

Envy scanned the mission and spied one square light emanating from the center of the complex. He squinted through the window and saw the Gambler slouched at his desk writing in a large leather book. The old gang leader picked up a cigarette from the dish on the table next to him. The Gambler took a long drag and fiddled with more strange looking objects scattered about the surface of the table. He exhaled with a plume of smoke and continued to write. Envy thought of what the Gambler said earlier. The sweat on his forehead and on the back of his neck grew frigid.

Envy went back inside of his quarters and put on his black leather duster over his white-buttoned shirt. He strapped his boots on and grabbed the lantern from the nightstand next to his cot. He lit it and stormed toward the light where Jack and Gabe still sat taking shot after shot of whiskey. The pair looked up as Envy approached. His boots were squishing and crunching loudly in the wet soil under his boots.

"Gabe, Jack, I-," Envy began.

Jack slumped down into his chair and snored loudly.

"Looks like I win this time, lightweight," Gabe laughed, "I think you arrived a second too late, Envy. Care for a shot or a smoke?"

"Sorry, I will not be here for long. I gotta take my mind off some things before I'm able to get to sleep again."

"Ah, yeah. I get how that is. I know we just met today, but do you mind if I ask what's troubling you? Maybe I can help. We'll have a drink or two… or three…"

Envy glanced around the shadowy mission for other men that might listen into their conversation. He looked back down to Gabe. Gabe looked up at Envy with bloodshot eyes and a dumb looking smile slathered onto his face.

"It might seem like I'm sober, but don't let my ability to form a full sentence lead you to think otherwise and don't worry about me remembering any of this shit, 'cause I won't be remembering a damn thing in the morning." Gabe declared.

"Whatever you say... Well, do you remember what the Gambler said earlier this afternoon?"

"Wait, which part?"

"When he was talking about how he found me in the middle of the desert... When he made me into what I am..."

"Yeah, sure."

"I- I just don't think I can take his word for it."

"He seemed genuine."

"But, don't you think there's something-"

"Nope."

"It seems like he's hiding something..."

"No, I mean you could be right… actually, you're probably right… the Gambler doesn't pay us to think. He pays us to sit, stay, and rollover… if you know what I mean."

Envy scratched his head.

"I mean, we're his dogs… as long as we get fed and get our treats, we shouldn't and probably aren't going to question a damn thing," Gabe said.

Envy nodded, "I get it…"

Gabe looked off into the distance, still swaying back and forth in his rocking chair, clutching the bottle of whiskey.

"…What I don't understand is how you're able to speak without slurring your words at this point… how much of that have you had?" Envy asked.

Gabe looked down at the bottle of alcohol with a thin line of liquid sloshing at the bottom as he moved.

"This bottle was full when we started and as for my speech, well, I have no rightly idea…. Just gifted, I guess… I definitely had more than Jack did."

"How can I take your word for it?"

"For my speech, what I told you, or how much I actually drank?"

"…The first two."

"Hmmm… I think that people… at least me… I'm always the most truthful when I'm drunk, 'cause it's a lot harder to lie and keep a straight face."

Envy looked back up to the window of lantern light where the Gambler sat. He maintained a stern expression and his brow furrowed.

"Thank you, Ga-"

Gabe was already slumped into his chair with his mouth hanging open just like Jack's. Drool crept its way out of his mouth and collected on his duster. The bottle slid out of his grasp and clanked onto the wooden floor of the porch. Envy gave the two sleeping men a weak smile and put his lantern back up in front of him to guide his way through the night.

Envy slid up to the window. His eyes darted through the window and at the Gambler who still sat writing inside. Envy peeked through the window at the gang leader who looked down at his large leather-bound book, focusing hard on its contents. The Gambler looked up and scratched his beard. He caught a glimpse of The Gambler's pupils.

Envy's eyes flickered as he changed into the Gambler. Thousands of images and flashed through his Envy's mind and were seared into his memory bank. He fell hard onto his knees and grabbed at the sides of his head. Tears flowed from his eyes and his jaw quivered.

Envy wiped his tears and clenched his fists. He stood up and an uncontrollable anger welled up inside of him. He let himself take his original form. Envy stormed over to the front of the building. He took a deep breath to calm himself down. He opened the doors of the building and eyed the Gambler whose head shot up from his book. He sat behind his desk straight across from the entrance where Envy entered. A lantern was perched on the table next to him. Two men stood in the corners of the shadowy room. They had their arms folded as they looked at Envy. They had their revolvers holstered at their hips.

"Envy," The Gambler grunted, breaking the silence.

Envy looked at the Gambler and said nothing. He walked over to one man in the corner.

"Do you mind rolling a cigarette for me? I ran out of tobacco earlier today," Envy requested.

The guard nodded and reached into his pockets for his papers and his tobacco pouch. Envy reached down to the man's hip and pulled his revolver from its holster. Envy looked behind him, leading with the barrel of the revolver. He pointed it to the guard in the other corner who fumbled at his weapon. He put two rounds in his chest and turned back to the guard in front of him who dropped his smoking supplies. He reached for something in his chest pocket. Envy fired a round under his jaw and didn't stop to watch him fall to the floor. He raised the revolver and pointed it at the Gambler. The old silver haired man's hands dropped into his lap and under the table. The Gambler laughed to himself and let a smile spread across his face.

"WHY…" Envy yelled, his voice trembling.

"I figured it was only a matter of time," The Gambler replied.

"Answer the goddamn question, or I'll-"
There was an explosion of light. The loud crack of the Gambler's revolver sounded from under the desk. A bullet tore a hole through the wooden back and through Envy's gut as he came crashing down.

The Gambler rose from his seat and looked down at Envy. The old man pointed his revolver at him. Envy still held onto the pistol and swung the barrel at the Gambler. The Gambler put another round into his arm and the weapon in envy's grasp fell. More men came running into the building, but The Gambler held his free hand up to them. They nodded, pulled the doors closed, and went outside.

The Gambler casually walked over to the sin. Envy's good arm shot over to the weapon on the floor next to him. The Gambler kicked it away before he could get a hold of it.

"You already know why. You know everythin' that I know. I knew I recognized that handsome old face through the window," The Gambler said.

Envy rolled onto his back and held the wound in his stomach. He glared up at the Gambler.

"So, you tell me. Why?"

Envy writhed on the floor, "I don't know why, you twisted son of a bitch, all I get is a bunch of images," He hissed, "You never saved me. You never saved any of us. You tracked us down with that goddamned book and ruined our fucking lives!"

The Gambler laughed more and leaned against the front of his table, still facing the bleeding sin and listening intently. Envy glared at the Gambler.

"What, you can't interpret reason from what you saw?"

The Gambler's smile grew wider, "… I butchered your family right under your nose, Carlos. You were gettin' well water for your mother and father. I lined 'em up for one shot just to save me the ammo. By the time I left, you saw the result and ran into the desert. I followed. I helped yet another desperate, distraught person in need."

Envy swallowed as the blood pooled underneath him and his eyelids drooped.

"Even knowing the truth… who… what I am, you'll still serve me, Envy."

"I'd sooner kill you… by dying," Envy replied weakly.

"I wouldn't bet on that."

Envy laughed, "I saw it… in your books… in your memories… centuries of hoodoo secrets."

The Gambler stood, waiting for Envy to finish his sentence breath by labored breath.

"By killing me, you've undone this curse… The caster who destroys his own hexes will have his power stripped… and you will wither away. Your age will catch up with you and your gang will die. You won't hurt anyone anymore. My family… the families, the people you've fucked with… the people you've destroyed and enslaved will have their vengeance," Envy finished.

Envy crawled, struggled toward the gun in the floor. The Gambler walked over to his desk. He pulled a book and some powder from the lower drawer. He flipped through the pages and muttered something. Envy's pupils expanded, turning his eyes a pitch black. The smile faded from Envy's face and his laughter was cut short. His limbs tightened up. The Gambler waved his hand up. Envy stood up. He tried to scream, to run, but Envy's body refused to listen.

"If you've seen what I can do… everything these books can do, then you've already seen that I have the ability to do what I'm about to do…"

The Gambler circled back behind the table and picked up his large leather book, muttering more gibberish and throwing powder onto Envy's wounds. The pain in the sin's gunshot wounds vanished. The bleeding stopped. The Gambler walked over to Envy, stopping inches from his face.

"You asked to know why I've done all this, why I do it… all of these terrible things."

Envy's eyes bulged from his head and his heart pounded. No amount of rage or desperation made him budge. The Gambler pulled a worn red poker chip from his front pocket. Envy sensed the Gambler's breath in his ear and sensed the want in his voice.

"I needed seven… seven sins slain… I needed someone strong… someone powerful… someone so incredibly, so inexplicably prone to slaughtering, to bloodshed, to unparalleled rage. I needed one ruthless enough to take down the six as a mere man. I needed my wrath. It's funny that I think of it now. His name is Shepherd. The one from Montana we spoke of today. It's almost like a goddamn prophecy. The shepherd gathers his flock… lambs to the slaughter."

The Gambler poked Envy in his forehead. The sin remained motionless and standing at attention.

"Once Wrath kills the last of you, he has to spill his own blood as a sin… the seventh. Then I'll have the power to get recover somethin' I lost a long… long time ago. I'll be able to bring her back. She's all I care about… I've done terrible things… things that I'll never forgive myself for… and I'll still do anythin'."

"Now," The Gambler smiled, "It's all comin' together."

The Gambler went back to his desk and flipped through one of his books as he did before. He fiddled with the drawer and pulled tobacco from it.

"I'll have to thank Greed for acquiring this rare edition. Shame I wasn't able to dig it up and study it until recently. You sins would've been a lot more… agreeable. Maybe I could've had her already, but first things first. Nathaniel Shepherd… Wrath is going to tie up those loose ends I created out there... 'cept for you, Envy. You're one loose end that'll serve me 'til you the day you die."

The sin tried to raise his hands. He tried to scream. He tried to run. All he could see was the sheer horror of his control being ripped away. He fought hard in his mind, but his body remained perfectly still.

Envy felt his lips move and his vocal cords vibrate on their own, “With Pleasure.”

Chapter Sixteen: The Boy, The Butler, and The Book

-Port Chandeleur, Southern Louisiana-

-1812-

A grey marine layer haze lingered over the harbor like an unwelcomed visitor with its boot wedged firmly in the threshold of the door. Ship hulls cut through darkened ocean water at a crawl. The vessels meandered through, passing back and forth at full sail. The muggy Louisiana day refused to give the trading vessels a strong push. Bored looking sailors worked at the same pace as the wind teasing their sails. Even distant orders barked by sea captains sounded halfhearted and less than half authoritative.

Marcus tapped his shoe on the dock impatiently. Sweat pooled underneath his suit. He pulled at the cuffs of his undershirt and realized that they were stained yellow. He hurriedly tucked them under his dark grey coat sleeves. The sweat he wiped off his forehead seemed to vaporize. It mixed with the similar scent of salt in the air. He could almost taste it on his tongue. Small and lazy waves lapped the beaches. They filled the air with a soothing, constant sound.

Marcus let his facial hair grow out to a patchy and tar colored goatee. Youth prevented it from growing out full and bushy. The man's eyes were sharp and as green as sea glass. He had thick, untamed eyebrows of roughly the same bold color.

While he waited, Marcus glanced over his shoulder. Boxes upon boxes of his tobacco lined the rickety pier. Behind them, his workers were ready to take his next order, waiting for the ship from France to arrive at its proper dock. Marcus looked to his assistant Jean with his arms crossed and his brow furrowed.

Jean stood a few feet behind Marcus. He was dressed as formally as ever in his butler's attire. Marcus scratched his head, trying to discern whether his servant was overdressed, or just better dressed than he was. Marcus thought they were both going to die of heat stroke before their pickup came. Jean's dark complexion could not save him from the sweltering humidity of the Louisiana coast. He wiped sweat from his brow as he pulled a pocket watch out from the front of his coat.

"Jean, what time is it?" Marcus asked.

"It's twelve thirty… our buyers should have been here about an hour ago," Jean replied through a bored sigh.

"Master…" Jean continued.

"Please, Jean," Marcus replied, "I told you not to call me that."

Jean nodded understandingly, "As you wish, but what would you prefer me to call you from now on?"

"Marcus is fine."

Jean stifled a nostalgic laugh, "You're just like your father in that way… He was never one for title-"

"Jean, please… it's too soon. Let me focus on this and we can talk about him when I'm ready, okay?"

Jean nodded again.

The pair continued their wait for the tardy traders with many of Marcus' other servants. Conversation seemed to bring their business partners from the open ocean to the pier in front of them.

A shoddy frigate docked, and its crew came spilling out. They appeared to be as dirty and miserable as the craft they disembarked from. Long travel left them in a zombie like state. They moved in synch with the slow Louisiana day.

A mariner they recognized approached them. He wiped snot from his nose with his sleeve. When he realized he didn't get all of it, he leaned over the side of the dock, held one nostril down and exhaled as hard as he could, launching the snot from his nose into the harbor water. The sailor held his hand out to shake. Marcus held up his index finger, gesturing for the man to wait. Marcus pulled a white rag from his coat pocket and gave it to the trader. He wiped his hands thoroughly. Only then, did Marcus greet him with a handshake.

"Laveau of Laveau plantations, I presume," The disgusting individual grunted with a thick Bostonian accent.

"Benjamin of… any harbor that has a bar, I presume," Marcus replied with a wide and warm smile on his face.

"Indeed, I am," he beamed proudly, "Do you have what my employa has asked you so kindly for?"

Marcus kicked one of the lids off the boxes closest to him, revealing the contents to the seaman and merchant.

"Five thousand pounds of fresh tobacco ready to be under distributed and overcharged to thee fine citizens of… where is that again?"

"Doesn't maddah, the less we know about each other, the beddah… The way my boss talks, this trade is kinda shady."

"This trade is shady only of you try hard to make it seem shady... or if you speak loudly in a crowded harbor about it being shady. Have you considered that?"

"Oh. I apologize mister Lavah. It's hard to speak quieter when you have to yell in taverns in your off time ya know?"

"That's Laveau…"

"Right, that's what I said… Lavo."

Marcus rolled his eyes at him and held his hand out to the Northerner. The Bostonian rifled through his many pockets with great effort and pulled his money out. He placed it in the plantation owner's possession and waved at the men behind the tobacco boxes to load the ship up with their tobacco. Marcus studied the currency closely. Satisfied with the amount he held, Marcus nodded. His workers helped the others load the tobacco onto the ship.

As Marcus stuffed the piece of money into his coat, he turned back to Jean with a half confused and half frustrated look on his face.

"Jean, I can't help but shake the feeling I'm forgetting some-"

"Renee," The butler replied.

"Goddamn Renee!"

Marcus waited impatiently for his workers to finish loading and thought about what he was going to say to his sister as soon as they returned to the plantation.

…

It was unorthodoxly quiet around the house. Even though the wide halls and the thick carpets did well to dampen a majority of noise, there were usually servants rushing about the house, cooking and cleaning. The slaves usually toiled outside, ramming the earth with varying farming tools, depending on the work they had to do when the situation called for it. There were also usually farmhands giving orders and galloping about.

The hustle and bustle from the plantation's workers was a familiar series of sounds that leaked through the windows, but this day was different. Many the people who worked there had gone to the coast on business, leaving the household in an eerie silence except for a group of young women.

The five women squinted at each other from across the green, felt covered table. Renee's friends sat all around her, giving each other strange, untrusting looks. Renee played with her long black hair and tucked it over one of her ears. Behind her ear was her lucky chip, a simple, red, flat, circular piece of wood. She gave her cohorts a smirk as she caressed the betting token. She placed her cards down on the playing field. Everyone but Renee rolled their eyes when they saw her hand. The four that had lost had a tired look, having already lost several games to her. One of Renee's friends drew in a breath to suggest something else they could have fun doing at her brother's plantation, but she let the idea go. She felt as though he had already suggested the notion merely minutes ago… and that maybe… just maybe she could win her money back. Renee scooped up the cards, shuffled them, and dealt a new round.

Then Renee and her fellow poker players paused and listened. Their ears twitched at a soft thumping coming up the stairs. Renee gaped at the rest of the group concerned. Renee's pals shrugged at each other and looked to Renee to explain. Before they could say anything, the approaching footsteps grew louder and louder with each passing moment, silencing them. They could tell it was Marcus… An infuriated Marcus. Renee rolled her eyes and took her brother's smoking tools on the table in front of her. She readied herself for the verbal onslaught she was about to receive.

One of the Renee's friends spoke up, "What's that stuff for?"

"Marcus sounds mad already by the way he's stomping around… Once he sees I ditched his trade this mornin' for a poker game, he will be livid. Smokin' always calms him down."

Her southern accent was as dense and heavy as the humid Louisiana. Her voice was as smooth as the manner in which she flicked the cards in her hand.

Marcus Laveau stomped into the room. He charged over to Renee. She held up his pipe and tobacco as a shield.

Her brother paused, grabbed the supplies, and readied his pipe for use. Renee said nothing and watched her brother angrily search for something to light his pipe with. He did so while struggling to breathe.

Renee sat up suddenly. Marcus coughed and wheezed wildly. He braced himself on another table nearby.

"Are you alright, Marcus… you've been coughin' a lot more lately… I'm worried about you," Renee said, trying to comfort her brother.

Marcus collected himself and wiped the blackened spittle from the corners of his mouth. He ran a hand through his wavy black hair and rubbed the sparse black whiskers on his face. He stifled another coughing fit as best as he could and mustered the will to speak without making his sister worry any more than she already was. The young man found a lit candle and grabbed it. He stuck the wick of the candle into the pipe and lit it.

"I'm fine, Renee, there's nothin' to worry about, it'll pass," Marcus replied between labored breaths, "I was goin' to assume that you forgot about the trade today, but now I see you were fuckin' around, I've concluded that you completely blew it off."

His boyish voice seemed to have, overnight, turned to a deep, gravelly growl from smoking his pipe so often.

Renee scratched her head, "I assume you also forgot about me this morning. I woke up and you had already left. Did you expect me to walk all the way down to the coast?"

"Well, I- … you… you caught me there," Marcus yelled, trying to let his fury subside, "You still could have woken up and met me in front of the plantation before we left. I told you about it the last night!"

"Why didn't you or Jean come and wake me up? Both of you forgot about me, didn't you?"

Marcus sighed, "We were already waitin' for the traders at the port by the time either of us remembered."

Renee clicked her tongue in half serious disappointment and raked her winnings in from the last hand she played.

"Renee, I still want you to learn the business… how everythin' works here, and it seems like you'd rather be goofing off with your friends… no offense, ladies."

"None taken, we love goofing off," the group laughed.

Renee sat with her arms folded, staring up at her brother. She gestured for her buddies to leave. They threw their cards down and left in a huff.

"This isn't over, Renee, we'll have our money back the easy way or the hard way," one of them playfully shook a fist at her.

Once the room had emptied, Marcus sighed and sat down next to Renee. He stared at the floor. There was disappointment in his voice.

"Renee, I'm not going to be around forever."

"Are you dyin'?"

Marcus was taken back by the sincere concern he heard in his sister's voice. He composed himself and continued.

"No, but the business is growin' and I need someone I can trust to oversee the expansion and run a plantation without me bein' there, do you understand?"

"So, you're sendin' me away? To where?"

"No, Renee, I am leavin' eventually, but not very far. I've purchased some new land a few hours away by coach. I want you to look after things while I am gone."

"For how long?"

"It may take me quite a while to find somebody to fill my shoes, but I think I'll only be gone for a few weeks… a month at most."

Renee looked down at the floor uncertain of what to say to her brother… uncertain of what to say about her impending responsibilities.

"Marcus… a woman plantation owner… that's ridiculous, I can't-"

Marcus hugged his sister, "Don't worry, you are a Laveau. If any of those traders give you lip, they'll have to deal with me. I am leavin' you in good hands. Jean will take great care of you as he has with me. Even if you aren't comfortable in your new position, Jean will be there to guide you. He's been at my side since father died, and he'll be at yours."

"Damn it, Marcus, you know how much he hates me… he treats you like a god, but he has no respect for me."

"He will, you just have to earn his respect… although, I've never seen him treat a woman decently… if he gives you trouble in the future, let me know. I'll have a word with him before I go."

Marcus left as fast as he entered. Renee looked back at her hands and hid them from sight. She noticed them tremble with each of her racing thoughts. The same sensation coursed throughout her feet as she shuffled out to the hall where her gambling friends stood waiting for her, leaning against the wall like a group of thugs.

Renee crossed her arms and returned the mean look that her group gave her, "Are y'all ready to lose more of your money?"

They merely looked her up and down with confident expressions upon their faces. They refilled the room. Renee lingered in the hall for a moment. She wore a look of genuine worry.

…

-Laveau Plantation-

-Several Months Later-

The study boasted one of the few wooden floors in the entire Laveau estate. Marcus' tall bookcases were supported by even taller wooden walls. A fireplace roared from across the room. It filled the space with a constant sound. Otherwise, the space would be silent. Orange light flickered about. Candles lined numerous surfaces for reading in various places.

Jean sat by the study's large window at Marcus's immense wooden desk scratching his head with his brow furrowed in frustration. Renee stood impatiently, tapping her foot on the floor to the hastened pace she had set for herself. It felt as though it had been hours since she was waiting there for her brother's servant to be done with him.

The sound of her taps and the crackling logs in the fire seemed to echo about the room, making it appear vaster than it was. The orange lights did their best to fight off the blackness that the night brought, but it was an uphill battle with the amount of space the meager lights had to fill.

Jean clapped his hands over his face after tossing the parchment back onto the desk, letting them become unorganized. He reached over to his right and grabbed a bottle of rum. Instead of pouring the darkened brown liquid into a glass, Renee was shocked to see Jean pulling straight from the bottle. The black man slammed the bottle down. He looked up at the young woman with a fierceness that Renee had rarely seen before. Jean licked at the residual rum that caked his lips.

"Renee," Jean said, "How long have I known you, your brother, and your father? How long have I worked on this plantation?"

"I've known you all my life, Jean. What's this about?" Renee replied.

"In spite of my role as a servant in this household and the color of my skin, I know more than you do, child. If you want me to continue helping you, I suggest you lose your attitude now."

Renee buttoned her lip and waited for Jean to finish what he had to say. She had her arms folded and a frown suck to her face.

"I have worked my fingers to the bone on this plantation for more than your entire lifetime…"

Renee watched Jean and nodded, indicating to the servant that he was still listening closely.

"… Needless to say, I have learned this business from every side. I've seen it from the perspective of a slave and from the point of an owner… as well as everythin' in between. Even though I've tried with the best of my ability, I can see now that your arrogance and your sheer unwillingness to learn has made you impossible to work with. Your brother wanted me to make you fit to run this place on your own, but it is clear to me that this is something you do not want."

Renee's look grew more intense.

"All you ever wanted to do is play around. Your brother thought you could do it, but he is wrong. I am the one who can run the plantation. I am the MAN who deserves to run it. I've earned it. All you've earned is pennies at the poker table. A woman could never fill the shoes of a man... a man such as your brother."

Renee tried her best to speak up, but she could not get a word in. She could feel the hate coursing through her.

Jean continued, "I brought you in here to inform you, first and foremost, that I am very disappointed in you. The job you are doing is poor at best. I have told your brother the same exact thing."

Jean's expression of annoyance and anger faded into something far more melancholy. He threw more rum down his throat.

"How dare you. I know you mean a lot to my brother, but that does not give you, a slave, the right to speak to a white woman in that manner. My brother will hear about this and then, I swear, we'll see you workin' back in the fields with chains and lashes. We'll see you wither away in the box for weeks, do you understand?!"

Jean nodded solemnly, "Yes, I apologize, miss Laveau… I forgot my place. I'll take my punishment as you and your brother see fit, but I beg you, please allow me to stay in my current position and out of the fields."

"What else do you have to tell me, Jean?" Outrage was replaced by worry in her voice.

"Marcus has returned."

Sudden excitement welled up within Renee, but Jean's demeanor whisked that feeling away.

"… He is not well," Jean continued.

Jean led Renee through the halls of Laveau manor until they reached Marcus' bedroom. It was dark in there except for a single candle resting on the nightstand next to Marcus lay in bed sweating and covered in his sheets. He looked over with a smile on his face and tried to greet the two, but his words turned to coughing, pained gagging, and gasping for air.

To his horror, Marcus saw something come up. He saw dark red globs of blood splash onto the carpet with blackened spit. He could taste the iron and tobacco residue on his tongue. Marcus managed to cease his coughing fit. He wiped the thick warm liquid from his lips and looked at his family, a weak and delirious look on his pale face.

"Renee, its so good to see you," Marcus wheezed.

"Marcus," She sobbed, "Are you… is everything alright?"

"I'm afraid not. That's why I came back home. I've been seein' some Doctors for a while now over at the other plantation… they say there's nothin' they can do for me."

Jean bowed his head and Renee cried.

"Marcus, I'm sorry I couldn't be the owner you wanted me to be. It was just… something I never wanted… I'm so sorry," Renee said.

Marcus reached over and touched her face, "I know. I could tell from the day I told you I was goin' away. I was too stubborn to let you have your own way. I thought you could learn to love it, but… it's okay, Renee, I thrust it upon you when I shouldn't have. I'm sorry…"

Marcus looked over to Jean and got his attention, "Jean, Renee will remain the sole heir to the Laveau plantations and estates. I want you to continue teaching her at a pace she sets… No pressure, Renee… Until she learns, you'll oversee operations here and find a suitable replacement for me at the other planation. I may seem like a horse's ass for giving you this responsibility, Renee. I am, but you must understand, you're going to be the last living Laveau. Pass the plantation on to your children when you have them one day. Do you think you can do that for me?"

“No Marcus,” Jean interjected, “You will not die, and Renee won’t be forced into anything.”

. . .

-Laveau Plantation, Slaves’ Quarters-
-The Next Night-

Marcus seldom visited this side of the plantation in recent times. There were occasional passers by, but their workers and farmhands were in this area far more often. There was little need for them to visit consistently with the exception of planning renovations or new buildings being constructed in the area. The young man struggled along by himself, coughing and hacking as he walked. Jean took Renee earlier in the day to assist him by shopping for ingredients. Jean neglected to tell him what exactly the ingredients were for, but based on what he said the night before, Marcus assumed it aimed to let him live.

Louisiana mush made each of his steps squelch loudly. He scoffed as he brought his lantern down to see the muck covering his boots. Both moonlight and lantern light helped illuminate the tall reeds and grass jutting out from the bayou. The pale orb in the sky appeared to dance on the surface of the black swamp water.

In spite of the dreary dark, the night was alive. Several sets of eyes glowed at Marcus from around the swamp, filling him with an overwhelming sense of unease. Thousands of bugs and insects filled the dark with their chirps, and their buzzing. Nocturnal animals called out in search of one another or perhaps as warnings to each other to stay far away. Marcus could nearly taste the bog on his tongue. The smell of the swamp assaulted his nose with a smell so strong that it reached his pallet.

Marcus could see he was nearing a small cottage due to fiery light leaking from cracks and abrasions in the walls. A pit formed in his stomach. His hands were sweating on a contract and a handwritten letter despite the frigid iciness spreading throughout his body.

Before he knew it, Marcus reached the shoddy cabin door. The young man took a deep breath and opened the door. Jean shook a tin full of orange powder as he moved about the cabin floor so that the powder came out in a thin line. Marcus watched the servant draw what looked like hieroglyphics enclosed by a large circle. The boy's heart pounded in his chest and he couldn't hide the fright from showing on his face.

The cottage had two rooms. The first was empty except for a chair in the middle of what Jean was drawing up. There was an old table behind it. The surface had many jars and sacks of ingredients and a series of candles that dimly lit the area, a caged rat, a single large knife in its center and under the knife, was a large and ancient looking leather-bound book. The cottage lacked any windows. It had a back door the opposite of where Marcus entered. The second room was much smaller and had its door closed, making it impossible to see what was inside.

Jean looked up at Marcus, continuing his work and gesturing for him to come inside and shut the door. Marcus did as he was told. He stared dumbstruck until Jean was finished with whatever it was that he was doing.

Jean stepped over his work and stood at the table, reading the contents of that large leather book.

"Are you ready, Marcus," Jean asked. He refrained from looking up and kept his focus on the strange symbols adorning each page.

"Y-yes," Marcus replied.

"Come foreword."

Marcus stepped into the sigil. Jean nodded. He picked up the knife from atop the old leather book and unlocked the rat's cage.

"Wait, what's going to happen to me?" Marcus shouted.

"No. No questions. Stand still... in the middle of the circle."

Marcus fixed his posture and made sure he was where Jean instructed him to be. The slave opened the rat's cage and picked up the animal. It squealed and squirmed in his grasp as he brought the knife to it. Jean's words were muddled and unfamiliar to Marcus. He spoke them so rapidly it was hard to decipher one phrase, one word from another.

Jean plunged the knife down the middle of the rat. Its blood and entrails squirted out like someone squeezing an overly ripe tomato. Jean picked up what fell out and threw it in the center of the circle in between Marcus' feet. With the rodent's blood coating his hands, he walked over and drew on Marcus' face. The young man stayed as still as he could and continued to watch Jean, growing more nauseous and more nervous with each move he made.

Jean walked back to the book and uttered one last unintelligible phrase. Marcus felt humid Louisiana winds find their way through the cracks of the building. It crept up his arms and along his shoulders until it entered his mouth. Hot air rushed into him and filled his lungs to the point of bursting. Marcus exhaled and watched blackened smoke erupt from his mouth. Like a serpent, the plume coiled and slithered about the cottage until it found an exit. As quickly as the wind entered, it had left.

Jean looked at the boy, "Breathe," He said.

Marcus did as he was told. There was no itching in his throat and no more pain in his lungs and no more wheezing noise coming from his windpipe.

Jean stood proudly behind the table and waited.

"How do you feel, Marcus?"

Marcus took a few more deep breaths to test out his newfound health, "Jean… How?"

"No questions, Marcus."

Marcus looked at his feet and stepped outside the circle, "My God, Renee is goin' to be thrilled! Where is she? Is she here? In the other room?"

Marcus ran in there with his newfound liveliness and energy. Jean remained silent. His expression grew grim. The boy doubled back in horror. Renee hanging from the wall bound and gagged. Fresh tears dripped down her blue-grey skin.

Marcus pulled his father's pistol from his side and whipped it toward Jean. Jean blew dust into Marcus's face, blinding him. The young man heard him yell more of the gibberish. Marcus could no longer move. He tried to pull the trigger, but his finger was stuck along with the rest of his body.

Jean took the knife and held it to Marcus's throat. The servant saw the terror in Marcus's eyes and chuckled. He pulled the knife away and peeled the pistol from Marcus's hand.

"I always knew she loved games and gambling, Marcus," Jean said with a laugh, always betting high in that wagering game, what's it called? Poker… She played games with MY plantation. MY hard work, and what did YOU do?! YOU gave it to her… you gave it all to her… So, now… I'm going to take it all from you."

Jean put the knife to his palm and let the blood drip onto the floor in a new circle around Marcus with a new series of symbols. Every part of Marcus' psyche screamed out, but no physical part of him moved. Jean tossed her to the floor next to Marcus. Jean reached into Marcus's mouth and grabbed his tongue. He uttered another phrase. Marcus felt his jaw come back under his control.

Jean stepped out of the circle and pointed the gun directly at Marcus's head, "Make a wish."

Marcus gaped at his sister's lifeless and bleeding corpse, "P-please," he quivered, "I just want to live."

Jean kept his eyes locked on Marcus. The boy met the servant's gaze.

"Coward… As you wish."

Jean spoke his strange gibberish in a chant, over and over, louder and louder, faster and faster.

The young man sensed something wash over him. A sensation he had never felt before. His breath become softer shorter. The strength in his body faded. His whimpering boyish cries became a low and aged growl. His vision blurred. The hair on his head and face grew outward and became silver. He watched his skin wrinkle, and his youthful tone become pale.

Jean tossed the pistol into the room, with Renee. He knelt down and took her lucky chip from her hair. He placed the betting chip inside of Marcus's frozen hand.

"Have fun living the rest of your life knowing you could've prevented this… knowing I'm still out there somewhere. Living forever as a withered old man. Here's little something to remember me by… A little something to remind you never to gamble with somebody else's life."

Jean snapped his fingers. Marcus came clambering to the floor. Marcus' limbs shook as he tried to bring himself up. He was weak. His bones and his muscles ached. Marcus looked up from the floor.

Jean scooped up his large leather book, snapping it shut with a large thud. The black man rushed from the cabin, not even stopping to look at what he had done to his master. Marcus chased after Jean, but his bones felt brittle underneath his own weight. Jean turned a corner, out of sight.

"Wait," Marcus croaked.

Marcus managed to get outside. He was tired and winded. Jean was already gone. The old man meandered wearily into the night until he heard water splashing underneath his feet. Marcus fell to his knees in the soft bayou mud.

He worked the chip around in his grasp. He looked upon it. It filled every inch of his body with remorse. Jean's words echoed in in his mind. He put the chip into his coat pocket.

The water at his legs was cold despite the sweltering humidity in the air. Once he felt the water stop lapping at his legs, he knew it was still and he could see what Jean had done.

Two spherical yellow flames flickered and glowed upon the surface of the water, the eyes adorned a grim and wrinkled face. His once youthful skin drooped and sagged over his bones. Marcus' eyes had dark circles around them and bags underneath them. His hair turned from shiny, clean and black, to dry, crispy, and silver-white.

Brilliant light suddenly filled the night. It caught Marcus' attention. The old man's heart sank as he watched his plantation erupt into flame. He smelled the tobacco plants burning along with the structure of his home… of everything he had left.

Marcus dragged his ancient frame back up to the estate as fast as his new body would allow him to. He passed black men and women cheering as they watched the symbol of their tyranny burn. Marcus' destruction was the symbol, the beacon of their freedom. Others ran amuck escaping the plantation before anyone with authority over them arrived to apprehend them. More slaves took the white farmhands and held them down for lashes, for vengeance.

Marcus scanned the area for Jean. He was gone. The old man marched past his former slaves and rushed into his burning mansion. With one arm raised over his mouth, he braved the inferno. Flames licked just about every surface of the halls. He reached his room and tossed a large painting from his wall revealing a safe. Marcus unlocked it, nabbed as much money as he could carry and left the way he came. The structure collapsed behind him. Somehow, he escaped with his earnings in hand and pocket.

Marcus did his best to hide the money from his revolting slaves as he walked toward Jean's quarters. The shack was separate from the slaves' quarters, close to the Laveau mansion. The other slaves set fire to that building. They were jealous, no doubt, of Jean's higher slave status.

Marcus ran in and scrounged up what he could of Jean's writings and other clues he could use to find him. The old man picked up a small book from Jean's desk. He doused the flames it its edges and ran back out.

Marcus left his plantation before any of his slaves attacked him. Past the gates, he watched everything he had burn. A surge of hatred flowed through him. He flipped through the pages of Jean's tome. Lines of a forgotten language adorned the page. English translations were jotted sloppily at the side of each page.

Ingredients, How-to's, blessings, curses, and hexes were listed before him. The old, silver haired man smiled insidiously. He stuffed the book into his coat pocket. Marcus pulled the chip out from the same pocket, flipping it between his fingers.

Chapter Seventeen: The Flock

-New York, Shepherds' Ranch-

-1837-

Clouds churned and spun like a thick stew stirred at the whim of the winds. Nathaniel and Daniel watched from the window of their room as purple forks formed in the sky and disappeared within the same instant. Flashes of light flickered across their eyes. Natural electricity brought the horizon to life. It revealed, for a second, the far-off shapes of the city's skyline and the hills surrounding the distant city. A rolling boom reverberated through the rest of the house. The sound followed the forks of brilliant light but struggled to keep up.

The two boys watched horses run panicked in their pasture. They galloped away from John who rode along behind the spooked herd. Nate and Dan could barely hear their father's calls to the animals. He tried, in vain, to guide them back into their stables. The two boys laughed as their father struggled, fell, and continued to yell behind the herd. John got himself and his clothes soaked with rain and mud. The brim of John's hat drooped sadly, a direct representation of his mood.

John managed to push the last of the herd into the stable. He closed the door to the stables behind the rest of his horses and ran clumsily toward the house, slipping in the mud every now and then. He held his hat to his head as the wind took it and slung rain into his face.

Christine folded her arms and shivered. She barked orders at John from the safety of the awning that protruded out of the side of their house. John shrugged at her and shook his head. The two boys watched their mother put a towel over their soaking wet and shivering father. John and Christine walked back inside. The door slammed behind their parents.

"Nathaniel, Daniel! Dinner is almost ready, get dressed and come down. Your father and I are cold and starving, so hurry up," Christine yelled!

The boys looked at each other with excitement on their faces. They scrambled over to the door of their room and opened it in a rush. The smell of seasoned pork chops and garlic-mashed potatoes overloaded their senses. The pair drooled. As they ran, they shoved each other playfully. Nate and Dan hurried down the hall and down the staircase. The two put on the facade of well-behaved children as soon as they knew they were within earshot of their parents.

Servers and butlers wandered around the table as Nate and Dan approached the dining room. John wandered into the room exhausted. His hair was darkened and wet from the rain outside. His cheeks were red from the warmth of a new set of clothes and the shawl draped over his shoulders.

Christine followed her husband. The four Shepherds sat down at their dining room table. The servers brought the family their meals on silver platters and promptly removed the lids. Nate's stomach growled. He and Dan ogled their meals. They picked up their napkins and set them on their laps. The boys greedily picked up their silverware and brought them toward their delicious looking morsels. Steam rose off the freshly cooked and pork. A small golden square of butter melted in a sea of white and creamy potatoes dotted by islands of green chives.

"Wait, you two," John said.

Nate and Dan flinched and froze in their places, hunched over their platters, longing for their food.

"Grace," John continued.

The two boys rolled their eyes. They dropped their forks and knives back onto the table and folded their hands in front of them with their elbows planted firmly onto the table.

"Oh Lord, we thank you for the gifts of your bounty which we enjoy at this table. As you have provided for us in the past, so may you sustain us throughout our lives. While we enjoy your gifts, may we never forget the needy and those in want and may the Shepherd always protect his flock. Amen."

Nate looked up from his plate to his father who picked up his fork and his knife, ready to tear apart the meal in front of him.

"Dad…" Daniel said over the clutter of fine china and silverware.

"Yes, son, what is it," John asked in reply.

"Whenever you say grace before we eat…"

"What about it?"

"Is that last part actually the lord's prayer?"

"The Shepherd bit…?"

"Yeah, where is that in the bible?"

John worked his knife back and forth over his steak and brought a large square into his mouth.

"It isn't in the bible, son… well, not that I can remember…"

"So then why do we say it?" Nate piped in.

"It's an old family saying."

"I had no idea," Christine said. She wiped her mouth with her napkin.

"Could've sworn I told you this story already," John mumbled.

Nate, Daniel, and Christine shook their heads silently at John. He looked around the table quizzically.

"Alright, well," John began, "The bit in the prayer we say before we eat was in my family for as long as I can remember. My father recited it in his prayers and so did my grandfather. Your grandfather's father without a doubt said it in his prayers too… or so I was told… When I was just a young boy like you two, I didn't really understand why we said it all the time, so it didn't really have any importance to me."

"Why do we say it," Nate asked again impatiently.

"I was getting to that, son. Give me a minute. So… your grandfather gave meaning to the phrase for me. That's why we still say it before dinner."

"What makes it so important, dad?" Daniel asked.

"Yeah, please tell us," Nate begged.

"Okay, but it might take us a while to get through it. Are you sure you want to hear it now, or do you want to wait until after dinner?"

Christine, Nate, Daniel, and an eavesdropping servant girl all nodded their heads eagerly. The mother and her two sons stuffed their dinner into their faces absentmindedly while the server set salt, pepper and other spices onto the table in the same manner. They all maintained eye contact with John, finding it difficult to contain their interest.

"Okay, so, I was about your age. It was… maybe thirty years ago… give or take a couple years. The land west of here was wild and untamed. Savages still ran rampant on the plains and ambushed unsuspecting folks like us. Older settlers either lost their horses or set them free on the plains where they became wild and bred out there themselves. That's how your grandfather and I would get our livestock and breed more of them. It just so happened that your grandfather needed more for the ranch. We couldn't buy and trade livestock from other breeders back in the day. We had to go out there and rustle some up ourselves when we needed more. The problem with going out there and getting them ourselves was the Iroquois Indians. They took them and broke them mostly for riding, but if they had enough already, they would kill and take what they could from the horse like its hide, its meat and whatever else they might be able to use or trade. So, one day, Grandfather Nathaniel… your namesake, Son…"

John looked warmly at Nate and continued his story.

"…He dragged me along to get some horses from the plains. It was an unusually hot day especially for the northeast. Grandpa and I were riding alongside one another. We were sweating through our clothing. I remember there wasn't a lick of wind out. The browning grass reached up to our rides' knees, it was so tall! The stuff only moved when our horses walked through it. There wasn't even a cloud from horizon to horizon. Endless blue on top of grass as far as the eye could see.

Grandpa held up his hand and we stopped moving. I couldn't hear a thing for a minute or so, but he sat still like he was listening for something. I was about to ask him what it was we were waiting for… that's when I heard it. The beat of hooves filled the air like slow and faint thunder rolling through a storm cloud. Grandpa drew his old six-shooter and looked in the direction of the distant sound. Just then, they appeared from behind a knoll, a herd of wild horses galloping along through the plain, trampling the grass as they went. I looked over at Grandpa Nate. He sighed and put his gun away. He glanced at me and told me to stay close. I nodded and grabbed my reigns. He took up his lasso and started after the herd.

After a while, Grandpa managed to lasso up a couple of them and had me hold on to the ones he caught while he went back to get some more… Before I knew it, the sky turned a soft purple and the sun had begun to set. My skin turned bright red and stung like hell all over.

Grandpa Nate had caught four horses and handed them to me one by one as he caught them. They stirred a bit while I held onto them, but they were all calm, especially for just being rounded up.

All of a sudden, I heard that familiar pounding of hooves in the ground approaching, so I looked up. Grandpa Nate rode toward me. He rode fast, and as he got closer, I could see was panicked. He had his revolver drawn and pointed up in the air. He yelled at me to return to the ranch. Over the knoll behind, him dozens of Iroquois riders followed, firing their bows at him. I spurred my horse and tugged at the ties of the four wild horses for them to giddy up, but they reared and bucked. They refused to move. Grandpa caught up to me and fired a shot into the crowd of Indians. He hurriedly ripped the ties from my hands.

But what about the horses?! I asked him.

He said, leave them and Run!

We spurred our rides and ran as fast as we could from the Indians at our heels. Arrows flew inches past us. I snuck a peek back. Some of them split off to catch us, but most of them still gave us chase. Grandpa Nate fired another shot at them and one of the savages fell from his horse.

An arrow whirred into Grandpa's side. He doubled over in pain. I shouted at him as my horse took an arrow in its rear. It began to limp and slow down. Grandpa looked over at me. He screamed back at me. He tossed his revolver away and pulled his horse as close as he could over to mine. He grabbed me by the collar of my shirt and hoisted me to the front of his saddle. I peered over my shoulder at my ride and it fell to the ground as another arrow hit it. It let out a high-pitched cry.

Grandpa Nate grunted loudly. His arm fell to his side as he held onto me and clutched the reigns with his one good arm. Yet another arrow lodged itself deep into the top of his shoulder of the same wounded arm. Still, Grandpa kept spurring the horse and kept shielding me with his body. He glanced down at me. Then he looked ahead. I tried to look but Grandpa blocked me from seeing. We were too fast for those Indian bastards and they stopped chasing us after a while.

Eventually, Grandpa and I made it here to the Ranch. It was already dark outside by the time we returned. He dismounted and stumbled a bit as he landed on his feet below me. I remember blood dripping out of his arm in a few places, but more so from his side. With two loud and deep grunts he snapped the arrows at their backs. I began to cry.

It's alright, John, he said to me weakly. Go ride into town and grab the nearest doctor.

I hesitated, paralyzed in fear.

I'll be fine, Son, they're just scratches.

To which I replied through my tears, *Dad, you didn't have to shield me from those arrows, I could've-*

Then he interrupted me by shaking his head. He looked up at me and said, *No, John, Shepherds always protect their flock...*

Then he slapped my horse with his good arm and sent me flying toward town without another word. I've remembered how important the saying is ever since that day."

Christine, Nate, Daniel and more of the servers accumulated at the table. They let their jaws hang loosely from their faces as they stood and sat around John.

"I hope none of you have to experience the importance of this saying quite like the way I did and I hope you boys understand what I mean when Grandpa said the phrase… and of course, when I say it from now on… and maybe one day, if you boys have a family of your own, you can tell them this story and you can tell them that no matter what… Shepherds always protect their flock."

…

-New York City, New York-

-1843-

"Nate…" Daniel said from behind a display of dried fruits.

Nate looked over at his brother. Then studied the various candies in front of him. The entire wall of the store that Nate faced was littered with different taffies, chocolates, peppermint sticks and many other sugary treats. The rest of the store had the regular bland assortment of groceries and goods that anyone might typically find in a general store.

Other customers wandered around the store in a trance like state, slowly and wearily picking out the foods they came for, shuffling between shelves and displays with sad looks glued upon their faces.

"Nate," Daniel said again, louder this time.

"What," Nate replied.

"Mom needed us to pick up vegetables for supper tonight, not candies. Put 'em back where you found 'em."

Nate looked down at his hands. He had mindlessly grabbed two handfuls of wrapped candy from the display in front of him and held them clenched in his fists. Without another thought, he put the candies where he found them.

Nate glanced over at the storeowner who peered at him suspiciously. Nate stuffed his hands in his pockets and walked over to Daniel who checked potatoes to see if they were past ripe or not. Daniel stuffed the good spuds into a burlap sack and eyeballed the onions in the display next to him. He glanced over at Nate who still eyeballed the store's owner.

"Why the hell does Jim stare at us like that whenever we come in here, we're just buying stuff, not stealing it," Nate hissed.

"If you hadn't noticed, you almost stuffed all those damn sweets into your pie-hole in front of him and not to mention, we're still in our uniforms from school today. You know how much he trusts students after what Gregory pulled last year."

"Gregory who," Nate asked.

"Greg Martley. He ran outta this place with as much candy and food as he could carry. Hasn't come back since."

"Oh, yeah…" Nate said giggling at the memory, "So what, he just thinks all the school kids are thieves now?"

"Yup, every single one of us that walks into his shop wearing the uniform, at the very least… we're all Gregs to him."

Nate and Dan shared a laugh as Dan checked the onions for rot or anything else weird on the outside. Daniel took the list out of his pocket and scanned it one more time to see what else they needed before they could leave.

"We still need beets and carrots for tonight. Can you go get them while I buy the rest of the stuff on the list," Daniel asked Nate.

"Yeah, sure. How much more do we need?"

"Two or three more items on the list after beets and carrots. I'll go get 'em and then we can head back home."

"Finally…"

"Oh, and grab couple of big carrots and three of the biggest beets you can find. We're having soup for supper tonight."

"Damn it… why the hell are we having soup? It's hotter than hell outside… It's way too hot for soup."

"I don't know. You can ask mom when we get back to the house. I'm sure she has a good reason for it."

Nate let out a long sigh. He shuffled over to the carrots much like the rest of the lifeless and dreary customers around the general store. Nate inspected the carrots as his brother did. No matter what angle he looked at the vegetables from, he still had no idea what he was looking for. He picked up two of the largest carrots he could find and headed toward the display where the beets were. A loud voice with a strong Bostonian accent came from behind Nate and stopped him.

"Empty your pockets."

Nate turned around and saw Jim the store clerk looming above him with his arms folded and his brow furrowed.

"Uhhhh… are you talking to me," Nate asked in response.

Jim rolled his eyes, "No, I'm talkin' to the other stupid kid that had his grubby hands full of my goddamn candy."

"Jim, C'mon, you saw me put all of it back into the basket right where I found it. Dan and I are just-"

"Just what, trying to steal my fuckin' vegetables too?"

"Jim, we're not stealing anything, I promise you."

"Okay," Jim nodded, "Empty your pockets… We'll see if you're lying your ass off to me or not."

"Fine, you crazy bastard, I'll empty them. Dan and I aren't stealing a damn thing, look, there's nothing in-"

Nate pulled a single piece of candy from the pocket of his pants and smiled sheepishly up at Jim.

Nate and Daniel hit the curb as Jim threw them out of his store by their collars. Jim took all the vegetables and threw their empty bag back at them. People walking by stopped to watch the shoplifters receive Jim's own brand of justice.

"You two stay the fuck out of my shop. Next time I won't be so nice about it, you understand me?"

"Jim, it was an accident. We need all of those vegetables for dinner tonight, just please let us in," Dan pleaded.

"No. I don't negotiate with thieves…. Especially goddamn students."

"Please, Jim. Our mom will kill us if we don't come back with those vegetables. Look, we have the money," Dan said.

He hoisted a messy wad of one-dollar bills from his pocket and waved them desperately at the angry storeowner.

"Good, I hope she murders you two little bastards. There's no way either of you are ever coming back into my shop."

Daniel got up and brushed the dirt off his uniform. He looked down at Nate and shook his head. He stormed off in the direction of the ranch and left Nate sitting in the dirt in front of the general store with Jim still standing in the doorway, making sure they wouldn't return to steal more.

A group of three students walked toward the shop entrance. Their uniforms seemed too tight on them due to their unorthodoxly large size. Nate recognized them as soon as they waddled up. Jim held up a hand at them. They stopped at the door in front of Jim.

"Hey Jim, what's going on, we gotta get some stuff inside here before we go home," One of them said.

"Sorry, no more students. First, Martley and now this asshole. I gotta make a living by selling my food, not having it stolen." Jim grunted shortly, pointing at Nate.

Jim turned and walked back through the door of his shop, leaving Nate to deal with the three unusually large and unsatisfied students.

"Nathaniel Shepherd," Phil said.

"Cut the shit Phil, are we doing this or what?"

"You don't even know what we want yet…"

"I have no money and no food, but I think I have a damn good idea about what you and your two enormous ogre friends want."

"Well, we wanted some goddamn chocolates before we went home today, but then your dumb ass came along."

"Come on, Phil I told you to cut the shit, are we going to fight or not?"

"Nah, we ain't gunna fight. There won't be one. Me and my friends here are just gunna beat on you until we forget about the emptiness in our stomachs."

"You think I'm not gunna fight back like the rest of those cowards at school, you're dead wrong."

Nate got up and brushed the dirt off his uniform. He raised his fists at the three massive kids, ready for a fight. Phil walked over and hit Nate right below the sternum. All the air in Nate's lungs was knocked out of him. He fell to his hands and knees, into the dirt again. A wave of shame ran through him. He wheezed and squeaked audibly, trying to get air into his lungs.

Phil and his two friends picked Nate up and dragged him into a nearby alleyway where they wouldn't be seen. They threw him on the ground where he gasped for air. The three teens kicked and punch Nate as he fought to breathe. Nate tried to get up and fight, but one bully held him down. He swung violently, trying to break free, but he didn't budge. Each strike stung him more after every hit. He could feel his flesh swelling and bruising already as he lay there in the dirt, writhing.

Heavy footsteps came charging down the alleyway. Nate looked up. Daniel flew into the fray. He dove and tackled two of the large bullies off Nate. The third stopped and took notice to the new fight that was taking place behind him. Daniel got up and swung at the pair of bewildered bullies while they got back on their feet. The third stared down at Nate.

Nate's fist collided with the bully's face and sent him doubling over to the right. Nate got up and wiped the blood from his nose and from a cut on his cheekbone. He looked down at the bully he punched. Nate kneeled on the teen's chest and grabbed his shirt, bringing his head up off the ground. Nate brought his face close to the bully's. Nate's lips curled revealing his bloodstained teeth in a snarl of a grin. He cocked his right arm back and clenched his fist until his knuckles turned white. There was fire in his eyes. They bully quivered, seeing the anger in him. Nate hit him as hard as he could. He felt the skin splitting over his knuckles and the bones in his hands straining. He ignored the pain and struck the boy over and over. Nate's world was tinted red. His fist flew after and harder with each punch as the boy's skin split open and bleed. Blood flew from his fist as he punched again and again. The dark wooden walls of the buildings sported small globs of red from flurries of punches. He ignored the bully's pleas for him to stop. Nate eyed the boy's mouth and plunged his fist into it until he could see pieces of the boy's teeth scattered about his mouth… until he no longer heard his pathetic cries for help.

Nate stopped swinging and let go of the boy's blood-soaked shirt. He let the bully flop unconscious into the dirt. Pieces of his teeth rolled from his mouth and down his uniform, into the dirt.

Nate's head darted over to Daniel and the other two bullies. They stood over Dan with their backs to Nate, punching and kicking Daniel while he tried his hardest to guard himself from the blows on the ground.

Nate looked to the bully he knocked out. He lifted the large boy's leg up and slid the shoe from the unconscious bully's foot and charged toward the two bullies with the shoe in his right hand. Nate brought his hand over his head and swung the heel of the shoe onto the temple of the bully on the left. The boy's arms drooped, and he fell limply to his side. Nate tossed near the bully as he too fell to the dirt.

Phil paused and glanced up at Nate who loomed over him. Blood dripped from Nate's facial cuts and into his teeth, bringing a red tinge to his fierce grin. His eyes were wide and darted at every target on Phil's face. Nate still clenched his fists as blood dripped gently from his knuckles and into the dirt.

Phil scrambled backward, kicking up dirt with him as he retreated. He froze and put his hands up with a look of panic. Nate took his crazed eyes off Phil to extend a hand to Daniel. Nate hoisted his brother onto his feet. Daniel rubbed the bridge of his nose and wiped the blood from the corner of his mouth with his sleeve.

"You okay," Nate asked between his breaths.

Daniel nodded as he studied the ferocious look Nate wore. Nate looked down at Phil and approached him.

"Nate, take it easy… y-you know me," Phil asked shakily.

Nate ignored his begging and kept walking toward him with that same crazed look glued to his face.

"D-Dan, talk some sense into him… we're friends, right… right?!"

Dan grabbed Nate by the shoulder and stopped him. Nate looked at his brother and his anger faded. Dan walked past Nate toward Phil and held his hand out to the bully to help him up.

Phil gracious accepted and took Dan's hand. Dan lifted the bully up and brought his fist across Phil's face as he lifted him up. Phil's two front teeth soared across the alley and hit the wall with small taps. Daniel cocked his fist back again while the bully hit the dirt. Tears formed in Phil's eyes as he desperately held his arm in front of his face, desperate to shield himself from the Shepherd brothers. Phil spat blood into the dirt and tried hard to hide his tears from Nate and Dan.

"Please, I give up," Phil pleaded.

"Quit your fucking blubbering and think," Dan said.

"W-what?"

"What happened to you and your friends, Phil?"

"I get it. Don't fuck with the Shepherd brothers. I-I'll tell everyone, just please don't hurt me."

"Close. You shouldn't have fucked with us, but try again… What happened to you and your friends?"

"Uhh…. Uhhhh… we fell. Yeah, we fell… down the stairs after we were messing around near the school."

"Good boy. Wait for your friends to wake up and tell them what happened. You come after my brother again; you and your buddies will fall down a bigger set of stairs. Maybe I won't be here to stop Nate… Do you understand me, Phil?"

Phil nodded and wiped more fresh tears from his face. Nate and Dan walked past the blubbering bully as he sat motionless. Nate looked down at Phil. Phil gaped up at him. Nate cocked his fist back and watched the cowardly bully flinch and hide behind his knees and arms, whimpering.

Nate offered a scoff and followed his brother out of the alleyway. He caught up to Daniel and walked along beside him. They both wiped the blood and sweat from their faces with their sleeves, but it did hardly any good.

"Nate… you okay?" Dan asked.

"Yeah, I'm okay… just cuts and bruises, they'll go away soon," Nate replied.

"No, I mean… I've never seen you like that. I was on your team and you were scaring the hell out of me. Is there something going on?"

"Remember dad's story a few years back, the one with grandpa and the Indians?"

Dan searched his memory. It didn't take him long to find the moment. He nodded in response.

"It's something that really stuck with me…" Nate continued, "… Ever since that night I wanted to be like grandpa. I want to be the man that he was, but how can I be when I can't even fight off dipshits like Phil and his goons? It just… it makes me mad on a whole 'nother level when somebody steps on my pride like that. What does that say about me when I can't stand up… even for myself?"

"Nate… grandpa was a fully-grown man… and a badass when that whole Indian thing happened to him and dad... We're kids…"

Nate shook his head and stared, sulking, into the dirt.

"Promise me you'll at least try not to let things like that get into your head."

Nate said nothing.

"There's more to life than pride, glory and living up to an expectation you set for yourself… besides, you think you're the only Shepherd around that has to protect his flock?"

Nate cracked a smile.

"I'm glad I jumped in there when I did. Those dipshits did a number on you, Nate," Dan said.

"Could've been worse," Nate replied with a sniff.

"…But I'm also sorry I didn't come earlier."

"Don't worry about it, Dan. I didn't see those assholes coming either. I didn't think you were coming at all."

"You're lucky I heard the ruckus from those three beating on you… I'll say it again for the sake of name-calling… Shepherds always protect their flock… even if the flock is your dumb-thieving-ass."

The brothers laughed and cleaned themselves up as best as they could. They walked back home, readying themselves to face the wrath of their parents.

…

-Seeley Lake, Montana, Nate's Ranch-

-1869-

The walk from the house to the stables was a short one. It was too short for Sofia's liking. She took a deep breath through her nose as she looked around the ranch at the edge of the forest.

The sun hung in an endless blue sky and gave her comforting warmth wherever the rays touched. A breeze blown from the waters of Seeley Lake cooled her and shook the branches of the pines surrounding the ranch and throughout the forest. The wind brushed past her clothes, making them dance on her. The pine needles and grass crunched underneath her boots as she strode.

As she got closer to the stables, the smell of the horses' manure hit her like a brick wall. She staggered back before opening the gate of the pasture and closing it behind her. No matter what she did, she was never fully prepared for that smell. She observed the horses lying about, running and standing around the pasture. Sofia smiled and directed her attention to the stables. She waved a hand in front of her face, but the smell of manure only grew stronger. She leaned against the threshold of the entrance and eyed her husband. He brushed a stallion while it stood in its stall. He looked up at Sofia with a dumfounded expression. Sofia tilted her head and folded her arms at him.

"What, didn't expect to see me down here," Sofia asked.

Her thick Mexican accent had died down over the years, but not entirely. It put a wide smile upon Nate's face.

"No, it's just…"

Sofia raised an eyebrow at him. She waited for the appropriate response from her husband as he wore a smile he couldn't control.

"Just, what," She asked again.

"You get more beautiful every time I see you."

Sofia laughed and rolled her eyes, "You know flattery won't get you off the hook today, mi amor."

Nate nodded while he continued to brush. He looked back to the stallion. The animal offered a loud grunt as Nate brushed him on the neck.

"Work before play, Sofia... you know I would never put off spending time with you."

"How much work do you have left today?"

"I'm just finishing up cleaning this guy up, so he can run around and get all dirty again. Give me about ten minutes or so and then we can go riding, I swear!"

Sofia was caught off guard. A beige mare had walked up behind her and nudged Sofia with her head, knocking her off balance. Nate looked over and laughed.

"Sofia, meet Willow."

Sofia rubbed Willow's face and neck. Willow seemed to nod with her approval.

"Is she usually this-" Sofia began.

"Oh, yeah she's a complete sweetheart. As a matter of fact, I want you to her out with me today."

"Well, we get along nicely…"

"Don't get used to her, though."

"Why the hell not?" Sofia frowned.

"She's awful popular with every customer that comes by… A lady that came by a couple weeks ago was especially fond of her. She's coming back as soon as she scrounges up enough money to buy her."

"Can we hold on to her?"

"I'm sorry, Sofia. I already promised that customer I'd keep her until she returns," Nate sighed.

"Damn it, Nate… I really like her…"

Nate rubbed the back of his head. He opened the door to the stall, letting the stallion wander out of the pen and into the pasture. Nate walked over to his wife with his arms open. She wrapped her arms around him as they both looked out into the distance over the pasture.

"Letting them go is always the hardest part, especially with horses like Willow. One of the nicest damn creatures I've ever met… God Damn it," Nate said.

Nate left Sofia's embrace and whistled loudly as he walked out into the pasture. A large white and black spotted horse with a saddle on it came running toward him. Nate mounted his ride and squinted at the main gate.

The clean stallion pulled from the top of the gate and opened the gate just far enough to squeeze out. The stallion ran into the woods near the ranch and past the tree line.

"That's the second time that asshole has gotten out. Smart bastard. I thought I tied the fence gate down there when I got in here."

Sofia stared at the ground with guilt while Nate looked onward toward the forest.

"I need you to stay, Sofia."

She eyed him and shook her head, "No, Nate it's my fault he got out… at least let me come with you."

Nate shook his head back at her, "It's not safe out there. I was at the saloon a couple days ago and Robert said somebody saw the body of a sizeable elk up in the woods close by here."

"So?"

"So, some big bear or cougar or something killed it. Please stay, Sofia, I want to know you're safe."

"Wait a second, at least-"

Sophia cut her sentence short and ran into the stables. She grabbed Nate's belt with his revolver hanging loosely by its holster. She ran outside and handed him the belt. He looked down at his waist and nodded at her, tying the belt hastily and sloppily around his waist.

"Thanks. I'll be right back. Hopefully it's not a bear lurking out there, or this measly thing will just piss it off."

"Nate!"

"What?"

"Why would you say t- … forget it and come back in one piece or I'll finish the job for whatever hurts you out there."

"Okay, just please close that gate behind me before any of the other horses notice it's open. We'll go on that ride I promised you after I get this horse back here."

Sofia nodded and watched her husband ride off toward the trail leading into the forest. She followed him the gate of the pasture. He rode faster and faster, his belt jostled more and more. She watched as his revolver flew from its holster and hit the dirt with a loud thump behind him. She grabbed her forehead and closed her eyes, letting out a long and exaggerated sigh. He rode off without noticing.

"Dios mío… idiota…"

She looked into the stables. She stared at the weapon on the rack. Willow walked up to her and nudged Sofia's hand with her face.

…

Nate studied the dirt trail as it flew by. He spied the stallion's fresh hoof prints in the dirt. He dug his heels into Ghost and held onto his neck. The horse let out a loud whinny. Trees and bushes whirred by as he rode through the forest.

"Alright, Ghost, just a little further, I know it," Nate said over the pounding of Ghost's sprint.

Nate glanced back down at the trail. No more of the stray hoof tracks could be seen. He pulled on Ghost's reigns

"Whoa, easy."

Ghost stopped as suddenly as he could and bent his head down as Nate used the stirrups on his saddle to dismount. Nate left Ghost near the trail and looked around the area. He held a horse tie in his hand and walked down the trail.

"So, looks like you're a creature of habit, huh…"

Nate recognized the area from the first time the stallion ran from the pasture. The right side of the trail descended into a grassy creek. A thick layer of bush lined the stream on the opposite side.

The stallion stood near the other side of the creek with his head bent down, drinking water. He hadn't heard Nate approach and kept drinking. Nate readied the tie in both of his hands. He walked carefully up to the horse and looked at the ground for dry leaves and twigs to avoid spooking the stallion. Nate ducked behind a nearby tree. He took a deep breath, spying the trail and Ghost in the distance. Nate peeked out as carefully as he could.

The stallion let out a loud cry. A cougar pounced from the brush, sinking its claws and teeth into its prey. The stallion scrambled and squirmed on the grass until the beast sank its fangs into the stallion's neck. The escaped horse was suddenly silent and motionless.

Nate heard the sickening noises of flesh being chewed and torn paired with the snapping of tendons and bones. Without looking down, Nate brought his hand down toward the revolver on his belt. He searched his empty holster and cursed to himself. He stuck a sliver of his head back out to the stream. There, the cougar munched happily on the stallion as the dead horse's blood spurted and flowed into the water. Red lined the edges of the predator's mouth and coated its paws.

Nate held his breath and looked down at the ground. He placed a foot in front of him as quietly and as softly as he could in the direction of the trail. He swiveled his head to the stream and stepped down on a twig. With the noise, the cougar's gaze locked on Nate and the large cat growled at him. It approached Nate from only fifteen feet away. The cougar kept its body low and ready to pounce. It circled Nate. The predator had a fierce look in its eyes. Nate faced the cougar and backed up slowly toward Ghost and the trail. The beast hissed in between its growls. Nate held his hands up at it in a vain attempt to calm it down. The cougar charged at Nate and leapt into the air. Nate flinched and braced himself.

A loud boom echoed across the woods and a bright flash came from Nate's left. Sofia fired a twelve-gauge shotgun into the big cat. Sofia fell backward with the butt of the shotgun in her shoulder. The cougar flinched in midair and fell just short of Nate, tumbling to a halt. The cougar lay motionless with several gaping, holes in its side. Nate looked over to Sofia. She laid in the grass, still barely holding onto the gun, its two barrels belched smoke from the shots. He raced over to her. She sat up onto her hands and let the gun fall into her lap. Her black hair was draped messily across her face. She puffed her cheeks out and tried to blow the black strands off to the sides.

Nate took the shotgun from her grasp and brushed the hair from her eyes. She wore a grimace on her face. Sofia brought her hands over to her shoulder where the butt of the shotgun was when she fired it. Nate cradled her and brought her upright as best as he could.

"Sofia…" Nate began.

"That thing has a lot of kick…did I hit it?"

Nate looked at the dead cougar with the massive bleeding hole in its side and back to Sofia.

"Yeah, I think you got him… are you okay?"

Sophia stopped and raised her eyebrows at him.

"Am I okay?! Look at you, Cabrón! Almost killed by that goddamn thing…"

"How did you know I needed you?"

"I saw your revolver fall when you and Ghost were just leaving the ranch, so I had to come make sure you were safe out here. I took Willow over. I heard you and that culo cat down here by the creek."

"Why'd you bring the twelve gauge?"

"You said it could've been a bear, so I wanted to make sure…"

Nate looked up at the trail where Willow and Ghost stared blankly at them, fidgeting impatiently.

"You know something?" Nate asked.

Sofia shrugged as Nate lifted her from the grass and back onto her feet. He brushed the leaves, dust and twigs from her. He held her against him.

"I was probably going to die until you showed up and saved my sorry ass."

"No damned giant pussycat will take my husband away from me…"

Nate reared back in laughter as he grasped her hand. He picked the shotgun up from the ground and clutched it as they walked toward the trail. She eyed him with a confused grin on her face.

"What's so funny," She asked.

"That giant pussycat was terrifying," He laughed, "You make it sound so harmless."

Sofia's smile grew.

"Sofia... If I died here today… If I-"

She stared intently at him and held her index finger up to his lips. He looked into her warm brown eyes.

"You never have to think about it, mi amor," She whispered with that wide and warm expression still on her face, "Because Shepherds always protect their flock."

. . .

-The Battle of Chickamauga-

-Near the border of Tennessee & Georgia-

-1863-

Nate turned to look at his prey, a look of pride on his face. Nate's skin turned white under the dried blood caked to his skin. He fell on his back. Nate felt vomit well up from the icy cold pit of his stomach. He flipped himself over on his hands and knees, retching what little food he had eaten the day before the battle.

Nate eyes were stuck open wide with shock. A pain like he had never felt consumed him and brought rage along with it. He felt his eyes leak and his vocal cords tear in a silent scream. Panic made his heart leap from his chest. He tried to un-see what he saw, he tried to pretend… he tried. Nothing could erase the image that was burned into his skull.

Nathaniel knelt. The far-off rifle and cannon fire no longer shook or startled him. The blood, gore, and carcasses around the battlefield brought no sickness or nausea. Nate gaped at his last victim who writhed and struggled to bring himself off the ground.

Private Daniel Shepherd coughed spurts of dark red liquid. It dripped down on his face and onto his already bloodied uniform. He stumbled back onto his feet, clutching his stab wound with one arm to stop the blood flow. He held himself up with his rifle. He looked into

Nate's eyes with a confused rage and pulled Nate's sword from his flesh.

"D-Dan…" Nate wept.

Daniel took his weight off his rifle and pointed it at his brother's head. He pulled the hammer back.

"I'm sorry," Nate wept.

The hammer of the rifle came down. The rifle clicked. Daniel wheezed and dropped his weapon. Daniel fell with it. Nate stared. Daniel no longer moved.

Before he knew it, Nathaniel was at his brother's side. He turned Daniel's body over. Daniel's eyes were stuck open. He hoped they still held life, any of that same old kind sharpness he knew when he saw them before. Nate knew better. With a shaking hand, he took Daniel's bloody letter from his coat pocket

Greif turned. Nate felt himself stand up with his muscled tightened and on fire. He felt an animosity come over him. One like he had never felt before, an undying rage at himself. He sprinted off. Hot tears flew off his face in gusts that felt colder than winter winds. His lungs burned at the effort. He felt his knuckles crack over the grips of his swords. Nate did his best to ignore the pain all over his body and in his heart. He tried his hardest to channel it and use it for the fight. The enemy knew not what was coming for them. Neither did Nathaniel. He lost himself.

Chapter Eighteen: The Lonely Shepherd

-Ojos Negros, Mexico-

-February1876-

-After the Fight-

Elaine watched from her room at the inn of Ojos Negros. Dark clouds rolled in from the Baja coast. She imagined them as dark specters that haunted and loomed over the desert and cast a shadowy veil over the landscape below. Her rifle sat propped up against the wall next to her, locked and loaded. She was ready for the Gambler to arrive with what remained of his gang and hired his guns. All she could do was sit there at the window, wait, and think.

I'll finish this and meet you back there in two days. Don't wait any longer.

His words still resonated in her ears. The first day came to a close. The setting sun illuminated the lingering storm clouds; changing their hue to a light gray until the sun fell behind the horizon. The clouds let loose forks of lightning shooting into the land below. The forked bolts illuminated Elaine in momentary flashes.

Her eyes split each second into minutes and made each massive bolt of electricity spread in slow motion. She sat guarding the window, impatiently staring out into the dark. A crack of thunder shook the room and woke Sara from her sleep.

Elaine turned her attention from the window to the tiny crying girl in the bed. Elaine walked over, lit the lamp next to the bed, and plopped down on the edge. She picked Sara up and held her in her lap, facing the window. The woman cooed to Nate's daughter with the wall at her back.

"Hey it's okay, Sara. It's only a storm. It won't hurt us… not unless we're dumb enough to go outside right now," Elaine whispered to Sara.

Another flash of lightning filled the room, followed by another boom. Sara nestled her face into Elaine's chest. The girl held onto her as tightly as her infantile arms could. Elaine wrapped her arms around Sara. She rocked the girl back and forth. Soon the storm faded, and the two fell asleep in each other's arms.

…

Elaine woke up to Sara stirring in her lap. She smiled and placed her on the bed, pulling the sheets over her. Elaine turned her head to the window. The sun painted parts of the storm clouds gold as its rays of light found their way to the earth. She peered through the window and saw a hunched rider bouncing at the pace of his horse He meandered over the horizon. Elaine grabbed her rifle and looked down the sights to see a familiar face bloodied and wounded. He was wrapped in cloth and bandages, fighting off unconsciousness as he rode into Ojos Negros. His head lulled. It bobbed from side to side.

"Nate," Elaine gasped as she raced outside.

Elaine burst from the room and ran as fast as she could out to him. She grabbed the reigns of the horse and guided it back to the inn where she hitched it next to hers. She threw his arm over her head and slid him from his horse, supporting some of his weight.

Nate's boots hit the ground, and he winced in pain. His skin was as pale and as grey as the storm clouds. Nate's lips were split and chapped. His eyelids fluttered open and shut and his legs shook under his weight. Nate's makeshift bandages were soaked in his blood.

"Elaine… is she… is Sara…" Nate whispered.

"Why don't ya see for yourself?"

She carried him to the room and set him down on the bed next to Sara who lay sleeping in the sheets. Nate coughed through a laugh and smiled as he watched his daughter sleep soundly. Elaine brought a water canteen to his mouth. He gulped it down and continued to gaze at his daughter.

"Nate, ya need help... Your wounds… I'll go find someone here that can treat ya."

"Open this… when you get there… thank you… Elaine…"

Nate reached into his coat pocket and pulled two cloth wrapped pieces of paper from it. He handed them to Elaine.

Elaine took the bundled slips of paper and stormed out of the room, calling for a doctor. The crack of thunder in the distance woke Sara up. Her eyes were fixed upon her father who still wore a large smile upon his face. Sara whimpered as she crawled into his lap. With shaking, bloody hands, Nate wrapped her in the blanket and in the bed sheets to keep her from getting wet while she rested on top of him. Sara grabbed his index finger with one of her tiny hands.

Tears rolled down Nate's cheeks and past his lips as she fell back to sleep in his arms. Nate's eyes grew heavier and heavier. His smile gently faded from his face. He too, let sleep slowly take hold of him, his breathing growing weaker.

"A Shepherd… always…"

…

Elaine stomped through the inn room door with the only doctor in Ojos Negros. She stopped dead in her tracks when she saw the father and daughter resting peacefully on the bed together. She watched Sara's chest rise and fall with her breathing. Sara laid in his lap, gripping his cold, grey finger. Sara grinned and shifted, nestling herself in her sheets on top of Nate. Elaine caught her tears with her sleeve as they rolled down her face.

Nate sat perfectly still with his eyes closed. His mouth hung open in a ghost of a smile. His chest neither rose nor fell. His jaw did not quiver. His tears no longer fell.

Scattered rays of sunlight grew in size and in numbers. They turned the droplets of rain into a brilliant golden-white shower of falling sparks. Thunder no longer rumbled in the sky. Elaine heard the gentle tapping of rain against the glass. She hung her head and looked at the little girl before her.

The sky wept for the lonely Shepherd.

-New York, New York-
-September 1876-
-Seven Months Later-

Elaine adjusted the strap on her shoulder. She hoisted loads of water and baby food as she rode along. Sara sat happily in front of her, holding onto the horn of the saddle. Elaine sighed in relief at the sight of New York's city skyline.

Late afternoon twilight was made brighter by the streets, awash with a bright orange light. Some of it was electric, but it was mostly lantern lit. She listened to the roar of the city goers. It volume was reduced to a whisper by distance.

Elaine didn't miss the wilderness or the small trading posts she dragged Sara through. She didn't miss having to watch her and Sara's backs as they went to the bathroom in the woods or wiping with leaves. She remembered city life… and she didn't miss that either. "We finally made it ya wee, bugger," Elaine said.

Elaine rustled the toddler's shiny black hair. Sara giggled and drooled at Elaine with a sparsely toothy smile. Elaine returned the expression.

"Let's get ya to grammy and pappy."

Her thoughts wandered to her own family. Elaine's smile was wiped from her face. She wasn't even sure if there were alive anymore, let alone in New York. She thought about the years of letters and packages of money she had sent to them without hearing a word from them.

Elaine and Sara searched the New York streets. Stagecoaches, pedestrians, and others on horseback zoomed all around. Everybody in the city had somewhere they needed to be even at such a late hour. Elaine took a deep breath in through her nose, embracing the familiar scents she grew up with, even if some weren't so enjoyable. Sara covered her nose and whined to Elaine.

"Better get used to it, sweetheart, this place is your home," Elaine shouted over the city noise.

Elaine parked her horse in front of a large brick building. Painted in large letters on the front was; New York Police Dept. Elaine wiped the sweat from her brow, hoping that she wasn't known across the country, hoping the Gambler kept her identity under wraps as much as she thought he did.

She took Sara from her seat atop the horse. Sara grabbed onto one of Elaine's fingers. The child's grip brought Elaine out from inside of her head. With one last deep breath, she led Sara inside. The girl gripped her finger tighter as they got closer.

Men in long blue coats ran amuck in the building. Some carried documents and others pushed defeated looking criminals along toward sections of the building labeled booking and holding. Desks made the halls narrow. Officers of the law sat vigorously reading signing and writing up mountains of paperwork necessary for them to properly do their jobs. To Elaine's amazement, there wasn't a single man without a thick mustache she could see.

While the commotion of the NYPD office was a blur to Elaine, stillness caught her eye. Behind a pane of glass was an officer staring at her and Sara. He waved them over.

"What brings you two lovely ladies in today?" The officer asked with a smile.

Elaine let herself relax. If they had any idea who she was, she'd be filled full of holes already.

"I'm lookin' for this little one's grandparents John and Christine. I was told they live near here."

The officer held up a finger and dug around in a shelf full of papers behind him. Elaine tapped her fingers on the countertop.

Eventually, he turned back around with a solemn expression, "I'm sorry, it says here that John and Christine Shepherd are deceased. Have been for years. Only a few months ago. The only other living relative they have is…"

"Sara," Elaine chimed in.

"Actually, that'd be a Nathaniel or Nate Shepherd who was last seen in Montana…"

"He's- … He died recently. I was working with him when he passed away."

The officer raised an eyebrow at her, "How did he-"

"We traveled a lot in Montana. Last winter, he went out during a blizzard and just never came back. Sara is his daughter."

"Not your's?"

"Nate's wife died a few years ago from… the flu."

"Papers," He said shortly, "We need to be certain of who she is. Do you have any proof that this kid is Mister Shepherd's?"

Elaine patted herself down frantically. She pulled cloth wrapped papers from her coat pocket and handed them to the officer.

The officer took them, nodded, and returned the papers to her.

He wrote some things down, "Are you her guardian?"

Elaine shrugged at him, "I've been lookin' after her for… a long time now, but I haven't signed any papers."

"Okay, so you have two choices; I can contact the people necessary to let you adopt her, or you can leave her here and the PD can take her to the orphanage. Your call." Elaine bent down and pet Sara's hair.

"You're goin' to be just fine here, Sara. I'll miss ya, sweet girl, but Aunty Elaine has her own family to track down and her own messes to clean up. I'll grab your food n' come say a proper goodbye," Elaine whispered.

Elaine started for the front door of the police department. She heard a familiar crying coming from behind her. It stopped her in her tracks.

"Aye, kiddo. Aunty Elaine'll come visit ya whenever she can," She swallowed the lump in her throat.

Without looking, Elaine continued her march back out to her horse. Mid stride, she felt that tiny, warm grasp around her finger.

"Ya bloody little gobshite," Elaine said softly.

The woman picked Sara up. She took the young girl over to the counter.

"Get those adoption people for me, would ya?"

The man behind the counter nodded and rushed over to one of his fellow mustached colleagues. Elaine played with Sara. She blinked the moisture away from the corners of her eyes as she played with Sara.

The officer rushed back over, "Now there's the matter of Ms. Sara Shepherd's inheritance."

Elaine turned her attention from Sara, dumbstruck.

"As her legal guardian, it will be your responsibility to maintain her property and ensure she receives it when she comes of age, given how young she is."

"Uhh, the house is-"

"Mostly Sara's, but also yours until she grows up… and as long as you take good care of her."

…

-Shepherd's Ranch-

-November 1881-

-Five Years Later-

Snowfall had already begun although it was still mid autumn. Brightly colored leaves dotted drifts of white powder, making the landscape look like a flatter version of vanilla ice cream dotted with candied toppings.

City noises dwindled to an eerie hush with the falling of the snow. The vanilla landscape had a colored glow to it thanks to the nightlife of New York City. The artificial light turned that pure white to a yellow French vanilla flavor.

Frost bit at Sara through her mittens and through her heavy coat. The six-year-old girl pulled at the school uniform she wore, trying to get the material of the skirt to warm her legs more. The thick woolen socks her aunt bought for her proved to do little against the cold. She shivered but fought through it. Liking the snow required at least a bit of tolerance for it.

Sara enjoyed the crunch beneath each of her tiny footfalls. It made walking more of a chore, but also more interesting to her, more satisfying in a strange way. She liked to pretend that she was so large and so mighty that her tremendous steps crushed the cold, white earth.

She found herself on a knoll near the house and past the stables. Golden light spilled from the house in wide, golden squares. Sara thought it looked like a game of hopscotch the way they were spaced out on the ground.

The girl hopped, skipped, and jumped until she came to a slab of stone protruding from the snow. Sara put her book bag down and wiped cold powder from its top and from its face until she was satisfied until she could see the names carved into it.

A shadow drifted from square to square of light. It brought Sara's attention to the house. Aunt Elaine searched frantically about the house. Sara put a hand on the stone with a weak smile.

Sara wheeled around. The back door of the house flew open, pushing fresh snow out of the way with a loud grinding noise. A flustered Irish woman barged out into the cold.

"Sara bloody Shepherd, did ya walk your little arse all the way from school again?! I was worried about ya!"

Sara said nothing. Elaine walked out to meet her. The pair stood silently looking at the stone.

"Aunty Elaine…" Sara began sullenly.

"I'm sorry, lass. I just don't want ya getting' sick, is all. I didn't mean to yell at ya."

"That's okay. I know how you worry. I was just thinking about them again… I wanted to see them."

"Tell ya what, let's get ya some hot chocolate inside and I'll tell ya some more stories about your mom and dad, sound good?"

Sara nodded. Elaine headed back inside and shut the door. The girl ran her hand along the gravestone once more. From her book bag, she pulled a blurry and worn photo. The grainy image showed a grizzled military man, a Mexican woman, and an infant all with wide smiles on their faces.

"I love you."

Sara Shepherd followed Elaine after a moment after reading the etchings underneath their names one last time.

The words made her smile along with her family's photo.

Shepherds Always Protect Their Flock